Praise for the

"Daniels is a perennial favorite, and I might go as far as to label her the cowboy whisperer." —*BookPage*

"Super read by an excellent writer. Recommended!"
—Linda Lael Miller, #1 *New York Times* bestselling author,
on *Renegade's Pride*

"B.J. Daniels has [the] unique ability to astound with her mystery and suspense." —*Under the Covers Book Blog*

"The action will set you on edge.... Daniels has created a story that has suspense to spare."
—*Fresh Fiction* on *Redemption*

"Romantic suspense that will keep readers guessing.
If you like *Longmire*, this is the book for you."
—*RT Book Reviews* on *Forsaken*

"Daniels is truly an expert at Western romantic suspense."
—*RT Book Reviews* on *Atonement*

"Will keep readers on the edge of their chairs from beginning to end." —*Booklist* on *Forsaken*

"Truly amazing crime story for every amateur sleuth."
—*Fresh Fiction* on *Mercy*

**Also by *New York Times* bestselling author
B.J. Daniels**

Look for B.J. Daniels's next novel
in the Powder River series
River Strong
available soon from Canary Street Press.

For a complete list of books by B.J. Daniels,
please visit bjdaniels.com.

B.J. DANIELS

DARK SIDE
OF THE
RIVER

CANARY STREET PRESS

CANARY
STREET
PRESS™

Recycling programs
for this product may
not exist in your area.

ISBN-13: 978-1-335-52304-4

Dark Side of the River

For questions and comments about the quality of this book, please contact us at CustomerService@Harlequin.com.

Canary Street Press
22 Adelaide St. West, 41st Floor
Toronto, Ontario M5H 4E3, Canada
CanaryStPress.com

Printed and bound in Barcelona, Spain by CPI Black Print

DARK SIDE
OF THE
RIVER

CHAPTER ONE

OAKLEY STAFFORD SPURRED her horse as she came bursting out of the ravine headed for the safety of the river bottom. Behind her she could hear the thunder of hooves, pounding as hard as her own blood. Only one rider, but he apparently was determined to catch her, to stop her. She knew that on horseback she could outrun him. That single rider, a cowboy who'd fallen in behind her as she came out of the ravine, wasn't who she was worried about.

The real trouble was in the sky behind her. The sound of a small-plane engine growing closer made her heart race. They were coming after her, determined to stop her at all costs. She was outnumbered and they had all the advantages. She could no longer hear the horse and rider behind her, but the sound of the plane's engine was getting louder. It was flying low, coming up fast behind her.

If it was the Piper Cub she'd seen earlier, one of the men had been shooting at coyotes from the open window behind the pilot. She knew she would make a much bigger target than a coyote. She was now easy prey.

The dirt ahead of her was suddenly pocked as a bullet struck it. Dust rose next to her horse, making it shy to the right. Ahead she could see the cover of the thick cottonwoods that lined each side of the Powder River. Once under that dark canopy, at the least the pilot and his passenger wouldn't have a clear shot at her. If they were the ones who'd just fired on her.

But the cowboy on the horse behind her was also armed—and maybe even more dangerous. She'd seen him as she'd come racing out of the ravine, getting only a glimpse before she'd heard him shoot. Her only chance was to make it past the trees and the river to the county road...

Spurring her horse, she leaned forward, urging the mare to go faster, desperate to reach the grove of cottonwoods. She heard the plane pull up and begin to circle, drowning out the sound of hooves behind her. But she knew he was still back there, determined to stop her.

She couldn't let him or the others catch her. They would kill her. She knew too much.

Cooper McKenna rested his arm out the open pickup window as he drove down the familiar county road. After being away this long, he was in no hurry to reach home. The late-June heat blew in along with grasshoppers that flew around the cab. Ahead, huge cottonwoods crowded both sides of the dirt road, making a shaded dark green tunnel. The sun pierced the green leaves to throw shadows across his path as he drove beneath them, the air in here cooler.

Overhead, puffy white clouds floated in a sea of deep blue above the treetops. He caught only glimpses of the river that began in Wyoming and traveled more than one hundred and fifty miles to empty into the Yellowstone.

Many claimed that the Powder River was a mile wide, an inch deep and ran uphill. The running joke was that it was too thick to drink and too thin to plow. Captain Clark of the Lewis and Clark Expedition had named it Redstone River. But the Native Americans called it Powder River because the black shores reminded them of gunpowder, and that had stuck.

The river, the lifeblood of those who lived here, passed right through the heart of the McKenna Ranch. Just the sight of it felt like home. This was where he'd left his heart. After two years of being away, he'd shaken off the dust of the places he'd been, this country calling him home like a migrating bird after a long winter. He'd felt an ache for the familiar, yearning for the rocky bluffs, the spring green of the grasslands and, of course, the river that ran through it.

He'd passed the ranch sign five miles back and still had another ten miles to go to reach the ranch house. The McKenna Ranch stretched as far as the eye could see, the county road cutting through the heart of it. His eyes were on the road ahead, but his thoughts were as dark as the shadows lurking in the trees.

The deep ache in his chest wasn't just for the land or for what he'd lost here. This place had broken his heart. Yet here he was, coming back. He smiled ruefully, knowing what kind of homecoming it could be. He was the middle son of Holden McKenna, a threat to his older brother, Treyton, the self-proclaimed rightful heir of the ranching empire the Holdens had built.

Cooper was the black sheep, the rebel cowboy everyone believed was a killer. The worst part was, he thought they might be right.

With a start, he caught movement out of the corner of his eye an instant before the horse and rider came flying out of the cottonwoods. The rider tumbled from the horse, going down hard in the middle of the road in front of the pickup.

Standing on the brake, Cooper was terrified he wouldn't get stopped quickly enough on the narrow dirt road. As the pickup shuddered to a stop, he let out the breath he'd been holding before throwing the truck into Park and jumping out.

Rounding the front of the pickup, he was relieved to see that he hadn't hit the rider, who was lying on the ground just inches from his bumper, back to him. The horse, wild-eyed and spooked, had run up the road and stopped to look back.

He spotted the brand. *Stafford Ranch?* What the hell was the rider doing on McKenna property with the bad blood between the families?

"That was a nasty spill you took," he said as the rider groaned. He knelt down, not adding that it had been a dumb-ass thing to do, riding out of the woods like that onto the county road. Picking up the fallen cowboy's hat, he asked, "You all right?"

He'd seen his share of cowboys hit the dirt, thrown from their horses for all kinds of reasons. He'd certainly had his share of unexpected dismounts. Cowboys usually just dusted themselves off, limped off to retrieve their horses and were on their way again.

Another groan. This one had hit the ground pretty hard and wasn't getting up. Cooper hoped he wasn't too badly injured. As he leaned over the cowboy, shock rocketed through him as he saw the rider's face.

Oakley Stafford? He swore under his breath. He'd just assumed it was a cowboy who'd come busting out of the trees riding way too fast. He'd known Oakley and her older sister, Tilly, all of his life—even though their families had been feuding for years.

So what the hell had she been doing riding a horse like that—let alone trespassing on the McKenna Ranch? There was no need for trespassing signs. Everyone knew the last place you wanted to get caught was on the McKenna or Stafford ranches without written permission.

As far back as Cooper could remember, there had been a war going on between their two families. The only thing worse than finding a Stafford on the ranch was for a McKenna to be caught on Stafford land—the equally large ranch that bordered theirs.

Oakley let out another groan of pain and rolled toward him. He'd been sure that she'd taken worse falls from a horse, so he hadn't been too concerned that her injuries were serious—until he saw that she was bleeding.

"Easy, take it easy," he said as he tried to see where the blood was coming from without moving her too much. "How badly are you hurt?"

Her eyelids fluttered. "Buttercup," she managed to whisper as she grimaced in pain.

He assumed that must be her horse. "Buttercup's fine," he assured her. "Where are you injured?"

"No." She tried to get up, letting out a cry before falling back in obvious agony. He realized she was hurt much worse than he'd originally thought. He couldn't tell where the blood was coming from, but it had soaked into the front side of her shirt on through to her denim jacket. All he could think was that she must have hit something in the road when she'd fallen.

"No. *Buttercup.*" She said it as if he just wasn't getting it. He wasn't. Her eyelids fluttered again, then closed, her head falling to the side.

"Oakley? *Oakley?*" He pulled out his phone to call 911. As he did, he leaned over farther to see that even the back of her denim jacket was soaked with blood. Startled, he saw a perfectly round hole in the denim. He stared in shock. It made no sense, no sense at all. Oakley hadn't gotten hurt falling off her horse.

She'd been shot.

CHAPTER TWO

EVEN AS COOPER made the 911 call, he found himself looking toward the woods in the direction Oakley had exited at such speed. "Oakley Stafford's been shot. I need an ambulance on the county road, about six miles into the McKenna Ranch. Please hurry. My name's Cooper McKenna. Just…hurry."

As he disconnected, the hair quilled on the back of his neck as he peered into the thick cottonwoods now deep in shadow. How the hell had she gotten shot? Why? He remembered her flying out of the trees like she was airborne and onto the road as if…as if she was being chased. What had she been running from? Who? He felt his skin crawl at the thought that her would-be killer could still be in the dense stand of cottonwoods. Watching them? Waiting?

Rising, he hurried around to his open driver's-side door and pulled a T-shirt from his duffel, grabbed a roll of duct tape from under his pickup seat and returned to Oakley. He balled up his T-shirt, pressed it to the front where he could see a lump under the skin where the slug hadn't exited. He duct-taped the T-shirt in place.

The late-June afternoon was hot. Taking off his own denim jacket, he slipped it under her head. Then he took off the T-shirt he was wearing and pressed it against her left side in the back where the bullet had entered. As he did, he listened for any sound. He could hear crickets chirping somewhere deep in the grove. But it was another sound that made his skin crawl.

Cooper realized he'd heard it earlier, the buzz of a small-airplane engine. The plane was growing closer. He stayed where he was, leaning against the front bumper of the pickup and keeping pressure on Oakley's wound.

The plane grew closer and closer, the sound louder and louder, until he felt the dark shadow of the Piper Cub pass over. The plane flew so low over the road that it barely missed the treetops. He tried to see the call numbers on the side, but only got a glimpse as the plane suddenly veered to the right and disappeared over the trees.

When he looked up the road, he saw that the plane must have spooked Oakley's horse. It was no longer standing a dozen yards away. It had either run into the trees or on up the road. He knew he shouldn't be so worried about the horse. But he kept thinking of Oakley's urgent expression and the one word she'd uttered before she'd passed out. *Buttercup.* He was convinced she'd been worried about her horse.

As the buzz of the plane engine died off, he heard another sound. This one brought comfort. Sirens. He checked Oakley's pulse, half-afraid they would arrive too late. With relief, he felt it. As the sound of the sirens grew louder, he found himself feeling jumpy. He pulled out his phone and quickly took photos of the scene with his free hand, including the tracks coming out of the trees and Oakley lying in front of his pickup.

He wasn't sure what exactly had made him nervous. Maybe it was the memory of being in a position a lot like this before. Only that time, the cops believed that the woman had been murdered and he was the only suspect.

Here he was again with a woman's blood on him, no one else in sight and his guns in the pickup he was leaning against. He had an inherent distrust of the law since he knew how they could jump to conclusions.

As the ambulance roared up in a cloud of dust, he pocketed his phone. A sheriff's patrol SUV pulled up behind it, but Cooper paid the cruiser little attention. He was anxious for the EMTs who jumped out to get to Oakley quickly.

"She's been shot," he told them as the two techs pushing a gurney hurried to her. "She also took a tumble when she fell off her horse. I didn't move her but secured the injury to prevent blood loss best I could."

"Shot?" Cooper turned to find a young deputy sheriff had joined them. "You shoot her?"

"No," he said irritably. He moved to help the EMTs load Oakley into the back of the ambulance and felt a hand clamp down on his bare shoulder.

"You aren't going anywhere."

"I wasn't planning to," he said, turning back to the deputy as he tried not to lose his temper. The deputy's name tag on the new-looking uniform read Ty Dodson. "You want to hear what happened, or do you want to just make it up as you go?"

The deputy's jaw tightened as he pulled out his note-book and pen.

"You have a gun in that pickup of yours?"

Cooper swore. "Yes, I have legal weapons, but I didn't shoot her. I was coming down the road and she came riding out of the trees as if someone was chasing her. If you look over there, you'll see her horse's tracks."

"She was on horseback?" He glanced around. "So where's her horse?"

"A plane came over and spooked it worse than it was already. I think it might have gone on up the road. I'm not sure." He'd seen that same skeptical look on an officer of the law's face a few too many times and groaned inwardly.

"As I was saying, she came flying out of that grove of cottonwoods onto the road and fell off her horse. I hit my brakes… I thought at first that she'd been riding too fast and had just been unseated from her horse. But when I got the truck stopped and jumped out, I saw that she was bleeding and that it was Oakley Stafford and that she'd been shot."

"You recognized her? That how you know her name?"

"I know her." Cooper didn't mention that he recognized the brand on her horse first before he'd knelt down beside her and, leaning over her, had finally gotten a look at her face.

"You say she came riding out of those trees." The deputy glanced in that direction. "Isn't that McKenna Ranch property?"

"You know it is," he said, trying not to roll his eyes.

The fact that a Stafford had been on the McKenna Ranch brought up all kinds of questions—and problems.

"That's when I realized that she'd been shot."

"Who do you think shot her?"

"I have no idea, but she was shot in the back." He could feel the deputy's intent, suspicious gaze on him.

"Let's see those guns of yours." Dodson started toward the pickup.

"How about we give the sheriff a call."

The deputy stopped and looked back. "Why would we do that?"

"I guess I'd just feel better if we did."

Turning, the deputy came back to stand within inches of him. "You know, I don't think I caught your name."

"You never asked. It's Cooper. Cooper McKenna."

The deputy's gaze flipped up from his notebook to bore into him. *"McKenna?"*

"It's just my last name."

"Right. And you just happened to be driving down this road that goes to the McKenna Ranch."

Cooper said nothing. "Just call the sheriff. He knows me."

"I'm going to do you one better. I'm going to take you to see him. I haven't been in Powder Crossing long, but I know about the bad blood between the Staffords and the McKennas. I'm going to have to take you in."

"You're arresting me? On what grounds?" He quickly backed off. "Look, I need to find her horse and make sure it's safe. She was worried about her horse."

"How do you know that?"

"I'll get a shirt out of my pickup. Then I'll go find

her horse and bring it down to the sheriff's department. Call your boss—"

The deputy had his hand on the weapon at his hip. "You aren't going to give me any trouble, are you, McKenna?"

HOLDEN MCKENNA KNEW why the sheriff had called him so quickly. A Stafford woman being shot on his ranch? He rubbed the back of his neck, at a loss for words for a moment. "You're sure Oakley was shot?" It wasn't that he'd misheard. He just couldn't believe it.

"Shot in the back. It definitely happened on your property," the sheriff said. "So far, I have no idea what she was doing there. We're going to be treating the ranch as a crime scene, which means I need to get men in there."

"Of course. How is she doing?"

"Serious condition."

That was when he'd heard something in the sheriff's voice and had waited for the other shoe to drop. "Cooper found her."

Cooper? He'd thought at first that he'd heard wrong. Cooper, his son who'd been gone for more than two years? "My deputy is bringing him in for questioning. I wanted you to know before it's all over the county."

"Wait—why is Cooper being brought in for questioning?" He felt that other shoe drop.

"He was the first on the scene. Don't worry. I'll get it sorted out."

Holden felt his stomach roil. Cooper had found her on his way to the ranch? He felt as if he was having trouble keeping up. It had been the second troubling call he'd gotten today.

"I don't have all the details yet. I just thought you'd want to know since it happened on your ranch."

He wanted to assure the sheriff that no one on the ranch had shot her. Not to mention Cooper, the one who'd apparently found her, Holden thought. But there would be plenty of time to deny accountability before this was over. "Yes, thank you, Stu, for letting me know."

"I called earlier and talked to Treyton. He said you were on a call. I wasn't sure if you got my message, so I called back."

He hadn't gotten the message. Just before he'd taken the sheriff's call, he'd seen Treyton take off in one of the ranch pickups driving too fast. He'd wondered what that was about. Now he knew. The question was whether his hair-trigger eldest son had taken off because of Oakley Stafford's shooting. Or because the sheriff had told him that Cooper was back in town?

Holden rubbed his temples. "Has Charlotte Stafford been notified?"

"I called, but Mrs. Stafford was out on a ride. Talked to CJ." The tone of his voice said what they both knew. Chisum Jase Stafford was a lot like Treyton, a hothead who needed little to set him off. Stu didn't have to warn him that CJ could be paying him a visit before the day was over.

Holden was less worried about CJ than he was about his own son. Cooper was back after all this time? He had to wonder why, even as he felt such a wash of emotion. He'd hoped and prayed that Cooper would return. Was he home to stay?

His thoughts quickly turned to Oakley, then her mother, Charlotte Stafford, as his thoughts often did. She would have to be told.

SHERIFF STUART "STU" LAYTON was as blond as Cooper was dark. The two of them had grown up together. Close to the same age, they'd been in the same grade in the small rural school for years. Cooper couldn't remember when they'd become best friends. There were rough times over the years when they'd fought over ball games or girls, but they'd lasted as friends. Stu had always had his back—even in the worst times.

Deputy Dodson had insisted on hauling Cooper into town in the back of his patrol SUV. The town of Powder Crossing hadn't changed much since he'd left two years before, he noticed. It was a typical small Montana town, but back in its day it was a stage stop for travelers from Deadwood to Miles City.

Back then, there was the Belle Creek Hotel, still standing today, but little else. Now Powder Crossing had a community church, a café, a bar, a grocery and a convenience store that sold gas out front and muck boots, overalls, rope and feed in the back. The hotel had its own restaurant that served drinks and bar food, and a part-time post office.

Along with a sheriff's department, the town had a small community hospital, with a couple of nurses and one semiretired doctor. For serious injuries, patients were flown to Miles City or Billings. Oakley had been taken to the local hospital. Doc Joe Hammond had taken care of his share of gunshot wounds over the years, along with delivering babies and mending broken bones. Residents of the county trusted him more than those big-city doctors who they swore charged an arm and a leg.

Cooper figured Oakley was in good hands, although her mother might not agree. He wouldn't have been surprised if Charlotte Stafford had her daughter flown to Billings.

After repeating everything that he'd already told Deputy Dodson about what had happened, the sheriff said, "Oakley didn't say anything else before she passed out but the word *buttercup*?"

That was the one thing that Cooper had left out of what he'd told Deputy Dodson. "She seemed worried about her horse."

The sheriff nodded. "Knowing Oakley, makes sense. Sorry about Deputy Dodson. He's new."

"Not that new. He seemed to know a lot about the McKennas and Staffords," Cooper said, but let it ride. He was still angry about being forced to leave his truck, give up his guns and being driven to the sheriff's department in the back of a patrol SUV half naked—just short of being arrested. He'd been told in the past that he had a chip on his shoulder. Something about a cop uniform always set him on edge. Probably because he'd had enough run-ins with the law in the past to last him a lifetime.

"I really could use a shirt from my pickup," he said.

Stu reached for his phone. "I'll have someone get

you something to wear. I've seen more than enough of that six-pack of yours. Been doing some physical labor, have you?"

"Construction. Can I also have my phone back?"

The sheriff slid it over to him. "We're going to have to hang on to your guns." At Cooper's surprised and displeased look, he added, "It's procedure. I'll get them back to you as soon as I can."

"I took photos of the scene, something Deputy Dodson failed to do," he said, and opened his phone and called up the shots he'd taken.

"You took photos?" Stu looked concerned as he took the phone and thumbed through the shots. "Why?"

"Well, I didn't do it because I thought it would make me look guilty of anything," Cooper snapped. "But yes, I was covering my ass. I just had a bad feeling, even before your deputy started harassing me. It isn't like I haven't been here before. And now a Stafford was shot on the McKenna Ranch and I'm the one who found her?" He shook his head. "You think I don't know how bad that looks no matter how innocent I am or my family?"

His friend leaned back in his chair and studied him openly. "It's yet to be determined if your family is innocent. Have you met your brother Treyton?" He raised a hand before Cooper could argue. "What are you doing back here?"

He knew his friend didn't mean the sheriff's office. The truth? He didn't really understand what had brought him back to Powder Crossing. Just a need for something he couldn't put his finger on, an ache he couldn't define. "Seemed like it was time to come home."

The sheriff nodded, still studying him. "Have anything to do with this latest war between the families?"

"Which war is that? I've lost track."

"You really don't know about the latest developments?"

He shook his head. He hadn't been in touch with his family or anyone else in the Powder River Basin. He'd tried to put the past behind him. Problem was, he was a McKenna, something he'd realized he could never outrun no matter how far away he went, since family was in his blood.

"The Staffords drilled a coalbed methane well close to the property line between your ranches. Your father is suing, claiming the well dried up his artesian well near the property boundary." The Powder River Basin was well-known for being the single largest source of coal mined in the country. It was said to contain one of the largest deposits of coal in the world. But methane drilling was something relatively new.

He remembered that there'd been drilling twenty years ago. "Has methane become that big of a deal here again?" Cooper asked. He knew a little about it. The gas traveled with groundwater in coal seams. Extracting it required drilling a well and pumping out the water. That was where the trouble came in. All that water, millions of gallons, pumped to the surface, emptied aquifers and dumped the used water, now high in salt content, into the rivers and agricultural land.

"It's pitted families against each other for years," the

sheriff said. "The thing is, it's used in everything now from fertilizers and gas cookers to cars, ovens, water heaters…" Stuart shrugged. "So, a lot more wells have been going in around here. The Staffords and the McKennas aren't the only ones fighting over the issue."

Cooper sighed. "It's always something. Will always be something."

"And now Oakley Stafford was shot on the McKenna Ranch." Stuart sat forward, leaning his elbows on his desk. "You really have no idea what she was doing there or why someone shot her?"

He shook his head. "I just got back to town." But he knew that if a Stafford was caught on the ranch, one of the ranch hands or his brother Treyton could have done something stupid like chasing her and even taking a potshot at her. He figured Stu suspected the same thing.

"If she dies…" The sheriff didn't have to finish; they both knew what would happen. The county would see a McKenna-Stafford war like nothing before. The situation was a powder keg even now, and Cooper, as his luck would have it, was right in the middle of it because he'd been the one to almost accidentally run over her.

He got to his feet as a deputy handed him a shirt through the open doorway. "Am I free to go?" he asked, as he dressed.

His friend rose. "Your pickup has been searched, anything of interest taken. It's parked in the lot out back, keys in it."

"'Anything of interest'?" Cooper swore. "I'm sure you'll provide a list of what was taken." He shook his head. "You know I didn't shoot her." He could see that didn't matter.

"Going to have to hang on to the guns until we get forensics back on the slug I heard they removed from Oakley. Just trying to cover all the bases. You should thank me. I'm also covering your backside."

He knew that was true. Stu was following protocol and just trying to clear him as a suspect. There would be talk as soon as everyone heard that a McKenna found her coming out of his family's ranch land.

"How is she?"

"Came out of the surgery. Still in serious condition, but stable. If you hadn't come along when you did, she'd be dead. There is that."

"Right." He thought about Oakley's sister, Tilly, and hated to think what she and the rest of the Stafford family were going through right now. He and Tilly were close enough in age that they'd competed at every fair and rodeo as far back as he could remember. He recalled with embarrassment all the times she'd outridden him, outshot him and even out-pig-wrestled him. He found himself smiling at the memory. She was as competitive as he was.

"So you're sticking around?" Stu asked as Cooper started to leave.

"Are you telling me not to leave town?"

He smiled. "Just wondering what your plans were. Thought we might have a beer sometime. It's been too long."

Cooper felt himself relax a little. He'd had the kind of day that had his shoulder muscles so tight they ached.

"Sounds great," he said, returning the sheriff's smile. "I'll let you know my plans. At this point, I'm not sure where I'll even be staying."

"It's like that?"

Cooper laughed. "It's always like that with my family, you know that."

"Maybe this time will be different," Stu offered.

"Right," he said with a laugh as the office door was flung open and his older brother, Treyton, came storming in.

TREYTON STOPPED IN the middle of the room, his gaze riveted on his younger brother. "So it's true. You're really back?" He shook his head. "You're just walking trouble, aren't you?"

Cooper sighed. "Good to see you too, Trey. Talk to you later, Stu." Behind him, he heard the sheriff telling Treyton to sit and calm down. He heard Treyton yelling something about vandalism and trespassers on the ranch. He couldn't wait to get out of there. He was in no mood to deal with his brother. He'd already been having second thoughts about his choice to return.

Now he was thinking he'd made a mistake. Why not pack up his truck and hit the road? He found his pickup parked behind the sheriff's department, an old stucco building with a matching auto shop behind it. The keys were in it, just like Stu had said. Only in Powder Crossing, he thought, where people got shot more often than vehicles got stolen.

Climbing in, he noticed his glove-box door hanging open; everything inside it had clearly been gone through. *Thank you, Deputy Dodson.* Same with his duffel, its contents dumped on the passenger seat. But according to the list he'd been given, only his weapons had been taken.

Gritting his teeth, he put everything back where it went, closed the glove box and tossed his duffel behind the seat. He had no idea when he'd get his guns back but couldn't leave without them. It made him feel a little naked and more than a little uneasy. He'd grown up with a gun handy as a kid. Never knew if he'd need to kill a rattler or scare off a critter. He'd had a rifle and a handgun in his truck for as long as he could remember. The worst part was that he couldn't shake the feeling that he would be needing a weapon and maybe soon. Whoever had shot Oakley Stafford was still out there.

As he started the engine, he thought about all the questions he'd had to answer, first with the deputy before he'd been detained. Not officially arrested, but damned close. Then with Stu. He had even more questions himself about what had happened earlier.

He sat for a moment, engine running, thinking about Oakley's horse. Had they caught up to it? If so, had they taken it to the Stafford Ranch? He didn't think it had been injured. He hoped not.

He knew the horse wasn't his concern, but it had been Oakley's. At least he'd thought that was what she'd been asking about. When she regained consciousness, he didn't want her worrying about her horse.

Buttercup. Had to be the name of her horse. He considered calling the Stafford Ranch to find out if the mare had been returned and if there was any news on

Oakley's condition, but reconsidered. He was persona non grata, and not just because he was a McKenna. He and Tilly had gone head-to-head a few too many times. He remembered one wrestling match in the mud between the two of them when they were about nine. Not his best moment, wrestling a girl in the mud. He remembered the whooping he'd gotten when his father had found out. To make it worse, a sculptor from Billings had witnessed it and actually made a bronze sculpture of the incident.

He told himself to forget about the horse. He had bigger things to concern himself with—like facing his father after all this time, given the way he'd left.

As he started to back out, he had to throw on his brakes for the second time that day as a pickup came roaring into the parking lot. The driver apparently still hadn't seen him as the speeding pickup swung into the space next to him. In the mood he was in, Cooper knew things could go south if he hit his horn or, worse, got out to give the driver a piece of his mind.

Fortunately, he did neither as the driver's-side door flew open and a woman bounded out, her blond braid flying from her shoulder to trail behind her as she stormed toward the rear entrance of the sheriff's department.

Matilda "Tilly" Stafford. He'd recognize her anywhere.

He shifted into Park and jumped out, calling after her. "Tilly?"

She'd been stalking up the walk, but now stopped. He had no doubt that she'd recognized his voice as her back stiffened before she turned around. He saw her eyes narrow, her jaw set. She headed toward him looking as if she planned to take off his head.

He held up his hands to ward her off as she charged up within a few feet of him and stopped. He could see that she was furious but also close to tears. He'd never seen her cry, although he knew there were times in competitions that she'd wanted to. The fury he'd seen before. Right now, he could see that she was struggling with both as she approached him.

Before she could speak, he asked, "Did you get Oakley's horse back?"

She blinked as if that was the last thing she'd expected out of his mouth. *"What?"* she demanded impatiently.

"Oakley's horse. The deputy wouldn't let me go look for it and make sure the mare was all right."

The fury won over the tears as she spit out the words. "You're worried about her *horse*?"

"I'm worried about her too. But she was worried about the horse. So—"

Her eyes widened. *"She talked to you?"*

"No, just— I'm so sorry. I shouldn't be bothering you with this."

"I thought you left town. How was it that you were the one who found her?"

He shook his head. "Just dumb luck?"

The tears were about to win. She turned and rushed away as if she couldn't deal with him right now. He couldn't help being relieved.

But as she started away, he called after her. "What's the name of her horse?"

Tilly stopped again, her back to him. Even from where he stood, he could see that she was vibrating with that earlier fury. He felt as if he'd poked a bear and was about to pay the price.

But to his surprise, she didn't turn, she didn't storm back to him. He heard her mutter, "Him and the damned horse? What is wrong with him?" Her shoulders seemed to slump for a moment before she said without turning around, "Cheyenne. Her horse's name is Cheyenne." She shook her head as if he was a pesky bug and disappeared into the sheriff's department.

Cheyenne? He stared after her, frowning. Not Buttercup?

Then what the hell was Oakley trying to tell him?

CHAPTER THREE

AFTER PASSING TREYTON MCKENNA on her way in, Tilly Stafford headed for the sheriff's office, her body trembling with more emotions than she could handle right now. Fortunately, she'd avoided a confrontation with Treyton. He had stormed out so fast it was as if he hadn't even seen her.

Which was fine with Tilly. Running into Cooper McKenna had been bad enough. She'd thought she'd seen the last of him. Now he was back? He just happened to return today? Just happened to find her sister after she was shot? After all this time, he just happened to pick today to cross paths with her?

She marched toward the sheriff's open door, ignoring the dispatcher who was asking if she needed help.

Stuart looked up as she stormed in. Without a word, he got up, came around his desk and pulled her into his arms. "I'm so sorry." He rubbed her back as she fought the tears that she'd dammed up since hearing the news. She stayed there taking the comfort he offered for a few moments before she pulled back to look into his handsome face. She'd known Stuart all her life. Just as she had Cooper. The three of them had gone to the same rural school, often with the same classes, especially in high school.

"I need to know what happened," she said, wanting the man she'd recently been dating to be the sheriff now.

He nodded and offered her a chair as he went to close the door before returning to his desk. He cleared his voice. "I can only tell you what I know, which isn't a lot. I'm sure you heard that Cooper found your sister after she'd been shot and called 911. If he hadn't found her... He saved her life."

She felt a stab of guilt as she thought about the way she'd just treated him outside. He was a McKenna; she'd just assumed since Oakley had been found coming out of McKenna property that he'd had something to do with her condition. Or knew who had.

"Why would anyone shoot Oakley?" she demanded.

"I don't know yet. The investigation has just begun. More than likely it was an accident. Maybe a hunter or—"

"Or one of those ranch hands on the McKenna place," she snapped. "A hunter? Are you serious? It's the end of June. There's no hunting season open."

He leaned forward. "This is Montana. There is always something to shoot by people who need to kill something." He sighed. "It would help if we knew what she was doing there in the first place. Do you have any idea?"

She shook her head. "Even if Oakley was trespassing, the McKennas can't just shoot her and get away with it."

"Of course they can't. But we don't know that they

did. We don't know who shot her, Tilly. But I'm going to find out. Are you sure you don't know what she might have been doing there?"

She didn't. Scalding tears suddenly burned her eyes. Her sister was in the hospital fighting for her life, and what hurt was that Tilly had no idea why. She and Oakley hadn't been close in months. She blamed herself as the older sister, because she should have noticed her sister pulling away from her.

"She's been secretive lately like she was hiding something," Tilly said. "I just assumed it was a man she didn't want me to know about. Probably because I wouldn't have approved."

"You don't know who?"

She shook her head before voicing her greatest fear. "What if she had hooked up with someone from the McKenna Ranch?"

"You mean like Treyton or Duffy?"

Tilly didn't know which would be worse. The arrogant, angry Treyton, whom she'd passed on the way into the sheriff's office. Or the youngest male McKenna, Duffy, who at thirty was wilder than Cooper and just as irresponsible. "How long has Cooper been back?"

"He said he just drove in today," Stu said. "I have no reason to believe otherwise."

She mugged a face at that. Stuart was Cooper's friend. He'd always take up for him. Just the thought of Cooper reminded her of his interest in Oakley's horse. "Was Oakley's horse returned to the ranch? Cooper said she was worried about it."

"You saw Cooper?"

Tilly tried not to read anything into the question or what she'd thought she'd heard in it. Was he jealous of her tumultuous history with Cooper? Their wrestling match all those years ago was made famous by that sculptor who'd taken a photo that day. Her mother had threatened to buy the sculpture and destroy it, but the piece had sold before she could get her hands on it.

There was no reason for Stuart to be jealous. The two of them had been dating for only a few weeks. It wasn't serious. They hadn't even gotten intimate, although she knew he was hoping that was where they were headed.

"Cooper kept asking about her *horse*." She shook her head, wishing she hadn't brought it up. There was definitely something wrong with that cowboy.

"The horse is fine. I'm sure it's already been returned, but I'll double-check." As if he could see that she was still thinking about Cooper, he said, "He didn't shoot your sister."

She knew that on some level. No matter how many times she'd butted heads with Cooper, she knew he wasn't a killer.

"Tilly, anything you can tell me about your sister's recent activities would help."

"I'll talk to my brothers and my mother. They might know."

"I'll be speaking to them and the McKennas. It would really help if we knew what she was doing on the McKenna Ranch."

Slowly, she got to her feet. "I'll be at the hospital. If you hear anything…"

"I'll call you." He started to rise to see her out, but

she waved him back down and left. If he offered her more sympathy, she feared she wouldn't be able to hold back the tears any longer.

"Just find out who shot my sister," she said as she closed the door behind her.

As HOLDEN MCKENNA saddled his horse, he tried to talk himself out of what he was about to do. The sheriff had said that he hadn't been able to reach Oakley's mother because she'd gone for a horseback ride. While he didn't want to be the person to tell her the news, he felt strongly that it would be better coming from him.

He wasn't using this tragedy as an excuse to see her, he told himself as he swung into the saddle and rode toward the spot where the two ranches joined. That it was a favorite place that Charlotte Stafford often rode hadn't been lost on him. He reminded himself that he was probably on a fool's errand. By now, she could have returned to her ranch, heard about Oakley and was probably on her way to the hospital.

But as he rode through the thick cottonwoods toward the creek that flowed into the Powder River, he spotted her. She'd taken off her boots and socks, rolled up her jeans and was now wading in the warm water. The sight of her made him catch his breath. She was still a willowy beauty even after all these years. Her hair was still long, although there were strands of silver among the gold. She still usually wore it in a braid, one long, thick plait that hung almost to her waist. But today, she had loosened the plait, letting her hair float around her slim shoulders in a golden cascade.

She was a vision, taking his breath away. It made him realize how long it had been since he'd seen her like this, relaxed, in her element, possibly even happy.

Her horse, grazing nearby, lifted his head as Holden dismounted and started toward Charlotte. Transfixed by her, he was flooded by memories of other warm summer Montana days by this creek. He felt a familiar ache, an old longing that had eaten away at him for years.

As if sensing him, she looked up. It had been so long since he'd looked into those emerald eyes. The sun-dappled leaves of the cottonwoods rustled in the slight breeze, throwing shadow and light over her beautiful face. Their gazes met for an instant before she moved, without a word, to her horse.

For a moment, he thought she was going for a gun. He thought it poetic that he might die here at her hand. Instead, she pulled out a bullwhip. As she turned to look at him, she snapped the whip, knocking off his Stetson, the tip of the cattail slashing his cheek.

"Lottie," he said as she started to snap the whip again. The use of his nickname for her made her green eyes flare in warning. He moved swiftly to her, grabbing the whip before she could snap it again.

Taking it from her, he pushed her back against the trunk of a large cottonwood, aware that they were both breathing hard. Their eyes met in that instant before he kissed her, the passion between them hotter and more dangerous because of all the time they'd been apart and the betrayal between them.

He recoiled as she bit his lip hard, drawing blood

yet again. They stared at each other for a long moment before she kissed him with a longing he knew only too well. The sound she made sent a river of desire raging through his veins. She dug her fingers into his shoulders, clinging to him as if, like him, she'd been denying this for far too long. He'd never felt like this with any other woman, including his two wives. It had always been Lottie. Would always be Lottie.

At the sound of a rider approaching, they pushed apart, adjusting their clothing and their expressions as her ranch manager, Boyle Wilson, came riding up. A rugged, surly man in his midfifties, Boyle often had a scowl on his face. Holden had once seen him kick a dog. Boyle went after the animal as if he planned to kill it. Holden had jumped him, throwing the man to the ground as the dog scrambled away. Alfred Wilson, Boyle's father and then-manager at Stafford Ranch, had pulled Holden off his son. But not before Holden had seen a malevolence close to evil in that young man's face, the same look he now saw etched deep in the now-older Boyle's expression.

The ranch manager drew up sharply, reining in his horse in obvious surprise at seeing Holden not just on the Stafford Ranch—but with his boss. The one thing Holden knew about Boyle was that he was very protective of Charlotte, maybe a little too much so.

"I was just leaving," Holden said, shifting his gaze to Lottie. She had regained her composure more quickly than him. Now she stood looking regal, the queen of the manor, his nemesis and his neighbor, his once-lover, now his enemy.

"Hope I'm not interrupting anything," Boyle said sarcastically, clearly hoping the exact opposite. "There's been a shooting," he said, glaring at Holden as if he recognized the kind of tension roiling between them. "It's Oakley," he said to his boss. "She was shot on the McKenna Ranch. Cooper was the one who apparently found her."

Lottie glared at Holden as her fingers worked urgently to pull her long hair back into a tightly contained twist. "Is that what you rode over here to tell me?" she demanded.

"Cooper called 911 and got her to the hospital." He didn't mention that his son was taken into custody and transported to the sheriff's office. She'd hear about that soon enough. "Lottie," he said. "The sheriff told me that he'd been trying to reach you. I knew where I could find you."

She shook her head, her eyes warning him not to say his nickname for her again. He could see that she was already regretting that seeing him here had made her weaken, just as it had him. It had been too long since they'd seen each other completely alone in a place they'd once made love in secret. The difference was, he didn't regret that stolen moment of wild abandon. But he could see that she did. Now she hated him more than ever, her look said.

He nodded, turned and walked toward where he had ground-tied his horse, not sure she wouldn't put a bullet into his back. Swinging up into the saddle, he turned to look at her, his heart aching. If he hadn't known her so well, he might have thought that all that anger was for him.

But he could see that she would never forgive herself for kissing him back the way she had, for wanting him as desperately as he wanted her. He had enough self-loathing for both of them. He didn't want her hating herself for old feelings neither of them had been able to control.

"I'm sorry about Oakley," he said. He spurred his horse, riding away sick with worry about their families. He felt more regret than he'd ever known. He was responsible for the animosity between the families. Years ago he'd betrayed Lottie and lost her forever, creating this ever-widening chasm between them and their own children.

"Go back to the house," Charlotte ordered Boyle without looking at him. But she could feel his disapproving look, sitting up there on his horse, looking down at her, judging her. As if he could judge her more critically than she was doing herself. "Go!"

She crossed to where she'd left her socks and boots earlier, but didn't lower herself to the boulder to put them on until she'd heard him ride away. Sitting down heavily on the large, smooth stone, she started to lean over to pick up her socks. The pain and anger and fear came hand in hand, hard and fast, doubling her over. She opened her mouth to let out all the anguish inside her, but no scream emerged.

How much longer could she pretend she was all right? The wave of pity she felt for herself was what made her snatch up her socks and angrily pull them on over her sandy feet. Her daughter had been shot. Oakley, her baby. Who would do that?

Someone as angry as she often felt, she thought as she tugged on her boots. Why had she gone for the whip instead of her gun? Because she'd wanted to hurt Holden—not kill him. She promised herself if she ever caught him beside the creek at their old place again, she'd go for the gun—and she'd use it, ending this for both of them.

With a curse, she thought how much he looked the same. Older, just like her, his dark hair salted with gray, making him even more handsome. He still had the broad shoulders and slim hips, and she could attest to how strong he still was. But it was his blue eyes, what she'd seen in them, that had made her weaken.

She pushed the thought away and rose. Mounting her horse, she rode hard back toward the ranch house as if the memories were chasing her. Once there, she left her horse for Boyle to take care of, and she headed for the house and her cell phone.

But as she walked in, she saw Tilly and immediately knew that her daughter had been waiting for her. "Oakley?" Charlotte asked, heart rising to her throat.

"She made it through surgery, but she's in serious condition," Tilly said, her voice breaking with emotion. "I came home to get you."

Charlotte could see how upset her older daughter was. But she knew that if she tried to comfort her, she herself would break down. Neither of them needed that right now, so she didn't move. They had to get to

Oakley. "Just give me a few minutes to change," she said, feeling the sand between her toes and the taste of Holden McKenna on her lips. She had to get rid of both before she faced what was waiting for her at the hospital as she turned and headed up the stairs.

Now more than ever, she had to be strong. She'd shown enough weakness already today.

Stu CALLED IN the new state medical examiner, Frank Brewer. Powder Crossing was a small town without the kind of resources needed to investigate a shooting involving two families like the McKennas and Staffords. If Oakley died, Stu would be forced to call in the state crime investigators. He'd be glad to hand it over to them. But right now, it was still his investigation.

Brewer had flown to the local airfield, and the sheriff picked him up and brought him to the crime scene out on the county road. On the way, he'd filled Frank in on what Cooper had told him.

"It does appear she was being chased or thought she was, given the prints left in the earth under the trees," Brewer agreed once he'd seen the crime scene.

Deputy Dodson had been waiting. The three of them moved through the deep shadows of the cottonwood grove to the sound of crickets and grasshoppers. The dark canopy of leaves overhead had a suffocating feel, as if he couldn't draw enough breath. Stu was glad when they left the trees and entered the open area before the rugged badlands rose toward the sky. A ravine dotted with cedar and rock cliffs had carved a passage back into the mountains.

"She came riding out of there," Deputy Dodson said. He'd volunteered to protect the crime scene after dropping off Cooper at the sheriff's department. Clearly, he'd done some investigating on his own. "She wasn't alone. There was another rider with her—or at least behind her. I think it's someone she met back in there and things didn't go quite like either of them expected and he chased after her."

Stu shot him a warning look to shut up.

"She was already being chased through the ravine, from what I can tell," Dodson said, ignoring the warning as he turned to the medical examiner as if Stu wasn't even there. "What's odd is that when she came out, she headed for the woods. Whoever was chasing her followed for a ways, then went the other way back toward the McKenna Ranch house." They'd been following the tracks as they walked and now stopped at the edge of the opening that cut back into the mountains.

"Or the rider could have headed for the Stafford Ranch, since it is just beyond those hills over there," Stu said to Brewer, wanting to clarify that whoever was chasing Oakley didn't necessarily come from the McKenna Ranch house. As he did, he desperately wanted an excuse to send his deputy back to the road.

"If the other rider shot her, there is no indication here that she was already hit," Brewer said. "I haven't seen any blood. For her to make it all the way to the road as your eyewitness said, I'd say she must have made it as far as the trees before she was shot."

"Eyewitness," Dodson said, and scoffed. "My instincts are that Cooper McKenna's the one who shot her. Something about him bothers me."

His deputy had made his suspicions perfectly clear— no evidence to back it up aside.

Stu stepped away as he got a call from the lab. "Sheriff Layton," he said into the phone.

"You asked for an update on the bullet taken out of Oakley Stafford as soon as I had it," the lab tech said. "It's a 130-grain load from a 270 rifle. I'm checking to see if this particular rifle has been used in an earlier crime. I'll let you know."

Stuart figured it was a long shot that it had been used in another crime. He didn't believe that whoever had shot Oakley was a known criminal. But then again, he could be wrong.

"I'm going to have my deputies bring in some 270s to be tested. The sooner we find the owner of the weapon that fired that shot, the better."

"It's just me and another assistant. How many 270s are you talking about?"

"Not sure. Just do the best you can. Thanks."

The sheriff disconnected and called Judge Branson. "I need a warrant." He explained about the slug taken out of Oakley Stafford. "Thanks. Deputy Dodson will be stopping by to pick it up."

Dodson, he thought with a low growl. He wasn't sure how much longer he could take the young, cocky deputy. The slug that was removed from Oakley during surgery was from a 270 rifle, one of the most common makes in the valley. None of the weapons found in Cooper's pickup had been a 270. Nor did the caliber match.

Not that lack of evidence seemed to stop Dodson from his assumptions based on his impressions. Stu walked back to where the deputy was bending the medical examiner's ear. "I need you to go by Judge Branson's, pick up a warrant, then take Deputy Collins with you to collect all the rifles from both the McKenna and Stafford ranches."

"All of them?"

"All of them." He didn't want word getting out what model they were looking for. "Bag them and any ammo with them, identify the owner and owner's permit, if they have one, and take the rifles to the lab ASAP."

"What about the guns we took from Cooper McKenna's pickup?" Dodson demanded.

"None of them match what we're looking for. And, Deputy, I need you not to share any more of your suspicions or theories with anyone else."

Dodson looked as if he wanted to argue, but not in front of the state medical examiner, whom he'd been showing off for. Even though he looked as if he thought he was being sent on a wild-goose chase, he thankfully left without another word.

"Did I mention that he's new?" Stu said to the medical examiner.

Brewer sighed as they both watched Dodson disappear into the woods. "I hate to say it, but Dodson could be right about it being a romantic liaison, though I can think of more comfortable places to get together than in that rough, rocky terrain back there. Doesn't feel right, does it?"

No, Stu thought. It didn't. She'd ridden back into that ravine that went back into the mountains, but they had no idea for how long or why. But it was suspicious that the other rider headed in a different direction—one that could have taken him to the McKenna Ranch house or over the property line to the Stafford home.

COOPER ALREADY FELT as if he'd overstayed his welcome. But since the sheriff had pretty much told him not to leave town and he wasn't going anywhere without his guns, he headed for the ranch. He figured he might as well get it over with. By now, his father would have heard about Oakley and the man who found her after she was shot. No doubt Holden would be wondering why he hadn't already heard from him.

He hadn't seen his father in more than two years. They hadn't spoken since the last time he was at the ranch. They'd pretty much said all there was to say at the time—another reason he was unsure if he was even staying at the ranch tonight. The smart thing would have been to stay in a motel and let the dust settle.

But Cooper knew the dust wasn't going to settle for some time. The shooting would be the talk of the county. What made it more salacious was that a Stafford had been shot on McKenna land.

As he drove through the McKenna Ranch gate, he knew he couldn't put off the inevitable. He'd planned to sneak back into town, test the water, see if he was staying or not. But that hadn't happened. He would have to face everything, including why he'd left. Wasn't that why he'd come home? Because he was tired of running from it?

Still, it seemed like a bad idea to confront his father now, especially after what had happened earlier. When he'd gassed up the truck before leaving town, he'd heard the local speculation. Tongues were wagging as if the jury was already out. A romance gone wrong, and the obvious suspect was some cowboy from the McKenna Ranch. What was Oakley Stafford doing there if not meeting up with someone?

It did make sense. They were the same questions he was asking himself as he parked in front of the house. He doubted his father would have the answers, but he never knew since he'd been gone for so long. A lot could have changed. He shut off the engine and sat looking at the place where he was born and raised.

All the lights seemed to be on inside the McKenna Ranch house, making it look even more impressive than in the daylight. The sprawling three stories of wood and glass had withstood the weather and the years. His grandfather had commissioned the building of the massive place, clearly not just to impress but as the beginning of a legacy of McKennas who would work and add to this ever-expanding empire.

Cooper thought his grandfather, Edward Holden McKenna, had optimistically figured on a lot of sons passing on that legacy by having their own sons who were born to continue his work. Each son was to marry a rancher's daughter and bring her family's land into the McKenna holdings.

It was a dying legacy even on other ranches around Montana. This generation didn't have as many sons, and a lot of those sons wanted nothing to do with ranching, let alone being coerced into marrying a rancher's daughter for their land, just as it was rumored his father had done by marrying Margaret Smith. One of the Smith ranches was now part of the McKenna Ranch, so Cooper long suspected there was some truth in the rumors.

Climbing out of his pickup, he didn't bother to grab his duffel. He wasn't sure he'd be staying. He wasn't sure he'd be allowed to stay. With a sigh, he headed for the front door debating whether to knock, ring the bell or just walk in like he was a McKenna.

Fortunately, he didn't have to make that decision. He'd barely reached the porch when the door flew open and his sister, Bailey, ran out, screaming his name. She threw herself into his arms. He couldn't help laughing and feeling a little teary as his heart filled with love for his baby sister, who was now in her midtwenties.

He hugged her tightly before he pulled back to look at her. She'd only gotten more beautiful in the two years since he'd been gone. Her long dark hair, wavy and wild, framed a beautiful blue-eyed angelic face that hid her less-than-angelic nature. Just looking at her made his smile broaden. He hadn't realized how much he'd missed her.

"The prodigal son has returned," she announced, laughing. "Dad's probably out killing the fatted calf right now."

They both turned at the sound of someone clearing

his throat in the doorway. "Dad," Cooper said as Bailey stepped away.

"I should go see about something," she said with a grin. "Welcome back home, Coop," she said over her shoulder as she waltzed past their father. "I've missed you, if no one else has."

Standing on the dark porch, he could feel the night settling around him. He definitely should have stayed in town in a motel. To show up at this hour—

"Don't just stand there," Holden said. "Come on in." As he turned, he said, "You might want to grab whatever stuff you have from your truck. I had Elaine make up your old room."

Cooper stood for a moment, watching his father disappear into the house, his heart lodged in his throat. He wasn't sure what he'd expected after the words that had been exchanged between them before he'd left. He'd regretted their argument, ashamed of some of the things he'd said, no matter how true they were.

Now he felt chastised. His father had always been the bigger man. The surge of love he felt for him surprised Cooper as he turned to walk back to his pickup for his duffel. Holden McKenna wasn't the kind of man who hugged his sons or ever told them that he loved them. Most of the time, Cooper had suspected that he didn't even like his sons all that much and was constantly disappointed in all of his offspring, even Treyton. Not that anyone liked Treyton particularly, he thought as he grabbed his duffel and headed back to the house.

HOLDEN STOOD IN the living room with his back to the front door, staring out the window toward the river. There was just enough light that he could make out the rough outline of the nearby mountains against the deepening darkness of the night. How many times had he stood here contemplating his life and the mistakes he'd made? Too many times.

He turned at the sound of the front door closing to see his middle son standing there with a beat-up duffel bag and a sheepish look. Cooper was the more sensitive of his sons, having felt things more deeply. Holden loved that about him. But it also made Cooper restless. This son wanted more out of life, something Holden understood more than Cooper could ever know.

"It's good to see you," he said, thinking that his son couldn't have come back at a worse time in so many ways. He feared once Cooper knew everything that was going on, he would leave again. Holden wouldn't blame him if he did. He just hoped he'd stay. "Would you like a drink?" he asked as he motioned his son into the den and headed for the bar. "As I recall, you don't mind a shot of bourbon?"

"Thanks." He stepped in, setting down his duffel next to a chair but not sitting down.

Holden poured them both two fingers. Handing Cooper a glass, he motioned for him to sit and took a chair in front of the fireplace. He raised his drink. "I'm glad you're here." He took a sip; Cooper did the same and sat down in a nearby chair. His son didn't look as uncomfortable as Holden felt. Cooper was good at hiding his emotions, unless he was pushed too far—then he'd come out fighting. He wondered if his son knew how alike they were. He doubted it. He'd raised his family without their mother for so long that he feared he'd scarred them irrevocably.

But unlike his father, Cooper had a moral compass that was both admirable and unyielding.

"I'm not going to ask you how long you're staying or even if you're staying," Holden said finally. "But I do have to ask why you came back."

Cooper smiled, studied the bourbon in his glass for a moment before he raised his gaze and said, "I have no idea."

"Whatever your reasons, I'm glad you're here," Holden said, wondering how much he should tell him, then deciding not to get into it tonight. He didn't want Cooper walking out and never looking back this time.

At the knock at the front door, he rose to find two deputies standing on the porch. "We're here for your guns," Deputy Dodson said, and shoved a warrant at him.

CHAPTER FOUR

EARLY THE NEXT MORNING, Tilly found her mother sitting next to Oakley's bed at the hospital. She'd apparently been there all night. It was clear that her sister's condition hadn't changed.

She stayed for a little while, but left her mother beside Oakley's bed, unable to take any more of Charlotte's silent, dry-eyed fortitude. She had to do something besides sit next to her sister's bed, holding her hand and crying. She also had to stop thinking about the fact that her sister might not ever regain consciousness. She might die. Tilly couldn't comprehend that kind of loss.

She had to find the person who did this.

Earlier Stuart had stopped by to see how Oakley was doing and talk to her mother. He'd asked the same questions he'd asked Tilly. Her mother didn't know if Oakley had been seeing anyone. She didn't know what her daughter was doing on the McKenna Ranch.

"It doesn't matter what she was doing there," Tilly had cried. "They can't just shoot trespassers."

"Matilda." Her mother had reproved her and given her that disapproving look she'd withered under while growing up. For some reason, Charlotte thought she could make Tilly into something she wasn't—a replica of herself. From the time she was little, Tilly had more interest in being outdoors than in. She could be found out with the ranch hands learning to ride and shoot and rope, determined to be as good as the best of them. She hated being forced to stay inside and help with setting the table or, worse, being told to act like a lady.

Tilly had stayed long enough at the hospital to hear if Stuart had any leads. He didn't, apparently. His concern had been about the problems between the families and what this might lead to.

"Mrs. Stafford, I hope you can keep this incident from throwing more fuel on the fire between you and the McKennas," the sheriff had said, as if he thought her mother had any more control over Tilly than Stuart did himself. "Let me do my job without getting calls about your ranch hands or anyone in your family making this worse. Please just try to keep a lid on things so I can find the person who shot your daughter. That's all I'm asking."

Tilly had gotten the message, which had only made her angrier. She'd been glad when Stuart had left. When he'd said he would call her later, she'd only nodded, afraid what would come out of her mouth if she spoke. Did he really think he could tell her what to do after a half dozen dates? Or even as the county sheriff?

As she left the hospital, she kept thinking about Cooper and how he'd kept asking about Oakley's horse. The cowboy was dense as a cedar stump when it came to women, but he wasn't stupid. So why would he ask about the name of Oakley's horse?

All the way back to the ranch, it nagged at her. Once

home, she went straight to the stable. "Did the sheriff's department return Oakley's horse?" she asked the ranch hand brushing down one of the stable horses.

"I put her in her stall."

"It's the palomino mare, right? What's her name?" She could feel his questioning gaze. He knew the horses and their names better than she did, especially her sister's since Oakley changed horses the way some women changed shoes.

"Cheyenne. Are you all right?"

She turned to shoot him a scorching look. "My sister was shot and might die. No, I'm not all right." He had the good sense to glance away, mumbling *sorry* under his breath. But at her sharp words, she colored, realizing she was sounding like her mother.

At Cheyenne's stall, she opened the door and started to step in.

"I'm not sure I would do that," he said. "She keeps shying for no reason."

"There is a reason. Oakley was shot off her horse. Of course the horse is acting scared." Ignoring him, she stepped into the stall, talking quietly to the mare as she went. The horse shied, but she kept up murmuring to her in a soothing voice as she began to gently run both her gaze and her hands over the mare.

He was right—the mare hadn't been hurt. As she left the stables, she kept thinking about Cooper, his peculiar interest in Oakley's horse. She knew she wouldn't be able to rest until she found out why.

She took a chance and called the McKenna Ranch

as she was walking to her pickup. Bailey answered the phone. "Is Cooper there?"

She heard a laugh and Bailey say, "Women are already calling for you?" before a few moments passed and Cooper came to the phone. Fortunately, she hadn't recognized Tilly's voice.

"Hello?" He sounded leery.

Tilly groaned inwardly just thinking that he'd gotten the wrong impression. "Why did you ask me the name of Oakley's horse?"

It took him a moment since she'd apparently caught him flat-footed. He must have really thought it was some woman interested in him. What an ego.

"I can't talk right now. Could we meet somewhere?"

Her first instinct was to say no. It had been a simple question. But something in his voice made her hesitate. If he knew anything about who might have shot her sister— "At the café?"

"How about the rodeo grounds?" He was keeping his voice down, not wanting anyone to hear. That alone made her think that maybe he did know something. Something he wasn't even sure he wanted his family to know about.

"Thirty minutes?"

"See you there." And he was gone.

Tilly had reached her pickup. She pocketed her phone and climbed behind the wheel, frowning. The rodeo grounds were a few miles outside of town. He'd chosen a place where there wouldn't be anyone around for miles since the only time the place was used was when there was a rodeo or a fair.

She shook her head, reminding herself that Cooper McKenna had left Powder Crossing two years ago after being released on a murder charge because of a lack of evidence. Was she really going to meet him alone at the rodeo grounds—somewhere they would be completely alone—instead of at the café in town?

You bet she was, she thought, convinced he knew something about Oakley's shooting, and she planned to get whatever it was out of him. Cooper McKenna didn't scare her. Nor was she going to swoon when she saw him. She couldn't believe the way some women behaved around him.

WHEN SHE REACHED the rodeo grounds, she saw Cooper's pickup already parked at the gate. The grounds consisted of several barns, a few low buildings and a set of wooden bleachers. There had been a roof over the viewing stand until that bad windstorm last year. The town was planning to replace the cover before the Fourth of July. She thought they'd better get busy.

Cooper was sitting at the top of the bleachers.

She'd almost talked herself out of meeting him here as she started up the steps. A dust devil sent a cloud of red dirt into the air in the middle of the arena. She could hear crickets in the tall grass nearby and the creak of the wooden stairs as she climbed. She concentrated on her next step, but out of the corner of her eye, she could feel him watching her with those blue eyes of his from under the brim of his Stetson.

The cowboy was handsome—she'd give him that. He'd always pretended he didn't notice the way women acted around him. The thought made her smile since she didn't believe it for a moment. Cooper knew. It was one reason why she'd done her best to ignore him, pretending that she didn't find anything about him tempting.

Even if he hadn't been a McKenna, she would have kept her distance. He was a heartbreaker; any fool could see that. Tilly didn't mind tempting danger, but not when it came to her heart. Also, there was that black cloud hanging over him after his last girlfriend had either killed herself or been murdered. While the case had been closed as a suicide, there were still those people in the county who maintained it had probably been murder. A lot of people thought both the McKennas and the Staffords would get away with murder because of their standing in the county.

Cooper got to his feet as she approached. "Thanks for coming."

"You made it sound…important and secretive." She motioned to where he'd suggested they meet and gave him a questioning look.

"I'm probably just being paranoid, but your sister was shot, and I got the impression she was running for her life when she came racing at breakneck speed out of the trees and onto the road."

She thought about Oakley running for her life and now fighting for it in the hospital, and had to swallow.

He motioned for her to sit and lowered himself back to the bench. She watched him stretch out his long legs and lean back. He looked even better than when he'd left, his Western shirt stretched across what appeared to be rock-hard abs, the muscles in his shoulders bunching. He was tanned, some new lines at the corners of his eyes. His dark hair was longer, curling out from the edges of his hat.

Okay, she could kind of see some of the attraction, she thought as she sat on the edge of the seat a few feet away from him and looked out at the view, rather than at the cowboy. Miles of river bottom were intersected by groves of cottonwoods before the land climbed into rugged mountains dotted with cedar and, higher up, ponderosa pines and rocky cliffs. It looked Western to her, like the old cowboy movies her mother was fond of. Maybe that was the appeal. To Tilly, it had always been home on a ranch she planned to run someday.

"I know you thought it was odd that I asked you about the name of her horse," Cooper said, and she felt his gaze on her. "You're sure the horse she was riding wasn't called Buttercup?"

"Buttercup?" Tilly shook her head. "Why would you think that?"

"Because when I got to her, she was clearly in pain and under duress. She said only one word, *Buttercup*. I told her that her horse was fine, since that's what I thought she was worried about. Then she repeated the word as if I should know what that meant. It doesn't mean anything to you?"

She frowned. Buttercup? "That's all she said?" He nodded. "I have no idea." He looked disappointed and embarrassed, as if all this secrecy had been for nothing. "That was it?"

"All that she said."

Tilly heard the hesitation in his voice. "But not all that happened."

He met her gaze, holding it for a long moment before he said, "It's probably nothing, but I heard a small plane's engine just before your sister and her horse shot out into the road and she fell."

That did sound like nothing since there were often small planes around these parts, most usually crop dusters.

"As I was on the ground next to my pickup with Oakley, the plane flew over really low." He shook his head. "Like I said, it was probably nothing."

"Unless the pilot saw the person who shot my sister," she said.

"If he had, then he hasn't come forward, or we would have heard," Cooper pointed out.

"What kind of plane?" she asked.

"A blue-and-white Piper Super Cub."

"A two-seater, so it might not have just been the pilot in the plane when it flew over," Tilly said as she got to her feet. "There can't be that many blue-and-white Piper Super Cubs around, right? I want to talk to that pilot and whoever might have been sitting behind him."

"HOLD ON," Cooper said as she started down the bleacher steps with him at her heels.

"If there is even a chance that he or his passenger saw something," she said over her shoulder, "I plan to talk to them."

"Wait—" He grabbed her shoulder as she reached the bottom and spun her around to face him. "Maybe the pilot or his passenger did see something. Or maybe..." He wasn't sure how to say it, so he just spit it out. "...the passenger shot your sister." Her eyes widened. She opened her mouth to speak, but he cut her off. "It's illegal but not that unusual for a rancher to take someone up armed with a rifle to kill coyotes or other animals from the air."

"Take someone up like you?"

He looked away, remembering a time when killing an animal he didn't plan to eat hadn't bothered him. That had been a very long time ago. "What I'm saying is that the shooting could have been an accident, but even so, the pilot isn't going to want to talk to you. It might even be dangerous if his passenger had been armed and breaking the law."

She planted her hands on her hips. "Which is even more reason to find this plane and the pilot."

"I agree, but I would suggest not coming on like gangbusters."

The look she gave him was so familiar that he almost laughed. For years, while growing up, Tilly had been his biggest competition at every rodeo and fair. Every contest he entered, he ended up going head-to-head with her. He'd seen that determination burning in those green eyes of hers too many times.

"If you're afraid, don't worry. I was planning to go by myself," she said, and turned, already a few steps ahead of him.

"You're not going by yourself," he said as he caught up to her. "I'm going with you." She gave him a side-long look but said nothing. "Don't make me sorry I told you." In truth, he was sorry. He could see how much she wanted to find the person who had shot her sister. But now he'd given her probably false hope. There was a slim chance that Oakley had been shot from the plane.

At the same time, it was a relief that Tilly had taken what he told her seriously. He couldn't help feeling there was something suspicious about the plane. That the pilot had flown over him so low like that had nagged at him last night. He'd lain in his room at the ranch unable to forget seeing Oakley come racing out of the woods. He remembered the terrified look on her face. She had been running from something very dangerous.

He'd kept thinking about the way she'd tried to pass him a message. Buttercup. It hadn't made any sense. Still didn't. But whatever it meant, it was important at least to her. He suspected it was why she'd been shot.

"We'll take my truck," Tilly said. "I'll drive."

He wasn't about to argue as he climbed into the passenger side.

HOLDEN WATCHED HIS eldest son pace the living room floor. He knew Oakley Stafford's shooting had everyone on edge. But he couldn't help being surprised at how Treyton was taking it.

"They'll be coming after us," Treyton said as he paced. "They're going to make it look like one of us shot her. We need to be ready. I can't believe that you just let them take our rifles."

One of the biggest fears of most Montanans, Holden knew only too well, was that someday someone would take their guns. It had never happened, but it was a fear his father and grandfather had shared.

"This isn't that," he told Treyton. "The lab will run ballistics on our firearms. If one of them wasn't the weapon that fired the bullet that struck Oakley, then the sheriff will bring them back. Let's not turn this into something it's not," he said as patiently as he could.

Glancing at the time, he needed to put a damper on his son's paranoia and get going. He didn't want to be late for his appointment.

Yesterday, he'd gone out to the ranch manager's house. Deacon Yates had gathered the ranch hands for him. Holden had hated to ask, but he knew he had to.

"If any of you might know anything about Oakley Stafford's shooting, I need you to tell me," he'd said as he looked around the bunkhouse. He knew all of the ranch hands, trusted most of them. They were young and often headstrong. The older ones worried him more, especially when it came to the McKenna-Stafford bad blood.

"I know that after the vandalism on our ranch, some of you might have wanted to pay back the Staffords, even though we can't be sure they were responsible." Several men grumbled that they knew otherwise. The same individuals who had gotten into fights with Stafford ranch hands before.

"Even if a few hotheads from their ranch are responsible for the vandalism, I don't condone any kind of retribution," Holden said. "As I've told you, any hand caught continuing this vendetta will be fired. But this shooting is serious. I'm hoping that if any of you know something, you will come to me. I will help you any way I can, including hiring you a lawyer if you were the one who pulled the trigger, because I want you to have a fair trial."

The room had gone deathly quiet. "Violence is unacceptable. I can't say that enough. This has to stop."

"Tell *them* that," said Rusty Malone, one of the older ranch hands who'd been in the brawl in town with the Stafford men.

"I'm telling you, Rusty," Holden said, trying not to lose his patience. "If you have a problem with it, you know the road off the ranch."

Rusty looked as if he had more to say but was smart enough not to.

Holden told the men that the deputies had taken their rifles as part of the investigation. They would be returned. Then he'd thanked them all for complying with the warrant and left. Now he was anxious to get to his appointment.

"Treyton," he said, interrupting his son who'd been going off about something. He hadn't really been listening, worried about getting to his appointment on time and so much more. "I've already told the men that I don't want trouble. I don't want you stirring them all up. The Staffords are not coming after us, and we're not preparing for war."

"We're already at war with them," he shot back. "They do any more coalbed methane drilling and we won't have any water. The Staffords are trying to put us out of business. If we don't fight back—"

Holden rose. "I don't have time for this right now. Let me deal with Charlotte Stafford."

"Like you have in the past?" his son said sarcastically.

"Would you see to that fence to the north?" It was the farthest point from the Stafford Ranch and trouble. At least he hoped that would be the case. "Take a few men with you. Take Malone. While you're up there, check out the pasture grass. We might need to move that herd."

Treyton nodded but clearly wasn't finished. "What about Cooper? He back to stay? He planning on working for his keep or just—"

"Leave your brother to me. In fact, when I get back from my appointment, I hope to get you all together to discuss a couple of things."

His son looked surprised and suspicious. "If this has anything to do with Cooper's return—"

"It doesn't. Just a family meeting. It's time we had one, don't you think?"

Holden left to avoid further discussion. Everything would be clear when he returned tonight. Though he dreaded the outcome. Treyton was worried about the Staffords destroying the ranch?

What Holden had to tell them tonight could destroy his often tenuous relationship with his family.

THE CLOSEST AIRPORT with a paved landing strip was in Miles City. But Powder Crossing had its own small airfield that was used by crop dusters and other pilots in the area. Cooper had suggested they start there instead of making the four-hour round trip to Miles City.

The local airfield had a wind sock and a grass landing strip the last time Cooper had been there. A small plane was coming in as they drove up. He noticed several new hangars had been added since the last time he'd been out here.

"Who built the hangars?" Cooper asked as Tilly drove them to a small shack-like building that was apparently now an office.

"One of the mining companies, CH4," she said, pointing to a small sign on one of the hangar doors.

"CH4?"

"The compound for methane gas. You didn't take any chemistry in college?"

"Too busy going to keggers," he joked. He knew what the compound was. He was just surprised that the gas exploration and drilling company was working out of here so much that they'd built their own hangar. He'd seen that name in the news over a recent controversy about their methods for talking ranchers into drilling on their land.

As the small plane taxied to a spot in the open field, Tilly parked and they got out. There were two small planes already parked in the field, both crop dusters. "Any chance CH4 has been talking your mother into drilling more wells on your ranch?" he asked her.

She shot him a warning look. "We're looking for my sister's would-be killer. We aren't on the same team."

"Really? I figured you'd be against the drilling."

Tilly sighed. "I am. But let's stay away from talk about our families' plans, okay?"

He held up his hands. "You make it sound like we're on opposing football teams and discussing what our families are doing is trying to throw the game."

"We aren't just on opposing teams—we're on rival

teams that make the Brawl of the Wild between the MSU Bobcats and the UofM Grizzlies teams look like a picnic."

"Don't tell me you're a Grizzly fan."

She shot him an impatient look. "Seriously?"

"Sorry. Just so you know up front, I'm a Bobcat fan. But back to CH4. I suspect they've been coming around the McKenna Ranch too."

"Only your father's been chasing them off." She sighed. "We probably shouldn't talk about this, our families and their choices. It's probably what started this stupid feud years ago."

He knew she was right. "No judgment. Just curious."

"I'm a Bobcat fan," she said under her breath, making him grin as the pilot of the small plane that had just landed finished inside the cockpit and climbed out, briefcase in hand. As they approached him, they heard the sound of a vehicle coming up the road behind them.

"Nice flight?" Cooper asked.

"Pretty day for it," the pilot said, and held out his hand. "Bob Turner. You're a McKenna, right?"

"Cooper," he said, frowning as he took the man's hand.

"I did some legal work for your dad quite a few years ago."

"Bob's an attorney in Billings," Tilly said. "He flies back and forth weekly. How is your mom, by the way?"

"Good some days, not so much others. My wife stays with her now until…until we decide future arrangements."

Cooper knew he meant whether or not they would

be keeping the ranch once his mother died. "You own the Montana 360 Ranch."

"My mother does," Bob said. "There's my wife now." He started to step toward the SUV that had just driven up.

"We were wondering if you'd seen a blue-and-white Piper Super Cub around lately," Tilly asked before Cooper could. Bob hesitated. "Cooper's interested in buying it."

The pilot glanced at him. "I didn't realize you had your pilot's license."

"The craft would have flown in and out of here yesterday, but if you weren't around…" Tilly said.

"It's in the far hangar," Bob said. "But I didn't hear anything about it being for sale. If you'll excuse me. It's been a long day, and I'm anxious to see how my mother is." He stepped past, going to the car and climbing in the passenger side.

"I'm in the market for a plane?" Cooper said.

"I could have said the pilot and his passenger might know something about my sister's shooting, but he didn't seem anxious to give us any information as it was," she said as they turned to watch the SUV kick up dust into the late-June morning.

"I get the feeling he thinks we're interested in his mother's ranch," Cooper said. "Apparently our parents have a reputation for buying up any land that comes on the market even before people like his mother dies."

"That could be it," she said. "But in case you are unaware, the methane drilling has split this community as well as families. Everyone around here has an opinion about methane as well as those making a living drilling for it."

Tilly headed for her pickup and he followed, wondering what a CH4 plane was doing flying over the McKenna Ranch yesterday at the same time Oakley was shot. As far as he knew, his father was still standing firm against anyone drilling for methane on the McKenna Ranch. Maybe more to the point, did the plane and its occupants have anything to do with why a Stafford was trespassing on the McKenna Ranch? Or why she was shot?

"Your sister ever mention how she felt about the methane debate?" he asked as he slid into the passenger truck seat again. She gave him that look. "Come on—you have to be asking yourself the same thing. If you want to find the person who shot her, then we're going to have to talk about our families."

She had started the engine but didn't shift the pickup into gear. Nor did she look at him. He figured she was preparing for a fight. He thought it wasn't beyond the realm of possibility that he'd be walking back to the rodeo grounds where he'd left his pickup.

"You sure you want to go there?" Tilly asked as she looked over at him. He gave her what he hoped was a think-we-have-to shrug. She took a deep breath and let it out before she said, "Oakley was opposed to the drilling. She tried to stop my mother. I'm not sure that they've spoken since."

Cooper nodded. "Interesting, but it doesn't explain what she was doing on the McKenna Ranch, though."

"Maybe it does," she said as she turned to him. "I

happened to see your brother Treyton talking to one of the higher-ups from CH4 one night outside the Buffalo Bar in Miles City. Don't ask. It was a friend's bachelorette party. But I wasn't so drunk that I missed the handshake between your brother and the gas company bigwig. They definitely looked as if they were making a deal."

CHAPTER FIVE

AFTER A DAY of butting heads with members of both the McKenna and the Stafford families, Stuart couldn't wait to go off the clock for a few hours.

He'd done everything he could on the investigation, including leaving a dozen or more 270 rifles his deputies had picked up in their search of the two ranches at the lab for ballistic tests. He hated to think about the angry phone calls he'd gotten on taking the rifles— even for a short time. He just wanted a quiet evening at home with a beer, a movie and the woman he'd wanted for a very long time.

"How about we just stay in tonight and watch a movie?" he asked Tilly when he called. A week ago, they had talked about going into Miles City to see a band they liked there.

"Maybe another night. I'm sure you've had a horrible day too." She sounded wrung out. He knew the feeling.

"Seeing you would make my day better." No response. "Does this have anything to do with Cooper?"

"What?"

Stu knew at once that he'd stepped in it. "Sorry, I was just looking forward to being with you and having a normal evening together. I'm making popcorn."

He could hear by her silence that she was still upset, but thinking about his offer. "I even bought your favorite wine."

"I do need to talk to you." She sighed. "I'm on my way, but I'm not staying long."

She needed to talk to him? He didn't like the sound of that. He hated how jealous he'd been earlier. Tilly and Cooper had always had an adversarial relationship, fiercely competitive. If he hadn't seen the two of them together that one time... He'd never been able to get it out of his mind. They'd been standing outside the barn at the fair in the semidarkness. Cooper had her backed up to the wall, one palm pressed against the wood next to her head, the other tilting her face up to his.

It was the look that passed between them before they realized he was standing there. Tilly shrugged off Cooper's hand and pushed past him, saying, "That really doesn't work on me, McKenna." Cooper had chuckled, the moment passing.

But Stuart knew what he'd seen. There was something between the two of them, always had been, looking back. A denied passion that manifested itself as they tried to outdo each other competitively. It was why when he'd heard his friend was back in town, he'd felt his heart drop. Stuart had only been dating Tilly for a few weeks. He needed more time. More time without Cooper around.

Now, as he opened the door to her, he saw that Tilly was still upset. Of course she was. Her sister had been shot, was lying in the hospital, still in serious condition. He pulled her in for a hug, and she came willingly enough but was the first to break contact. He tried not to read anything into that as he led her into the kitchen, where he'd just finished making a big bowl of popcorn.

"Help yourself," he said, handing her a bowl. "I found a movie I thought you might like."

She put her bowl down on the counter without touching the popcorn. "I need to ask you about the plane Cooper saw after Oakley was shot."

Talking shop was the last thing he had wanted to do. But he could understand that it was probably the only thing Tilly had on her mind right now. He leaned back against the counter. "I have one of my deputies checking on it. Why?"

"Cooper and I went out to the airstrip. We talked to a pilot there. He said it belongs to CH4, that coalbed methane gas development group, the same one that has been drilling on my family's ranch."

She and Cooper? He knew he shouldn't have been surprised. "So?"

"Doesn't that seem suspicious to you?" she demanded.

"It's not that unusual since they are doing business here."

"That plane was flying over the McKenna Ranch."

"That isn't restricted airspace."

Her eyes widened. "Aren't you going to at least ask the pilot if he saw something?"

"Of course I am. Tilly, what are you doing?"

"I'm trying to find out who shot my sister!"

"So am I, only I have the badge, I'm an officer of

the law. It's my job. I don't want you investigating on your own, especially with Cooper."

She drew back. "I beg your pardon?"

"He's a McKenna, you're a Stafford. I'm doing my best to keep a lid on this, but I shouldn't have to tell you how your brothers would feel about your attempts to track down a possible killer with the man who found Oakley."

She looked as if steam might come out of her ears. "What are you saying? You can't believe that Cooper had anything to do with—"

"Of course not." He held up his hands. "We already checked his guns. He doesn't even own a 270, so he definitely did not shoot Oakley."

"She was shot with a 270?"

He swore. "I misspoke. That information cannot get out." He sighed. "Do we really have to talk about this tonight? I'll talk to the pilot, see if he saw anything. I know what I'm doing." Her look questioned that. He took a step toward her. "Tilly."

She took a step back. "I can't do this. Not tonight." With that, she walked out, leaving him mentally kicking himself for getting into it with her. Was it Cooper he was angry with for coming back or for getting Tilly involved in the investigation? Right now? Both.

HOLDEN CLEARED HIS throat as he got to his feet. He'd gathered the family in his den. His daughter, Bailey, was staring at her phone screen. His youngest son, Duffy, was squirming after mumbling, "Let's make it quick. I have a date." Treyton had refused to sit and was now standing next to the fireplace, tapping the fingers of one hand impatiently on the mantel. Cooper was slumped in one of the chairs, fiddling with his Stetson balanced on one knee of his crossed legs, his mind clearly elsewhere.

His family, Holden thought, aware of the mistakes he'd made as a father. Worse, he feared he was about to make a huge one right now.

"I have some news," he said, raising his voice to make sure he had all of their attentions. The problem was that he didn't know how to say it, so he just blurted it out. "We're going to have a new member in the family."

Well, the blunt statement worked. They frowned at him, shared questioning glances at each other, then moved from him to Cooper.

"Who'd you knock up?" Treyton demanded of his brother.

"It isn't one of you," Holden said quickly, which brought their gazes back to him. Treyton swore and started to walk out. "It isn't me either," he said. He was doing a terrible job of this.

"Her name is Holly Jo Robinson. She's twelve and she's going to be living with us."

"Why?" Bailey asked, glancing up from her phone. "Is she an exchange student or something?"

"Tell me she speaks English," Treyton said.

"Too bad she isn't old enough to date," Duffy joked.

Holden had thought about telling them everything. He knew he was covering his bets by keeping the truth to himself until he saw how this was going to work out.

That he was even thinking that filled him with shame. He'd made a promise years ago, one that he now questioned but, come hell or high water, he was bound to keep.

"Holly Jo lost her father, a man I knew, and now her mother has died. I promised years ago that I would help any way I could if I was ever needed."

"Do you really think bringing her here to live on the ranch is the best way to help?" Treyton demanded.

"It's what I've decided. I want you all to make her feel at home. I'll be bringing her back here tomorrow. I'm depending on all of you to make this adjustment easy for her. Keep in mind, she's lost both of her parents. Maybe we could show her a little compassion?"

"Sounds like a bad idea," Treyton said. "But whatever. Shouldn't we talk about Oakley Stafford?"

"From what I've heard, she's still in serious condition," Holden said, but should have known that wasn't his son's concern.

"What was she doing on our property?" Treyton demanded. "Don't you think we should get some answers?"

"I think we should all pray that she survives," Cooper said.

"Because you had something to do with her getting shot?" Treyton wanted to know.

With a sigh, Cooper got to his feet. "It's been a long day. If you'll all excuse me." He started out of the room.

"Cooper's right," Holden said. "I think that's enough for tonight."

"So that's how it's going to be?" Treyton pulled an

angry face. "We don't get any say about who you let into this house? Cooper leaves for two years and you just welcome him back with open arms. Have you forgotten why he left?"

"Treyton—"

"Well, I haven't. Now he might have killed another woman—"

"Stop!" Holden hadn't meant to yell. "I never want to hear you say that again. Cooper is your brother. He's back. Let it go."

Treyton shook his head. "You're making a huge mistake." With that, he stormed out of the room.

"Guess that's it, then," Duffy said as he walked out. "I've got a date."

Bailey was still looking at her phone screen.

Holden appealed to her, hoping to have at least one member of his family backing him. "I was hoping you'd make this transition easier for Holly Jo."

His daughter looked up and smiled. She was beautiful. Spoiled rotten, but he only had himself to blame. "If you think we're going to do each other's hair and sit on my bed and talk about boys, you're delusional. She's *twelve*. Just tell her to stay clear of my room," she said, getting to her feet. "I catch her in there and there is going to be trouble." With that, she walked out.

"Great," he said to the empty den. In a way, things had gone better than he'd hoped. He told himself that he would pick up Holly Jo tomorrow, bring her back, get her settled in and then deal with everything else.

Every day seemed like a battle to save not just the ranch, but this way of life. Lottie was making it more difficult. After what had happened yesterday, he figured things were going to get much worse.

With that cheerful thought, he poured himself a drink and told himself that maybe having a tween in the house was exactly what they all needed... Bailey was right. He was delusional.

COOPER DIDN'T GO straight to his room. Instead, he went for a walk around the ranch as twilight deepened. The late-June night was clear and warm. Stars began to pop out overhead. A sliver of silver moon peeked out from behind the rugged silhouette of the badlands to the east.

As he walked along the river, he noticed that some of the leaves in the nearby cottonwoods were already starting to turn. Usually, it took a frost. This year it was the drought. He noticed how low the river was and now they'd lost one of their largest producing wells.

The ranch couldn't survive without water. A few more hot summers, no rain, more drought and he wasn't sure what they would do. He thought about Bob Turner and his mother's ranch. The Montana 360 Ranch had plenty of water. It would be a good addition to the Mc-Kenna Ranch if it came up for sale. But there would be competition for it, Charlotte Stafford the biggest one since that land fit nicely next to the McKenna and Stafford ranches like a missing puzzle piece.

He'd seen the worry in his father's face. Hard country made men tough, according to his father. Cooper disagreed. He thought it made them hardheaded.

There was no one more stubborn than his father or tough and determined. Cooper had seen that steely look in his eyes. He wouldn't give up this ranch without the fight of his life—even knowing that it was going to kill him.

He remembered the night he'd left here two years ago. His father had followed him out to his pickup.

"You're just going to turn tail and run?" Holden had demanded.

"I know when I'm defeated," he'd said, tossing in the duffel. "Do you?"

His father had shaken his head. "Only cowards run."

Cooper had laughed. "Or smart men who know better than to beat a dead horse."

"You're talking foolishness. You're a McKenna. We don't quit. We don't run. We take a stand."

"Is that what you did thirty-five years ago when you married Margaret Smith for her ranch?"

He'd seen his father's face fall, the low blow making the big man stagger back. Cooper had wanted to take back the words immediately. That he'd struck too close to the truth was obvious from his father's expression. He could have said he was sorry, but he hadn't because he'd been about to ask what he really wanted to know.

"What about thirty-two years ago?" He saw his father's eyes widen. "Don't you think it's time you put all the rumors to rest? Or at least tell me the truth?" Cooper had demanded. "Am I the bastard son?" This was something that had been skulking below the surface between them for years. Now it was out.

He'd wanted his father to deny it outright. But instead, Holden had shaken his head, turned and walked away, his spine rigid, but enough slope to his shoulders that Cooper had felt sick with what he'd done.

As he'd climbed into his pickup and started the engine, he'd feared that he'd burned the last bridge between them. He'd thought he would never see his father again, and that had been the way he'd wanted it. That his father had taken him back so easily didn't make him feel better about the question that remained between them.

But he had no idea how to get over it because there was still that question between them, a question only Holden could answer. Treyton had held it over Cooper's head for years, calling him a bastard, taunting him with the truth.

This life hardened everything, even hearts, he thought now. It drove families apart, sent mothers away, left the men bitter and alone, their sons coming up in their footsteps with even less hope of surviving it. Cooper could see that ranching, maybe especially in the Powder River Basin, was a dying way of life. More and more ranches had sold out to large conglomerates or the rich and wealthy, who seemed to be in a race to own more of everything—even land they would never use.

He could understand why some of the ranchers had bought into what the gas companies were selling, allowing the coalbed methane wells on their property for ready cash in the belief that it was a win-win proposition. The ranchers made easy money on the promise that they wouldn't even know the well was there.

Except that the process of getting the gas from the coalbed took gallons and gallons of water, lowering the aquifer, drying up ranchers' wells in a place where water meant everything. When the gas wells no longer produced, they were often abandoned by the gas companies to leak contaminated water into the ground.

It didn't escape him that Tilly had said her sister had been opposed to the drilling on Stafford property—and that one of the main gas corporation's airplanes had been flying close by when Oakley had been shot.

His cell phone rang. *Tilly?* "Hello?"

"I got the name of the pilot who was flying the plane. Want to go with me to talk to him in the morning?"

He hesitated only a moment while he reminded himself that whoever had fired that shot at Oakley might have been trying to kill her. Tilly could be going to meet a would-be killer who wouldn't miss the next time. "Of course."

"Good."

"How is she?" he asked.

"Same. Seven good for you? I thought we could meet for breakfast. There's something you need to know."

"In Powder Crossing?"

"Yes, at the Cattleman Café. Unless you don't want to be seen in public with me."

"See you there."

He waited for her to disconnect. When she didn't, he asked, "Is there something else?"

"No, we can talk tomorrow. Night."

As he pocketed his phone, he tried to imagine what she needed to tell him. Something about the case? He figured he would know soon enough.

Yet when he went up to his room, sleep was the last

thing he thought about. Grabbing his duffel, he unpacked what few things he'd kept. Moving a lot, he couldn't hang on to much, which was fine with him. If he was staying, though, he'd have to pick up some more clothes.

He put away what clothes he had, then went to stuff the duffel into another drawer, when he spotted something on a nearby shelf. He recognized the book spine, surprised the book was there.

When he'd left this room back then, he'd packed quickly, taking only what he considered necessities. Why did he still have Leann Hayes's favorite book? Because he'd forgotten about it after her death. For a moment, he was poleaxed by the memories of that horrible time in his life. It was bad enough that she killed herself, but the prosecutor at the time had been convinced Cooper had played a part in her death. When he'd left two years ago, he'd been in rough shape. He'd just been released from jail for lack of evidence in her death. No wonder he hadn't noticed that she'd put the book up there.

Swallowing, his throat having gone dry at the sight of the book, he realized that he now didn't know what to do with it. Throw it away? Put Leann behind him? It should have been easy. They'd hardly known each other, neither of them in love, both killing time in thinking they would leave one day—and not together. Dwelling on her death as he had for the past two years had gotten him nowhere. He still had no idea why she'd apparently killed herself, since her death had finally been ruled a suicide. Not that a lot of people believed it.

Yet he knew he couldn't just throw the book in the

trash any more than he could forget. He left it where it was, on the top shelf for the time being. Everything was for the time being, he told himself as he looked around his room. What was he doing back here?

Maybe more disconcerting was, what was he doing playing detective with Tilly Stafford? If not a recipe for disaster, he didn't know what was.

CHAPTER SIX

Tilly hadn't slept well after her argument with Stuart. She knew she shouldn't have gone over to his place in the mood she'd been in. Not that he wasn't equally responsible for the way things had gotten out of control. Had he really told her to stay away from Cooper as well as stop trying to find out who'd shot Oakley?

It's my sister. As long as she was trying to find Oakley's shooter, she didn't worry constantly about whether her sister would wake up or not. Tilly just needed to feel like she was doing something to help.

But she knew her butting into his investigation was only part of the problem. It wasn't her interfering in the investigation that bothered Stuart as much as her investigating with Cooper.

Stuart was jealous. Jealous of Cooper McKenna? Was he a complete fool? She and Cooper? Ridiculous. They could hardly stand each other. The only reason they were doing this together was that he was the one who'd found Oakley. He'd been there when she'd needed his help. No matter what Stuart said, she wasn't going to stop looking into her sister's shooting.

But meeting Cooper for breakfast was more out of spite. They had no reason to hide. If Stuart didn't like it, too bad. Nor was she going to stop looking for the shooter.

Yesterday afternoon, she'd made a few calls. Her mother had a number for CH4 since they were the company who'd put in the methane well on the ranch. She'd used her "sweet" voice and within minutes had the name of the pilot of the blue-and-white CH4 Piper Super Cub.

She could have gone to talk to Howie Gunderson alone, but she needed to see Cooper anyway. Also, if Howie's passenger had been the one who'd shot Oakley, then it might be nice to have the cowboy along for backup.

His pickup was already parked outside of the café when she arrived. It was early enough that there weren't many people inside. She found Cooper sitting at a small corner table in the back. There were two menus and two cups on the table. His cup was half-full of coffee.

He looked up and started to get to his feet, but she was too quick. She'd already pulled out a chair and sat down across from him. "You ordered yet?"

"I was waiting for you."

She tried to tamp down her annoyance. It made it easier to remember why she didn't like him when he wasn't being so polite. The waitress arrived with a pot of coffee, filled her cup and asked if they needed a minute.

"Chicken-fried steak, eggs medium, hash browns and whole wheat toast," she said in answer. It was going to be a long day, and she wasn't sure when she'd get to eat again. Also, she'd skipped supper last night. She'd lain in bed thinking about the big bowl of popcorn Stuart had made her and wishing she hadn't stormed out of there so quickly.

"I'll take the same," Cooper said, and handed the waitress the menus with his thanks as he made eye contact. The woman beamed, her cheeks reddening.

Tilly wanted to groan. Not that it was anything new, the way women responded to Cooper. "I've been dating Stuart." Why had she said that? She felt her own cheeks redden with embarrassment. It made her sound desperate that she felt she had to tell him she'd been dating someone. Not just someone. His best friend. After her argument with the sheriff last night, she wasn't even sure it was true anymore. But, she told herself, she'd said it because she didn't want Cooper to think she'd been keeping it from him.

"Okay," he said, showing no emotion.

"I just thought you should know."

"Okay." He looked confused, which only irritated her more.

"It's just that if we keep looking for my sister's shooter together…"

He seemed to be waiting to see where she was headed with that thought, as if almost daring her to finish it. If she saw even the hint of a grin, she swore she would dump his coffee over his head on her way to the door.

"So what's the name of the pilot we're going to see?"

COOPER COULDN'T HELP being confused. Had Tilly thought hearing that she was dating his best friend would upset him? He and Tilly had been adversaries from as far back as he could remember. Even in kindergarten he remembered the two of them competing when it came to everything. Even coloring. She had seemed to think that she was the only one who could color inside the lines.

He'd found himself mentally shaking his head, unsure why she had felt the need to tell him she'd been dating Stuart. Fortunately, he'd hidden his reaction. *Tilly and Stuart?* Sorry, but he couldn't see it. Stuart was his best friend, but the sheriff was analytical, approaching everything in life with caution—just the opposite of Tilly. Also, Stuart lived by the letter of the law.

Tilly was a free spirit, a wild young woman excited about life, willing to try anything, and while she had been able to color inside the lines in kindergarten, she didn't approach living that way at all. Which was probably why Cooper had always been drawn to her, he realized.

"Howie Gunderson," Tilly said, keeping her voice down although there weren't any patrons close by. He must have frowned as if he couldn't remember what they'd been talking about, because she added, "That's the name of the pilot. The plane is his, apparently, but he works pretty much full-time for CH4, flying their executives as well as geologists in and around the area."

"Do we know if he had a passenger with him that day?" Cooper asked.

"Not yet. That's why we're going to talk to him." She was all business again. When food came, she dug in.

He couldn't help but wonder why she seemed… What? Disappointed in his reaction about her and Stuart? How had she expected him to react? She'd said they were dating. He started to wonder exactly what that meant but stopped himself. None of his business. In fact, after talking to the pilot, he didn't see any reason he and Tilly had to see each other again. He thought of it as fraternizing with the enemy. Wasn't that the way Treyton would have put it, had he known?

That was another problem with him and Tilly doing this together. It would be hard to keep it a secret. Especially after having breakfast together here in town. It would be impossible for word not to spread throughout the county by noon. This kind of news moved faster than a grass fire.

His gaze went to Tilly. So why had she suggested meeting here? She wasn't trying to make Stuart jealous, was she?

"There's something else," she said between bites, as if just deciding to tell him. He braced himself. She and Stuart weren't getting engaged, were they? The thought hit him hard, harder than he would have expected. He tried to imagine what would be worse. Pregnant?

She cleared her throat and lowered her voice. "Stuart let it slip, so it's just between you and me?" He nodded. She leaned toward him. A teasing pleasant scent crossed the table. Not perfume. Maybe her body wash. Maybe her shampoo? He breathed it in a little deeper. "Oakley was shot with a 270 rifle."

That took him by surprise, but no more than how relieved he was that she and Stuart weren't engaged, let alone having a baby together. It would have just been wrong, not that he had a dog in the fight.

HOLDEN SAW THE girl's face at the edge of the curtains as he drove up in front of the house and parked. All he got was a glimpse of large blue eyes, short choppy dark hair and a mouth set in a grim line. He hadn't seen Holly Jo since she was born—the same day he made her mother the promise that he was now about to keep.

As he exited his vehicle, he looked up to see if she was still peering out. The face was gone. By the time he reached the front door, it opened.

An older woman stood, hands on hips, glaring at him. "You're late." He started to explain, but she cut him off as she yelled toward the stairway. "Holly Jo, get your scrawny butt down here. Now. Don't make me come up there after you."

She turned back to him. "That's her bag," she said, pointing to the single small suitcase on the floor by the door. "She cut up most of her clothes with a pair of scissors, all except a pair of jeans and an old flannel shirt of her mother's and what I could rescue before she ruined the lot."

"I'll buy her clothing," he said, wondering who this woman was to Holly Jo. He'd never asked if Holly Jo's father had family. He knew her mother didn't. He'd just assumed when her mother had agreed to Holden taking the girl that there wasn't anyone else.

"Are you her grandmother?"

"Good Lord, no! I'm a neighbor. It's been tough enough the few days I've had her. Well, she'll be all yours now." She crossed herself and turned to bark the girl's name but stopped as Holly Jo came down the stairs.

The girl was wearing a pair of too-short shorts, a tank top and flip-flops. Her expression was sullen and surly, reminding him of a junkyard dog that'd been put on a short chain. Her short dark choppy hair framed her face, making her blue eyes look huge when she wasn't narrowing them.

Holden reminded himself that she'd lost her father before she was born and now she'd lost her mother. She'd been apparently pawned off to a neighbor, and now she was being taken clearly against her will by an older man she didn't know.

"Hello, Holly Jo. I'm Holden McKenna. It's nice to meet you."

"I really doubt that," she said as she shot her caretaker a sour look. "Can we please go?"

He picked up her suitcase and motioned for her to lead the way. As an afterthought, he worried that might have been a mistake, letting her go to the truck by herself. What if she took off running? Would he be able to catch her? She was tall for her age, he thought, her tanned legs long. Her head up, back straight, there was defiance in her walk, but there was also something graceful about her as she climbed into his pickup.

After putting her suitcase in the back, he slid behind the wheel. "You hungry?" She shook her head. "We could stop at a drive-through. Would you like that?" She shook her head again, then turned to look at him.

"Didn't she tell you? I'm vegan. I don't eat that crap."

Holden wasn't sure what *vegan* meant, but he suspected that meant that she didn't eat the beef they raised on the ranch. *Pick your battles*, he told himself, as he started the engine and headed back toward the Powder River Valley.

He told her a little about the ranch, but his new family member kept her face turned toward the side window away from him, showing no indication that she was listening. He finally gave up and just drove.

The silent treatment didn't bother him in the least. He just reminded himself to keep scissors away from her. It was clear from the odd angles of her hair that her clothing wasn't the only thing she'd chopped.

HOWIE GUNDERSON HAD rented a place not far from the airstrip. The house was small and part of a larger ranch that had sold to a conglomerate from back East. The house was vacant since no one ever intended to live there again. Howie had somehow talked the organization into renting it to him while he was here working. The rest of the time, he lived in Billings with his family, flying home every few weeks or so, Tilly explained as she drove.

When she'd suggested they take her truck again, she'd thought Cooper might put up an argument. He'd shrugged as if it didn't matter to him. It surprised her. She'd thought he was one of those men who liked to control everything like her college boyfriend had. Brian couldn't walk into the room without picking up the remote control—even if she'd been sitting there watching something.

"Anyone else living here with Howie?" Cooper asked as the house appeared up the road ahead. He hadn't spoken since they'd left the café. She suspected something was eating at him, but she didn't ask, telling herself she didn't care.

Was it the news about her and Stuart? Probably not. She was mentally chastising herself for telling him. Cooper's reaction had been even more embarrassing. He couldn't have cared less, when all she was trying to do was let him know the lay of the land, so to speak. Transparency—wasn't that a big thing nowadays?

"I didn't ask who all lived there." She saw an SUV and a second vehicle parked in front of the house, a large pickup, and realized that was why he'd asked.

After parking between the two vehicles, they both got out and walked up to the door. Cooper looked at her as if to ask if she wanted to be the one to knock. She felt herself flush. Was he insinuating that she was pushy? Worse, controlling? She shook her head and bit down on her lip to hold back what might come out of her mouth.

The door opened almost immediately after his knock. No doubt the occupants had heard them drive up, although there was only one man standing in the doorway.

"Howie Gunderson?" Cooper asked.

"Yes?"

"Mind if we come in and ask you a few questions?"

"You don't look like cops," Howie said, perusing them both before returning his attention to Cooper.

"I'm Tilly Stafford and this is Cooper McKenna. We just want to ask if you might have seen something the day my sister was shot," she said, tired of biting her lip. "Your plane was seen in the area."

The pilot nodded in understanding and waved them

inside. "I have to leave soon for the airstrip, but can I get you some coffee, water?" They shook their heads.

"Just information," Cooper said. "Did you have a passenger with you that day?"

"A geologist. Tick Whitaker. I think his name is actually Alfred, which could explain why he goes by Tick." He smiled, offered them a seat and sat on the edge of a chair facing them.

"What were you doing flying over the McKenna Ranch?" Cooper asked, making Tilly cringe. Could he sound any more accusing?

"I'd just flown over a stretch of land Tick had wanted to see from the air on Stafford land and was turning to head back toward town and the airstrip when I saw what I thought was a cowboy on horseback come racing out of one of the ravines."

"Have you told the sheriff this?" Cooper asked.

"I told the deputy who asked. He was riding so fast it caught my eye. Tick spotted another rider coming out of the ravine. He seemed to be chasing the first one," Howie said, glancing at Cooper.

"You did hear that the first rider was Oakley Stafford and that someone shot her," Cooper said.

"I did, but when I saw her, she seemed to be fine, so I figured she must have been shot either in the woods or when she came out of them onto the county road."

It was clear that Howie had heard who'd found Oakley. The pilot also must have gotten Cooper's backstory, including the part about his former girlfriend Leann Hayes.

"Why did you fly so low over my pickup on the county road?" Cooper asked.

"I guess I was concerned," he said. "And curious. I had no idea the rider was a woman. I had no idea who you were," Howie said to Cooper.

"So you didn't contact the sheriff's department?" Tilly asked.

"I didn't know for certain what was going on. I could see that she was apparently hurt, but I never would have guessed that she'd been shot. I made a big circle after I saw you, thinking I might come back and check, but then I saw the flashing lights coming up the road from farther downriver. Whatever was going on seemed to be covered. When I heard someone had been asking around about my plane, I assumed it was the sheriff. Figured he'd be talking to me about it. Sorry I can't be of more help," he said as he rose from the edge of the chair, "but I really have to get going."

Cooper rose as well. "You didn't see the second rider again?"

Howie shook his head. "Tick said he thought the rider turned south either toward the McKenna house or the Stafford Ranch. But I didn't see him."

"But you think the rider was male," Tilly said.

The pilot chuckled. "Thought they both were. Assumptions, you know."

"Where can we find Tick Whitaker?" Cooper asked.

"He's staying at the hotel in town," Howie said as he walked them both to the door.

"Do you happen to have his cell number?"

Howie hesitated only a moment before he went to

find something to write on. A few moments later, he handed Cooper a piece of lined notepad paper with the word *Tick* and a number written on it. Cooper thanked him and asked to use his pen.

Tilly watched him write something on the note, then pocket it and hand back the pen.

As they stepped outside, she noticed that the other vehicle, the truck that had been parked next to them when they went inside, was now gone.

It wasn't until they were in her pickup that Cooper handed her the note with Tick's number on it and a row of numbers and letters that appeared to be a license plate number—or the call number of a plane.

She shot him a questioning look.

"The license plate number of that large pickup that was parked outside the house when we got there," he said as he leaned back, tilted his Stetson low over his eyes to shade them from the sun. "Maybe your boyfriend can find out who the rig belongs to."

CHAPTER SEVEN

TILLY SHOT A look over at Cooper as she drove him back to his pickup parked in front of the café. His comment about asking her "boyfriend" to run the license plate still annoyed her. Did he have a problem with her dating Stuart? Cooper didn't get a say as to who she dated. It wasn't like he'd ever asked her out.

The thought made her groan inwardly. What was it about the cowboy that had always set her off? She glanced at him again. He acted like he couldn't care less about anything, maybe especially her. Even when she beat him at some competition, he would just shrug and say, "Nice job." *Nice job?* The other contestants she had beaten—even some of the women—stomped off, wanted to argue about the outcome or gave her grudging looks. Cooper seemed to do everything he could to beat her, but if he lost to her, he always acted like he didn't care.

Maybe that was what annoyed her the most. He *did* care. It wasn't like he'd let her win. He was competitive. Why did she let him annoy her so much?

Like right now. He hadn't said a word since he'd handed her the note and mentioned Stuart. "Why are you being so quiet?" she demanded as they neared the edge of town.

He glanced over at her from under the brim of his Stetson. "I'm always quiet."

"Not like this. What's bugging you?"

Cooper seemed amused by the question. "Do I seem bugged?"

"If you wanted to drive your pickup, you should have spoken up."

He laughed as he pushed back his hat and sat up. "You think I'm upset about you driving?" He shook his head. "You drive well enough. I hardly feared for my life more than a few times."

She'd started to object at his "you drive well enough," but she was glad she hadn't. He was teasing her. She liked this Cooper who could tease. She liked his smile, and his laugh was contagious. This was a side of him that she'd never seen before. "You should laugh and smile more often."

"Give me a good reason to and I'd be happy to oblige."

The tension she'd felt earlier in the cab of her truck had dissipated by the time she stopped behind his rig in front of the café. The place was packed at this hour. She saw people at the tables along the window looking out at them. But if Cooper was uncomfortable with townspeople seeing them together, he didn't say anything as he started to open his door.

She wondered if this was the last of their investigating together. It felt that way, and to her surprise, it disappointed her. She'd gotten a glimpse of a Cooper

McKenna she'd never known. She wondered if there was more to him than she'd always thought.

"Can I see that note again for a minute?" Cooper asked.

She'd expected him to leap out of the pickup the moment he got the chance. His request surprised her. She dug out the notepaper and handed it to him. There wasn't much written on it. Tick Whitaker's name and his phone number, as well as the license plate letters and numbers.

"What are you looking for?" she asked as he held the note up to the light. From where she sat, she could see that the background was faint, the letters large.

"CH4," he said.

She nodded. CH4. "I don't get it. We already know that Howie works for the gas exploration company.".

COOPER STUDIED THE note as Tilly gave him a questioning look. He didn't like keeping anything from her. But what he'd seen had nothing to do with her sister's shooting. At least he hoped not. He'd seen on the back of the note how hard Howie had pressed the pen to paper. So it was no surprise that what he'd written on the piece of notepaper before the one he'd given them had left an impression.

The ghostlike indentation was a name: Treyton McKenna, and what could have been his cell phone number. The haunting shadow of Treyton's name on CH4 notepaper appeared to be a damning assumption backed by what Tilly had told him about seeing Treyton being friendly with a gas company man. Howie or someone else? Times like this led to betrayal even inside the family.

"I was just thinking I might go check out Tick Whitaker before I go back to the ranch," Cooper said. Tilly had said their families were off-limits. No reason to share this with her, he told himself.

"Not without me. Where were you thinking of looking for him?"

Cooper pointed across the street at the hotel. Tilly groaned when she saw what he'd seen. Parked out front was the geologist's SUV with Texas vanity plates that read TICK followed by numbers that could have been his IQ.

"You just think you're smart, don't you," Tilly teased as they crossed the street.

"Not particularly," he said, but couldn't help grinning at her. It wasn't every day that he could best her.

Inside, they headed straight for the hotel registration desk. "We're looking for Tick Whitaker," Cooper said.

"Check the bar." The way the clerk said it, he figured Tick had made himself so at home in the bar that he probably had his own stool. So he wasn't that surprised when he heard a loud Southern drawl and followed it to an attractive, large man who had a redhead cornered at the bar.

Cooper looked over at Tilly as if to say, "Wanna bet that's Tick?" as they advanced on the Texan. Tick was pouring on the Southern charm at an annoying volume. "Tick?"

"Not now," he said without turning around. "Can't you see that I'm busy?"

"Tick?"

At the sound of a sultry female voice, he turned, already smiling even before he saw Tilly. "Hey, honey. Where did you come from?"

"If you have a moment, we'd like to ask you a few questions," Cooper said.

"Not really the time," Tick said with a wink.

"We'll make it quick. Maybe we could step over to a table in the corner?" Tilly suggested.

Tick gave the redhead a questioning look. "Promise you won't go away?"

She smiled. "Order me another drink. I'll sip it while you're gone."

The geologist roared at that and motioned to the bartender. "Keep her well-oiled," he said over his shoulder as he followed Cooper and Tilly to the table. "What's this about?"

TILLY GLANCED AT COOPER, who nodded for her to take the lead. "Howie said you were the man to talk to."

"He did, did he?" Tick beamed. He looked to be close to fifty, with big brown eyes fringed with dark lashes and a full head of thick brown hair. He was broad-shouldered and athletic looking, and handsome enough that Tilly knew the redhead wasn't going anywhere until he returned.

"He told us that the two of you were flying over the McKenna Ranch the other day and saw the woman who got shot."

Tick looked from one of them to the other. "You cops?"

"No. She's my sister."

"Oh, sorry. She okay?"

"Not really. She's still unconscious."

"Oh, that's too bad."

"Can you tell me what you saw?" she asked.

"Sure. Didn't see much. Saw her riding out of the ravine like the devil was chasing her, so she caught my eye. Then this other rider came out, hot on her tail. I thought…" He shrugged. They all knew what he thought.

"The male rider, can you tell me about his horse?" Cooper asked.

"Truthfully, I wasn't paying much attention to his horse. Brown, that's the best I can do."

"You didn't happen to see the brand?"

He shook his head. "I was watching the woman ride into the trees. By the time she disappeared, so had the male rider." Tilly thought it interesting that he knew the first rider was a woman, while the pilot had thought Oakley was a man by the way she was dressed.

"What about later when the plane flew low over the road?" Cooper asked.

"Saw the pickup and the girl on the ground. Wasn't sure what had happened until later that night here at the bar I heard that she'd been shot."

"Can you tell me what you were doing flying over the McKenna Ranch?" Cooper asked.

"Checking for coalbed seams," he said, looking more relaxed now that they were on a subject he clearly enjoyed. "I can usually spot them from the air. If I see a good one, then we let the ranch owner know that he's got a potential moneymaker out there in those badlands that aren't all that much use for anything else."

Tilly saw Cooper clamp down on his jaw. That the geologist saw this land as useless for anything except gas exploration made Tick like a lot of men who'd come to the state to rape it of its treasures and leave. It was why Montana used to be called the Treasure State.

"If that's all," Tick said, glancing back at the redhead as he got to his feet.

"If you think of anything else." She handed him her business card with the ranch number on it.

"Stafford," Tick said, glancing at the card. "Right. The girl who got shot was a Stafford. So you're related to Charlotte."

"She's my mother."

"We just put a well on your ranch recently." Tick looked way too pleased about making her wonder if he wasn't more involved in CH4 than just their geologist. "Your mother made a smart decision. Hopefully some of these other ranchers will follow." He looked over at Cooper. "I just realized that I didn't get your name."

"Cooper McKenna."

"Related to Holden McKenna?"

"He's my father."

Tick nodded, his smile evaporating quickly before he turned to Tilly. "It's been a pleasure. Can I buy you a drink?"

She declined. Tick returned to the redhead, and she and Cooper left.

"Well, that was fun," he said as they reached their

trucks. He looked over at her. "It's been a pleasure," he drawled.

She laughed as she watched him go to his pickup and leave. They'd learned little today, and yet it hadn't felt wasted. She wondered if he would have agreed.

As she climbed behind the wheel, she looked in the Cattleman Café windows where they'd had breakfast. Like then, there were people looking in her direction. Hers and Cooper's. She was sure the two of them were already the talk of the town. She could feel her ears burning as she started the engine, put the truck in gear and pulled away. What could they say other than that she and Cooper had been seen together? Big deal.

But she did wonder what Cooper's father would have to say once the gossip reached him. Unfortunately, she knew exactly what her mother's reaction would be, no matter how innocent their interaction had been.

THE SHERIFF HAD been down the street when he'd seen Tilly's pickup go by with a large male shape in the passenger seat. He hadn't seen Cooper's face. He didn't need to. It was him.

He'd sworn as Tilly had parked at the café next to Cooper's truck. Stuart had seen Coop's vehicle there first thing this morning. Which meant it had been there all morning. At the time, there'd been no sign of Tilly or her rig. He'd realized when he'd seen them returning from wherever they'd been that the two of them had been together this whole time.

Stuart had told himself, blood pressure rising, not to make a big deal out of it. He'd told himself to drive on past, wave if they spotted him. But he hadn't been able to move from where he was parked. He'd sat, waiting for Cooper to get out of her pickup and go to his own. As sheriff, he was under so much pressure already that he didn't need this. He didn't have time to be worrying about Tilly. Not to mention Tilly and Cooper. What were they thinking? Right now he was trying hard to keep Oakley Stafford's shooting from turning into all-out war between the families.

He'd had CJ in his office earlier, demanding to know if he'd caught the shooter. He'd also had Treyton bitching about the McKenna Ranch crawling with cops and him demanding to know when it was going to end.

With relief, he'd seen Cooper finally get out of Tilly's pickup, but then she'd gotten out as well. He'd thought he would lose his mind as the two of them had walked across the street to the hotel. What the hell? He'd told himself to drive off, but he couldn't. Instead, he'd glanced at his watch.

This couldn't be what he thought it was. He was still mentally kicking himself for his argument with Tilly. He shouldn't have brought up Cooper. Tilly had thought he was just being jealous. He wished that hadn't been true. Tilly and Cooper. He kept thinking about that one time… Now the two had gone into the hotel together in broad daylight. What was he supposed to think? Was Tilly doing this to defy him or—

He'd checked his watch as the two came out of the hotel. They hadn't had enough time to even register, let alone go up to a room. His relief had him nauseous. What had he been thinking?

Tilly had admitted that she and Cooper were doing some investigating into the case. That alone was maddening enough. Neither of them had any experience. What was it they thought they could uncover that he couldn't?

But her hanging out with Cooper? He didn't even think that she liked him.

Stu tried to tamp down his irritation and worry as, up the street, Cooper climbed into his truck with no more than a goodbye to Tilly. She got into her own, but sat there for a while. He could see her behind the wheel. He desperately wanted to know what she was thinking.

Down the street, he could still see the back of Cooper's pickup. Was he headed back to the ranch or was Tilly giving him a head start before she met him somewhere? Stu hated the path his thoughts had taken. But Tilly and Cooper were making him think these things.

He shifted his patrol SUV into gear and drove down the street. As he passed Tilly, he didn't even look in her direction. Instead, he wanted to find out where his old friend was going.

Cooper hadn't gone far when he hit his brakes and turned into a parking space in front of the local real-estate office. Again, Stu pulled over down the street, his curiosity growing. Why would Cooper be interested in property? He was born into a huge ranch. That made no sense unless his father hadn't let him return to the homestead. He watched his friend go inside Beckman's Realty. Frowning, Stu couldn't imagine why, until he noticed a McKenna Ranch pickup parked next to the building. Someone from the ranch was inside the realty office.

Now even more curious, he waited.

Cooper came out of the office followed quickly by his older brother, Treyton. Even from a distance, Stu could tell that they were arguing. What had Treyton been doing in there? Finding out what the ranch was worth? Or investing in more property? Times were tough and a lot of ranchers were selling out. Not Holden McKenna, but then the rancher couldn't live forever, Stu thought as he watched Treyton and Cooper quarrel.

Whatever the reason, Cooper looked furious as he stormed off, got into his pickup and roared away.

Stu followed him at a distance, hoping his friend was upset enough that he wouldn't notice he was being tailed.

CHAPTER EIGHT

TILLY DROVE STRAIGHT to the hospital. She'd ask her mother to let her know if there was any change in Oakley's condition. That she hadn't heard anything made her assume her sister was still unconscious. In the intensive-care area, she saw that Oakley was in the same room as yesterday, hooked up to all the equipment, eyes closed. She looked so pale and small in the bed that Tilly felt her heart drop.

She'd been telling herself that her sister was strong, that Oakley could overcome anything, that there was no way she would die. But now, seeing her like this, she had to face the truth. Oakley might not make it.

Tears rushed to her eyes, a sob rising in her throat as she moved to her sister's bedside. Oakley's hand was cool to the touch. Tilly watched her face, hoping she would open her eyes, hoping she would come back and tell them who'd done this.

"Where have you been?"

She turned as her mother followed her accusing tone into the room. Charlotte held a cup of vending machine coffee in her hand. She looked as if she'd been here since the shooting, without sleep or a change of clothing.

"You haven't been home?" Her mother didn't answer, merely sat down in the chair next to Oakley's bed and took a sip of her coffee, making a face as she did. "You should go home, shower, change, get some sleep. I'll stay here with her."

Her mother's gaze lifted to hers, the answer in her eyes even before she shook her head and said, "Cooper McKenna?"

The entire under-a-hot-light grilling took place with those two words.

She bristled, pretending it was from her mother's implication that she'd been out having fun while her sister was fighting for her life here in the hospital. She knew better. This was about a McKenna.

"We're trying to find out who shot her."

"Isn't your lawman boyfriend doing that?" her mother asked.

Tilly felt bruised and battered enough with everything that had happened over the past few days. She wasn't up for one of her fights with her mother. Nor was this the place.

"Unless you're going home, I should see to the ranch," she said, and started to the door.

Her mother's words stopped her before she could reach it. "CJ and your brothers can run the ranch just fine without you."

Did her mother really believe that? She turned to look at her. Was it possible Charlotte Stafford didn't realize who loved this ranch, who would do anything to save it, who had been actively working the ranch?

But before she could speak, her mother seemed to shrink before her. The ramrod-straight back bent like a young willow in the wind, the hardened expression sculpted by an equally hard life softened, and tears filled those ocean-deep green eyes as she looked at her daughter. As she extended a hand, Tilly moved around the end of the bed to take it. The skin felt thin, mottled with freckles and ice-cold.

"We aren't going to lose Oakley," Tilly said, her voice sounding more confident than she felt. "We aren't going to lose anything."

Her look said that she'd already lost too much. Tilly knew that loss had nothing to do with Charlotte Stafford's last husband, who'd run off and hadn't been seen since. Tilly had heard the rumors, about her brother Brand being a product of an affair with Holden McKenna. She'd also heard that Holden's wife Margaret had a wild affair more than thirty years ago and that Cooper might not be his.

Tilly had always wondered if Holden had been the love of her mother's life—or if any man had that honor. She had always felt that her mother's only love had been the land that she would die trying to keep.

"Don't make this worse," her mother said, and let go of her hand. "Stay away from that McKenna."

Seeing her mother turn away from her, she felt a deep sadness. As much as she was determined to someday run the ranch, she didn't want to have the regrets she saw carved into her mother's face. Did it have to be a choice between the love of a man and the love of the land?

HOLDEN WAS GLAD that none of the family was around when he and Holly Jo arrived at the ranch. She sat staring dispassionately out the windshield as he turned off the engine. "This is your new home."

"Only until I leave," she said. "I'm not staying here, and you can't make me."

He wasn't going to argue the point. She was twelve. She didn't know how to drive a vehicle. He couldn't see her jumping on a bike and riding twenty miles into Powder Crossing and then what? Nor could he see her making the hike on foot, especially in a pair of flip-flops, the only thing she now apparently owned. "Come on. I'll show you your room. I'll see about getting you some boots tomorrow."

She made a gagging sound and didn't get out until he'd taken her suitcase out of the back and started for the house. He could hear her hollering something at him, but didn't turn. He was already missing her silent treatment.

Holden carried her suitcase up the stairs to the room Elaine had readied for the girl. It wasn't his taste, too frilly and pink, but she said a little girl would like it. He doubted Holly Jo would like anything here on the ranch.

Turning, he saw that she'd followed him upstairs and was now staring at the room in horror. "I'm not five," she said, clearly offended.

"Our cook and head housekeeper, Elaine, decorated the room for you. I don't want you hurting her feelings. We can change it to something you like better after a few months."

She raised a brow. "A few months?" She scoffed. "I won't be here that long."

"Well, then, I guess it will be fine the way it is." He headed for the door. "If you're hungry, come down to the kitchen. Elaine will make you something to eat if you ask nicely." Otherwise, as far as he was concerned, she could starve.

TILLY WAS COMING out of the hospital when she saw Stuart pull up. When he didn't get out of his patrol SUV, she knew that he was looking for her. She'd seen that he'd texted a couple of times and tried to call once. She hadn't checked her messages. She was still angry with him. Angry with Cooper as well. Men, she thought as she walked over to his driver's-side window.

He powered it down. "Get in. Please," he added before her eyebrows could shoot to the stars. He leaned over and opened the passenger-side door.

Going around the SUV, taking her time as she debated how she felt about Stu right now, she climbed in and closed the door.

"Did you get my messages?" he asked.

"I've been busy," she answered without looking at him. Okay, she was still angry about last night. Reminding herself of some of the nice things he'd done in the past, including making her popcorn last night, she turned to him. "I don't want to fight with you."

"I don't want that either." There was a tightness in his voice. "I was out of line last night about Cooper."

Interesting. "That's all?"

"As for you crime solving on your own, damn it,

Tilly, I'm the sheriff. I can arrest you for interfering in my investigation."

"So arrest me, because that is the only way you're going to stop me." They locked gazes for a long moment.

"This isn't a game," he snapped, angrily running a hand over his short blond hair.

"Don't you think I know that?" she snapped back. "I also know that you're understaffed, and you don't know my sister as well as I do." He raised a brow at the last and she had to drop her gaze, feeling her cheeks flush. "No, I don't know what she was doing on the McKenna Ranch or who shot her. I don't even know who she's been dating. But I know my sister." She took a breath. "I think it might have something to do with CH4, the gas company that drilled on our ranch. Oakley was adamantly opposed to the drilling. She and my mother fought over it. I think that's what was going on that day."

"That doesn't really explain why she would have been on the McKenna Ranch. There isn't any drilling going on there."

"What was the company plane doing in that area? We talked to the pilot and the passenger. Have you met Tick Whitaker? He's a good ole boy from the South, a real charmer."

"Are you saying your sister might have been involved with him?"

"Not in the way you think, if I'm right. It's just a feeling I have."

"This is exactly what I'm talking about. I'm the one who needs to interview these people. I'm working the case, Tilly, as fast as I can. I have the lab trying to establish the rifle used based on the slug taken out of your sister. My job isn't just about interviewing possible witnesses."

"My point exactly," she said. "How long before you know who shot her?" When he didn't answer, she groaned and threw open her door.

He grabbed her arm before she could get out. "I'll look into the methane gas angle, okay? But it's not the only one I'm chasing, all right?"

She stared at him. "If you know something—"

"Tilly, trust me. I'm going to find your sister's shooter, okay? Just give me a little time. I can't be worrying about you and what you're up to." His gaze met hers. "I don't want you getting shot too. We don't know if the shooting was an accident or if the person who pulled that trigger was trying to kill your sister. You don't want to find yourself in the crosshairs of a killer because you asked too many questions of the wrong people."

She felt as if she'd been doused with ice water. His words reverberated through her. She *had* forgotten that she could be chasing a would-be killer. "Aren't you worried that the person who shot Oakley isn't finished? What if he tries to finish the job at the hospital?"

"Don't you think I've thought of that?" he demanded, shaking his head. "She's in intensive care, where there is always someone on duty. The only visitors she gets are family, and even then, I've alerted the nurses to watch family in addition to strangers. I'm doing everything I can."

"I'm sorry. Thank you."

"I don't want this to come between us," he said quietly.

Tilly knew what he was also saying. He didn't want Cooper to come between them. "It won't," she assured him.

He reached over and took her hand, giving it a squeeze. "I hope not. I felt like you and I were just getting started." He sounded so serious. She liked Stuart, had enjoyed going out with him. They'd gotten close—just not as close as he would have liked since they still hadn't had sex. Her choice.

She had put the brakes on, and she couldn't say exactly why. Stuart was a good-looking man. Maybe it was because she'd known him all her life and yet lately this was the first time they'd ever gone out. She thought of him more as a friend. Maybe if they kept dating her feelings would change.

"Once this is over…" She pushed her door open and climbed out. "Call me if you hear something?"

"Be careful." She nodded, then walked to her pickup, thinking back to before Oakley was shot, before Cooper came home, before she'd gotten to see this other side of the sheriff. Had her feelings for Stuart changed? Or had he always just been a friend? A friend who'd been too possessive suddenly?

Whatever it was, she felt different about him, and that made her feel sad. It was like everything had changed the day Oakley was shot. Or was it Cooper coming home that changed everything?

HOLLY JO LOOKED at the hideously pink and frilly room and felt her eyes burn with tears. Angrily, she dared the tears to fall. She'd cried herself to sleep for months after hearing that her mother was sick and dying. She'd sworn that no matter how awful Holden McKenna and his ranch were, she wasn't going to let him see her cry.

Keeping her tears at bay only made her want to throw herself on the floor, kicking and screaming until she didn't feel like this anymore. "It's all part of the grieving process," the doctor had told her. "I promise that you will feel better. It just takes time."

He was old and his kindness made her hurt worse. He'd patted her head as if she were a child. She would be thirteen in a few months. She'd been told that she was tall for her age, wise beyond her years. She could pass for older once she got out of this place.

But in the meantime, this was her life, she said to herself as she looked around the room. She thought about unpacking her suitcase since she'd purposely brought only as much as she would be able to carry on her back once she left here. Just the thought of actually using the white wooden dresser next to the bed seemed like more than she could handle right now.

Her stomach growled. Maybe she would go downstairs and see if there was something to eat. She wasn't looking forward to meeting Elaine, the woman who'd apparently decorated her room, as she left and went downstairs. She had no idea where the kitchen was. This place was so huge it should come with a map, she thought as she wandered around, peeking behind closed doors until she found a massive kitchen off the back of the house.

So far, it was her favorite room since it was light and airy, with large windows that looked out toward the mountains in the distance.

"You must be Holly Jo," a voice said behind her, and she turned to see a small woman with bright blue eyes and a wide smile. "I'm Elaine. It is a pleasure to meet you."

She really doubted that, but she smiled and used the manners she'd been taught since she had a feeling this woman could be an ally. "It's nice to meet you."

"I'm betting you're hungry. I knew you were coming today, so I've been cooking all morning, but not knowing what you liked, I had to just make my favorites." She gave what Holly Jo would have called a belly laugh. To her surprise, it made her smile. She thought she could like Elaine, in spite of everything.

"Is this her?" said a male voice after Holly Jo had put away some deviled eggs, a pint of yogurt and a half dozen chocolate chip cookies.

The cowboy who came up to the breakfast bar was tall, broad-shouldered and handsome with his short dark hair and chiseled features. But his smile didn't reach his blue eyes. She knew at once that he wouldn't be an ally.

"This is Treyton," Elaine said. "He has no manners. This is Holly Jo." Elaine slapped the man's hand as he reached for one of the chocolate chip cookies on a small plate she'd said were for Holly Jo to take to her room. "Those aren't for you, Treyton."

Another cowboy came in laughing. "Don't let him take your cookies, girl. Hi." He had a great smile. "I'm Duffy." This man was much cuter and nicer than Treyton. He had longer dark hair and blue eyes that twinkled with mischief. She liked him and wanted to tell her friends back home about him. They would be so jealous.

"Duffy is an odd name," she said.

"He's an odd young man," Elaine said, but she was smiling. Holly Jo could tell that she liked Duffy better than Treyton. "Now you've met two of the McKenna men. You'll meet Cooper later, I'm sure."

"I wouldn't be so sure," Treyton said. "He might have already left again for parts unknown." He stormed out of the kitchen.

"I'm going to go get cleaned up," Duffy said.

"Another hot date?" Elaine asked with a laugh.

"You know it," he said, and winked at Holly Jo.

She'd made up her mind not to like anyone on the ranch. But she couldn't help liking Elaine and Duffy. Not that she would be staying long. Even if she did, though, she doubted she would ever like Treyton.

Back in her room, she unpacked her suitcase, putting everything away even as she planned her escape. Her mother had told her about the ranch. After the long drive here, she knew it was in the middle of nowhere, far from any and everything.

She moved to her window and pushed aside the

curtain. There were rugged-looking mountains, miles of prairie, huge trees next to a very lazy river. How was she going to get away? Then she saw the answer standing out in the field.

A horse.

CHAPTER NINE

"I THINK WE should ride up that ravine that Howie and Tick saw Oakley and the other rider coming out of."

Cooper had been surprised that Tilly would call at all. When they'd left each other earlier, he'd thought for sure that was the last time he'd be hearing from her.

"I'm not sure that's a good idea." He was driving to the ranch, getting fairly close to home, too aware that the sheriff had followed him partway out of town earlier. "I get the feeling Stuart doesn't want us investigating."

"Why? What happened?"

"He followed me out of town after I left you."

"The sheriff's just jealous. He doesn't like me hanging out with you."

He didn't miss that she had called Stuart "the sheriff." Distancing herself from her boyfriend? Or not wanting to remind Cooper that she was dating his best friend? "Another good reason not to keep getting involved in his investigation. It's still a crime scene out there. Also, it could be dangerous."

"Not with the sheriff's deputies taking all our families' rifles," she said, and laughed. She did have a point. If it was someone from one of the two ranches.

He was still surprised about what she'd told him at breakfast. The rifle used to shoot Oakley had been a 270. He was just glad that he didn't own a 270 and it wasn't one of the guns that the deputy had taken from his pickup.

Still, it worried him that Stuart would follow him out of town. Maybe the sheriff was just jealous. If so, maybe he was building a case against Cooper to get rid of him. The thought of an arrest reminded him of the last time he'd been hauled into jail. It hadn't been pretty. Nor had he done well behind bars.

He didn't want to go down that road again. He remembered the deputies coming to the house the other night. They'd taken all the rifles, but according to Tilly, they had really wanted just the 270s to compare to the slug taken from her sister.

"I think we'd better not give the sheriff any reason to arrest us for interfering in his investigation," he said now. He was sure that Stu didn't think that he'd shot Oakley. Then why was he following him out of town earlier? Stuart hadn't turned back until it was obvious where Cooper was headed—to the ranch. The whole thing made him nervous. Had it been anyone but his best friend, Cooper might have been worried that evidence would be manufactured that made him look guilty.

Then again, it could be what Tilly had said. Stuart wanted to know where Cooper had been headed because of her. He shook his head. There was nothing to be jealous of. Surely Stuart wasn't worried about him stealing his woman. If Tilly even was the sheriff's woman. He realized that he'd missed something Tilly had said on the other end of the call. "Pardon?"

"Tick. He called. He wants to buy me a drink to-night at the Buffalo Bar in Miles City. I think I should go and see what I can find out from him when it's just the two of us. There is something about him."

Something lecherous. Not that Tilly couldn't handle herself. She'd had enough cowboys try to take advantage of her over the years. If Tick did try, he would know the pain of defeat. It would probably have him limping for weeks.

So why was she calling him? It was odd. He'd known Tilly his whole life. She wasn't calling to ask his permission or his approval. He was sure she'd already made up her mind to go. So what was this about? Had she seen something in Tick that made her worry she might not be able to handle the Texan?

"Sure, if that's what you want to do." He made the decision in a split second. "Would you mind if I went along? I haven't been to the Buffalo in years."

She laughed, but sounded relieved, which made him realize that he might have been right. "I don't think a double date was what Tick had in mind."

"I'm sure it wasn't. That's why I'll sit at the bar, and when you get ready to leave, I'll make sure you leave with me. That way you can tell me what you found out on the way back to Powder Crossing." He waited to see if he'd overstepped. He knew how easy it was to get her back up if she thought he was trying to protect her. Or worse if she thought he was telling her what to do.

"You're just looking for an excuse to get away from the ranch, aren't you," she said.

"You guessed it. On the way I'll tell you about my new little sister."

"*Your what?* Your father?"

"It's not that. Truthfully, I don't know what it is. But Holden came home with this twelve-year-old girl. Apparently, she's going to be living with us and we're supposed to be nice to her. Has something to do with a promise he made. The girl's father's dead and her mother recently passed away."

"That's awful, the part about losing her parents. It's nice that your father is taking her in. Though I feel sorry for her. I know you'll be nice to her. But Treyton? He's not nice to anyone. I bet he isn't happy about the situation."

Just the mention of his older brother had him gritting his teeth as he recalled their argument at the real-estate office.

"What is she like?"

"I haven't met her yet, but I'm almost to the ranch now. Let me shower and change, and I'll fill you in on the way to Miles City. What time is your…date?"

It was an hour drive. They decided to leave by seven. He was hoping that going with her wasn't a bad idea. But he'd gotten the feeling that Tilly didn't want to go alone. Going with her, though, worried him a little because of Stuart. He needed to call him soon to go out for a beer so he could test the temperature of their best-friend status.

As he pulled into the ranch yard, he saw Deacon

Yates, coming out of the stables. He had a young dark-haired girl by the scruff of her neck and was hauling her toward the house. One look at the ranch manager's angry expression and Cooper figured this must be Holly Jo—and she'd already gotten into trouble. It appeared she was off to a less-than-auspicious start here at the ranch.

"What's going on?" he asked as he climbed out of his pickup.

"Tell him to get his hands off me!" she yelled.

"This little scamp was in the stables trying to saddle Midnight—of all our horses. It's a miracle he didn't kick her into next week."

"Let me go!" she yelled again, squirming to break free.

"I'm taking her to your father," Deacon said. "Let him deal with her."

Cooper studied the little scamp in question. "You must be Holly Jo," he said to her. "I'm Cooper McKenna. You ever saddle a horse before?" She glared at him in answer. "We have rules on the ranch, most of them for your own good. You're going to have to abide by them." Her look of utter defiance said she thought otherwise. "Have it your way. But when it comes to this ranch, my father won't put up with any shenanigans. Go ahead. Take her to Dad."

Cooper watched the girl go, kicking and squealing, and Deacon steadfastly hauling her to the boss. He had to wonder who this girl was and why his father had brought her here. He couldn't imagine the kind of promise that would have Holden McKenna raising a twelve-year-old girl at this time of his life.

When he reached the house, Holly Jo was getting a good scolding. Cooper heard the girl say, "I don't even know what *corporal punishment* is."

"I suspect you'll find out soon enough if you ever pull something like that again," he heard his father say before sending her to her room.

"Have a moment?" he asked his harried-looking father, who was sitting behind his desk in his office den. Cooper closed the door, wondering if his timing could be better. Too bad—this couldn't wait. "I ran into Treyton earlier in town at Beckman's Realty. He said he was looking at property for you." His father's expression gave nothing away. "I also heard from a reliable source that he was seen buddying up with one of the hotshots from the gas company doing all the drilling around here. I would have let both things slide, but I saw his name on a notepad at one of the gas company men's house."

"What are you saying?"

"I suspect he's up to something and has been for a while." Cooper shrugged. "Just thought you should know." He hesitated. "If you're thinking about letting them drill on the ranch, forget I said anything."

"Hell no, I'm not. How can you even ask that?"

"Because you don't seem that interested in why Treyton appears to be dealing with them. Was he looking into property for you?" This time, his father's expression gave him away. "Then I suspect he was there to find out what the ranch is worth on the open market. Are you thinking about selling?"

His father sat back in his chair. He looked older, as if weighted down by life. "I'm just trying to understand what was going on," Cooper said. He felt as if he'd walked into the middle of a movie, one he'd been edited out of. One thing was for certain: this definitely didn't seem like a good time to adopt a twelve-year-old orphaned kid.

"You're right," he said, even though his father hadn't said anything. "It's none of my business, but this girl..."

"It will be a transition for us and for Holly Jo, but I made a promise and I'm damned well going to keep it. As for the ranch, I intend to keep it too, right up to my last dying breath. Does that answer your question?"

He nodded. "It does."

He started to turn, when his father said, "As for Treyton, he doesn't agree with me about the methane wells. But I think he's too smart to try to go around me, don't you?"

Cooper wasn't so sure about that. His older brother had always been sneaky and often underhanded when he wanted something badly enough. "Probably me coming back just has him wanting to remind me that he is the eldest son. He's always liked to put me in my place."

"Where is your place, Cooper?"

He chuckled since his father had never answered that question. "You'd know better than me."

"This ranch is your place."

Was it?

"And now that you're back," Holden said, "any chance I could get you to teach Holly Jo how not to just saddle a horse, but how to ride? It seems she's determined to learn. It might be a positive thing."

He gave it a few moments' thought. "I could do that." He certainly hadn't stepped back into any roles here on the ranch since he'd returned. Instead, he'd wanted to tiptoe back in just to get his feet wet until he knew how deep it could get. "I'd be happy to teach her."

"She's a wild one."

Like Bailey, he thought, wondering why his sister had been so scarce lately. It made him think of Oakley, which made him worry about his sister. Both women were headstrong. "Is there some kind of local movement against the gas companies? It sounded like Oakley might have been involved."

His father frowned. "If there is, you're thinking of Bailey."

"I might look into it," Cooper said as he left.

CHARLOTTE MOVED TO stand at the hospital room window. The glare as the sun began to dip behind the mountains made her wince. It shouldn't be shining at all, the sky shouldn't be so blue, the birds shouldn't be singing. It felt as if the world should have stopped. Hers had. But all around her life was going on.

She turned back to her daughter's bedside, consumed by her own anger. She'd been like this long before Oakley was wounded, but some days all this pent-up fury wanted to overwhelm her, making her feel as if she might explode.

Seeing Holden the other day had reignited more than her desire. The memory of that kiss made her shudder at how she'd dropped her defenses, at how desperately she'd wanted what he was offering. What had she been thinking? She felt a wave of shame wash over her. She'd wanted more than even that passionate kiss. She'd wanted him right there beside the creek as if they were still teenagers. How could she have wanted him, let alone succumbed to her own desire with a man who had betrayed her? She felt humiliated, shocked by her behavior and worse. She'd hated that Boyle had shown up when he had and at the same time was thankful that she hadn't humiliated herself worse. How could she forget the devastation she'd felt when Holden, her lover, her soulmate, had married someone else?

"Char?"

She stiffened. Only one man called her that. Bracing herself, she turned and attempted a smile.

Alexander Forester stood in the hospital room doorway, the brim of his Stetson gripped in his thick fingers. "I came as soon as I heard." He stepped in. "I'm sorry I couldn't get here before now."

He opened his arms and she stepped into them. She pressed her face against his crisp, expensive shirt, breathing in his rich aftershave. Everything about Alexander felt like money. "Only first class for me," he often joked. He didn't flaunt his wealth, but he didn't hide it either. He made no excuses, saying that he'd started out dirt-poor. He took pride in his accomplishments. He promised her a better life. He'd offered her a way out of at least one of her problems, keeping the ranch going. If only she could fall in love with him, she thought as she stepped back. She'd married for all the wrong reasons before. She would never do that again.

"Thank you for coming."

He glanced toward the bed. "She the same?" Charlotte nodded. "Honey, just say the word and I'll fly her out to any hospital in the world."

She swallowed, tempted. "She just needs to wake up. Apparently, along with being shot, when she fell from her horse, she hit her head. She has a concussion. The doctor said that when the swelling in her brain goes down, she'll wake up. But when she does…" The doctors just didn't know if she would be the same or not.

"She'll be just fine," Alexander said. "You have to have faith."

Faith? She had to turn away, trying to remember how long it had been since she'd had faith in anything—or anyone.

At a sound at the door, she looked over and saw her sons standing there giving Alexander looks filled with animosity. He saw them and their expressions and said, "I should go. I have a big meeting tomorrow in Denver. But if you need me, I'll hustle right back up here." He placed his hand over hers. "You just call me."

She met his gaze and nodded. He leaned to her, kissed her softly on the mouth, then pulled back to smile at her. She knew what he wanted from her. Marriage. He'd come to Montana looking to buy a large ranch. He'd wanted hers and had offered more than she had ever imagined she could get for it. This part of Montana wasn't as desirable to most buyers as the mountainous, pine-tree-filled western part. That she'd been tempted to take what he offered along with money brought home how desperate she was.

"Thank you and thank you for coming." She hadn't called him. He seemed to have his ear to the ground when it came to her. She wondered if he'd made offers on any other ranches in the area run by women.

He tipped his hat on the way past her sons. She gave them a scolding look and turned away. It felt impossible to deal with other people right now, maybe especially her own children.

Brand came in, hugged her, then went over to say something to his sister. That Brand was her favorite was no secret to anyone. At thirty-two, he worked harder on the ranch than his brothers. He caused no problems. He was her gift—but also the talk of the Powder River Valley since everyone thought he looked like a younger Holden McKenna. He had blue eyes and darker blond hair and was drop-dead gorgeous—like his father.

Her eldest son hadn't moved from the doorway. She depended on CJ as much as Brand, often even more because she knew that he loved building the ranch as much as or more than she did. She knew that he would fight for it beside her no matter what she did. Not that he wasn't the most judgmental of her children and always had been.

"You okay?" Ryder asked as he walked over to Oakley's bed, put his hand on his sister's arm for a moment, then turned to her. "Two sheriff's deputies came to the ranch with a warrant. They took all of the rifles. Now the sheriff is checking our horses. Apparently, he's looking to match the hoofprints found at the spot on the McKenna Ranch where they think Oakley was shot."

"Stuart Layton thinks someone on our ranch shot Oakley?" Brand cried. "That's ridiculous. What do you want us to do?"

There was nothing to do. She shook her head. "Let them take our guns, let the sheriff look. We have nothing to hide." She saw a look cross CJ's face. "Do we?"

"You really need to go home for a while," Ryder said. Like CJ, he had the Stafford blond hair and green eyes. Like Brand, he was handsome, only unlike Brand, Ryder knew it and used it to his benefit. At thirty, he made no secret of the fact that he would much rather be chasing young women than cows. "We can stay with Oakley while you're gone."

She shook her head. "I'm not leaving until she wakes up."

"And if she never wakes up?" CJ said from the door.

She shot him a warning look. "Oakley will wake up. She will come back to us." Her sons shifted on their boots, clearly anxious to leave. "Go. Take care of the ranch."

Brand hesitated, touching her arm before following Ryder out. CJ, she saw, was still in the doorway, his green eyes on her. She wondered if she'd made him like he was, often so angry.

As Ryder and Brand went down the hall, CJ stepped into the room. "Why are you leading him on?" he demanded. She didn't have to ask who he was referring to. Alexander. "You aren't going to marry Al. Hopefully, you aren't going to marry anyone ever again."

"It's my business. Anyway, you don't know. I might remarry someday."

He let out a bark of a laugh. "I do know, though. There isn't a man on this earth that you could live with. Alexander? He isn't the type to stand back and let you run the ranch. The minute he took over, we both know what would happen. You want to go through that again? I sure as hell don't. Remember, I was there last time."

She would have drawn up to her full height, told him he couldn't talk to her like that, but she couldn't meet his gaze. He was right. She'd put her children through her last disastrous marriage. She couldn't do anything like that again.

But still, she couldn't have her son talking to her like that. Before she could get air back into her lungs to put him in his place, CJ had turned and walked out.

Grinding her teeth, she watched him go, hating that what he'd said was true. Would she have been happy with Holden, the one man she'd truly loved? She had never had a chance to find out, she thought bitterly, and now they were both alone—no doubt what they deserved.

But as CJ left, his words still burned inside her. Sometimes she thought he was the most like her, that brittle hurt part that always felt on the edge of breaking. Her excuse was that she'd been through too much, done things she'd never thought she'd do and survived by taking another breath when she just wanted to curl up in a corner and cry.

She watched CJ go down the hall to where his brothers were waiting for him. The eldest, CJ had been through more with her than his brothers. She hated to think how much he remembered, how much he actually knew. He knew enough to be suspicious, she reminded herself. Wasn't that enough?

CHAPTER TEN

AT THE BUFFALO BAR in Miles City, Cooper had been nursing a beer and keeping an eye on the table in the back where the Texan was doing his best to charm Tilly. He wasn't sure how much longer he could pretend to be drinking his now-lukewarm beer. Not only was he her designated driver tonight, but also he was here to protect her—not that he would ever admit that to her. For those reasons, he didn't want to drink too much.

"Cooper Frigging McKenna? You've got to be kidding me. I hope to hell you're lost."

Groaning inwardly, he set down his beer bottle on the bar. He'd known it was only a matter of time before he ran into Leann's brother. He turned slowly on his stool, knowing how ugly this could get, and quickly.

"Billy." Billy Hayes moved closer, towering over him since he was still sitting on the stool. But getting to his feet might be all Billy needed to throw the first punch in this crowded bar.

"You remember me?" Billy asked, frowning as if expecting more of a reaction.

"How could I forget?"

"I never liked you, ranch boy."

"I remember the feeling being mutual."

Billy chuckled at that, and Cooper saw that the man was drunker than he'd first appeared. Not that it would stop Billy from starting a brawl. "I thought you were gone for good. Didn't I threaten to kill you if you ever came back?" His voice carried. The crowd around them began to quiet, their attention turning in Billy and Cooper's direction.

He considered what he might say to try to defuse what was clearly coming. There were no words. He turned and picked up his beer, took a sip, but didn't set the bottle back down. He knew how Billy Hayes fought. Dirty. All-out annihilation. He wasn't looking forward to what was going to happen next.

"Excuse me." Tilly raised her voice. *"Excuse me,"* she said again, and pushed Billy aside to reach Cooper. "You promised my boyfriend, the sheriff, that you would get me home." She sounded more drunk than he thought she was. "He just called. He said unless you want him coming down here, you'd better get your donkey's be-hind moving." She practically dragged him up off the stool and toward the door.

"This isn't over, McKenna," Billy yelled after him.

Cooper said nothing as he left his warm beer and he and Tilly walked out.

"You're welcome," she said as she climbed in after he opened the passenger-side door of his truck for her.

"Thanks. Too bad you won't always be around."

"Yes, isn't it."

He started the engine and pulled out. As he did, she spotted Billy standing in the bar doorway watching them leave.

"How was Tick?" he asked, wanting to change the subject. If Billy beating him up would solve the problem, Cooper would have gladly let him. Unfortunately, that wasn't the case. Things festered with a man like Billy. Not that Cooper blamed him. If he thought a man had killed his sister, he'd be the same way or worse.

"Tick," she said with obvious disgust. "I'd rather hear about your new sister." On the way to Miles City, they'd talked about Oakley and the investigation and what Stuart had told her. "Did you finally get to meet her?"

He knew he could be dense sometimes, but clearly she didn't want to talk about Tick. Because she hadn't gotten any useful information out of him? Or another reason?

But he went along with it since he didn't have much choice. Tilly would tell him when she was ready. Or not. "Holly Jo. She's something." He told her about the kid's run-in with their ranch manager after trying to saddle Midnight, the wildest of their horses.

"What does everyone else think about her?"

He had the feeling that she was trying to keep him talking about anything but Tick. Why was that? "Depends on who you ask. Elaine says Holly Jo's delightful, but then that's Elaine. Duffy said she seems to be an okay kid, though he wished that if Dad was going to bring home girls that they were at least legal age." Tilly chuckled as if only half listening. "Our ranch manager says she's hell on wheels. He couldn't believe she'd try to saddle Midnight. Clearly, she has no experience with horses. She's a city girl for sure. She's lucky the horse didn't kick her in the head." Tilly nodded and chuckled, but he could tell her mind was elsewhere. He had a pretty good idea where.

"You going to tell me about Tick?" he asked.

"Sounds like Holly Jo's got gumption."

"You could call it that. I said I'd teach her to ride."

"*You're* going to teach her?"

"Sure—why not? If she's going to live on the ranch, she needs to have something to do. I reckon she'll be starting school soon too, catching the bus down at the road." Even as he said it, he wondered how she would like that.

He looked over at Tilly. She was chewing on her lower lip, something he'd seen her do since she was a kid. Usually, it meant she was brooding over something. Often it meant she was getting more determined. He realized that he'd been away from her for too long to know what she was stewing over.

Stu. Was that what was going on with her? Cooper decided to let her brood, telling himself it was none of his business.

AFTER HER VISIT from Alexander and her sons at the hospital, Charlotte had gone down the hall to the ladies' room to freshen up. They were right; she looked awful. She splashed her face with water, knowing that she should go home and at least shower and change her clothes.

But she couldn't make herself do it. She wanted to be with Oakley when she woke up. Her daughter would wake up. Oakley was a strong young woman, stubborn to a fault and more independent than any of the others. She'd been like that since she was a child, a loner. Charlotte had never known what her younger daughter was thinking. Wasn't that why she had no idea what Oakley was doing on the McKenna Ranch when she was shot?

As she'd returned from freshening up, she stopped dead in the doorway. Holden was standing next to Oakley's bedside. For a moment, she wanted to scream at him to get out, to get away from her baby. She watched him touch Oakley's arm. She couldn't hear what he was saying, but she could see the expression on his face. His sorrow clutched at her chest and brought tears to her eyes.

As she stepped into the room, closing the door behind her, Holden glanced at her, but quickly turned his gaze to her daughter again. She watched him brush a lock of Oakley's hair back from her face. The sight weakened her knees and her resolve to throw him out as it brought back the memory of how tender the man could be, how loving. Her heart felt as if it would break all over again. He made her remember how much she'd loved him and how badly she wished she still didn't.

"What are you doing here?" Her voice didn't sound like her own.

"I wanted to see how she was," he said without looking at her. "I didn't think you'd let me see her, so I waited until I saw you leave the room."

He'd been here in the hospital, watching her? She swallowed and moved to the chair beside Oakley's bed to collapse into it. He looked at her then. "When was the last time you had something to eat?"

She shook her head. "I'm fine. I don't need your..." She hadn't known what she was going to say, words failing her for a moment. For months she hadn't seen him even in passing, and then he rode up at their spot on the creek, and now this visit? "You should go. There is nothing you can do here." She could feel his gaze as if it were caressing her face. She couldn't meet his eyes. Instead, she kept her eyes on Oakley, wishing he would leave, wishing he didn't make her feel warring emotions that wore her out.

"I'll go," he said after a moment. He turned to Oakley again, touched her cheek, murmured something Charlotte couldn't hear—a prayer?—and then left. She waited until she was sure he was no longer out there watching her before she put her face in her hands. But no tears came, as if she'd cried them all out over the years. As badly as she needed to weep, to scream, to let it all out, there was no comfort for her, no release of her grief, her fear, her aching need to rewrite history so she would no longer hurt so badly.

For a few moments, she felt incapable of moving, she was so exhausted. She sat looking down at Oakley long after Holden had left. Then she straightened, picked up her purse, kissed her daughter's cheek and headed home. A woman had to know when she was beaten, she'd always said. She was. But good. She needed a bath, clean clothes and a decent night's sleep.

Tomorrow, she'd face all of this. Tomorrow.

COOPER DROVE IN silence through the darkness between the rocky, pine-covered mountains before the highway dropped down into the Powder River Basin. Tilly seemed lost in her thoughts, her face turned away from him. But he could see her face reflected in the glass. He could see her chewing at her lower lip, and he knew something had happened back at the bar that had upset her. "You don't have to tell me about Tick."

"It's not that," Tilly said, tugging at the bottom of her jean jacket for a moment as she sat up. "He made my skin crawl. All the time I was sitting there I was thinking that he could be the person who shot Oakley."

"I'm sorry."

She shrugged. "It was my idea. I mean, I knew where he was headed the first time we talked to him. I could have shut him down from the get-go. I certainly didn't have to meet him at the bar."

He could hear regret and something more. He glanced over at her. "Did he make a pass at you?"

She let out a startled laugh. "If he had, you'd have known about it by the way he hollered in pain. No. He just made me feel…icky. He's so slimy." She hugged herself. "Also, I didn't learn much. I suppose I'm disappointed, feel cheap for even agreeing to have a drink with him. The only thing he said when I mentioned Oakley was that my sister had the prettiest eyes he'd ever seen."

Cooper caught his breath, his gaze swinging to hers. "When did he see her close enough that he knew the color of her eyes?"

"I started to ask him that, but he said he misspoke, that he'd had too much to drink, that it was my eyes he was talking about. He said he'd never met my sister, but he sure hoped she'd be all right. I didn't believe him."

Cooper didn't know what to say for a moment. "I think I might know how their paths could have crossed. We need to find out if Oakley was involved in a group opposed to the methane drilling."

"You think that's how Tick met her?"

"I think it's a place to start. There's been rumors floating around about residents getting together and doing something about the drilling. I doubt we were the only ranch that lost one of our biggest producing water wells because of the drilling."

"The drilling on our ranch really did cause that?" Tilly asked, concerned. "I'm sorry. I tried to talk my mother out of it, especially so close to your place, but CJ convinced her otherwise. But I can't see Oakley involved in an anti-methane group... I'll look in her room when I get home. I don't even know if she keeps a diary or will have some item to give me an idea of what she's been doing."

He glanced at her as he drove. "Can you get into her phone? There could be something on her calendar."

"Stuart still has her phone. I'll see if he's gotten into it. Maybe I can talk him into letting me give it a try. I know Oakley's passwords."

He nodded, thinking of his one and only password. Ahead, he could see the lights of Powder Crossing, and the river silver in the starlight. "Maybe you should tell Stuart what you found out and let him take it from here. He is the sheriff." *And your boyfriend*, but he didn't say that.

She shook her head. "He's also understaffed and, if you must know, looking into other leads, he told me. He didn't say it, but it was clear that he thought I was wrong about the gas company having anything to do with this because of my bias. If you don't want to help me—"

"That's not it." He slowed on the edge of town and caught her eye. "I don't want to come between you and Stuart."

"Do you have any idea how arrogant that sounds?"

"You know what I mean. I don't want him thinking…"

"What?"

He could see the challenge in her eyes. She was already angry with herself and Tick. He knew that Tilly could be reckless enough, but when she was angry… He didn't want her doing something she would regret— and he might regret even more.

"I'm not bailing on you," he said quickly. "I just don't want him thinking there is more going on between us than there is," he told her, and saw that he'd put his foot in it again even as hard as he'd tried not to.

She sat back in her seat, turning to look out at town as they drove through. "My truck's right up here," she said, unnecessarily since he'd picked her up here not that many hours ago.

She was angry, and he wasn't entirely sure how much of it had to do with him. But he suspected it was because he'd made it sound as if there was no chance there could be something going on between them because he wasn't interested. That wasn't the case.

He clamped his jaw shut, determined not to put his foot in his mouth again tonight. He'd let her call him tomorrow if she wanted his help. Otherwise, he'd start teaching Holly Jo about horses. It would be for the best.

He liked Tilly, too much, and spending this time together had only made him like her more. He was afraid of getting too close because of his feelings for her.

But if she didn't call tomorrow and they quit working together, he'd be disappointed. He'd come to look forward to seeing her. He enjoyed being with her, something he wouldn't admit even under torture. They weren't Romeo and Juliet, and their families were definitely not the Montagues and Capulets, but it was close. He couldn't let this go that far. No good would come of it for either one of them.

He pulled up by her truck, glad this conversation was over. But Tilly didn't get out.

"Tell me about Leann."

Where the hell had that come from? His old girlfriend was the last thing he wanted to talk about. "You already know about her. Her suicide was all over the news, all over town."

She shook her head. "Did you steal her from Stuart?"

He swore. "You can't steal people without duct tape and a gun to their head. I really don't want to talk about this with you. It was a horrible time in my life. I certainly don't want to relive it tonight." He met her gaze. "Did Stuart tell you that?"

"No. I know a friend of Leann's. She doesn't tell the same story as the one Stuart told me. She said Leann was never in love with Stuart, that she dated him a few times and he became really controlling and jealous and—"

"Tilly. That's all water under the bridge."

"But is it?" She turned to him. "Stuart has been

acting really jealous, like he thinks you're trying to steal me."

Cooper held up both hands. No matter what he said, it would be wrong. "I didn't come back to town to get between what the two of you have."

"I know how Leann felt. Stuart and I went out six times in the weeks before you came back. Maybe it's Oakley's shooting or being around you, but—"

He stopped her. "Don't. Please don't."

Tears pooled in her eyes. "Tell me you don't feel anything for me, and I'll never bring it up again."

Cooper felt his heart fall like a stone into a bottomless well. "I will not come between you and Stuart."

"That doesn't answer my question."

He shook his head. "Please, get out of the truck. This isn't the time to get into…us. *Please, Tilly.*"

"I've never thought of you as a coward, Cooper McKenna," she said as she climbed out and slammed the door behind her.

He grimaced at her words. The thing about even the chance of history repeating itself was enough to keep him from calling her back and trying to fix this tonight. He shouldn't have come back home, and he sure as hell shouldn't have feelings for Tilly Stafford.

Rubbing a hand over his face, he waited until she drove off before he headed toward the ranch. His head spun with thoughts and emotions that felt as tangled as barbed wire and just as painful to try to unravel.

He hadn't gone far when he saw the flashing lights of a patrol car come on behind him. Swearing, he pulled over. He hadn't been speeding, he doubted he had a taillight out and he wasn't driving drunk.

That left only one thing. Stuart had seen him drop Tilly off at her pickup at this time of the night. Had he been sitting down the block waiting? Or did he just happen to be nearby? Cooper figured he was about to find out. He waited in his pickup as the sheriff pulled his patrol SUV up behind him, got out and walked toward him.

Cooper pulled out his license and registration, determined to keep this civil. But from the expression on the sheriff's face, it was too late for that. He whirred down his driver's-side window and did his best not to look guilty of anything.

TILLY HADN'T CRIED over a boy since high school. After she'd left Cooper, she'd been too upset to go home. She'd driven to the hospital, glad to see that her mother wasn't around. The nurse told her that Charlotte had gone home and wasn't planning to come back until morning. Even better news, Tilly thought.

Now, as she sat next to her sister's hospital bed, she let the tears flow. There had been a time when she and Oakley had shared confidences. She missed those long talks, when they'd covered for each other when one of them was in trouble, when they'd been close and shared everything.

"I can't believe I let this happen," she said to her sister in the privacy of the closed-door hospital room. With Oakley unconscious, she could pour out her heart in privacy. "Cooper McKenna. I know. You would have a fit if you were conscious. You'd tell me what a fool I am. How a relationship with a McKenna would never work. How Mother wouldn't allow it." She took a breath between sobs. "Not that it would stop *you*. You always were braver than me. What am I going to do? I like him so much it hurts. I know he likes me, but he's such a coward. He doesn't want to hurt Stuart even though I tried to tell him that it isn't like that between Stuart and me. Oh, I wish you'd wake up. I need to know about Cooper's old girlfriend, the one who killed herself. I wasn't paying that much attention at the time, but you always know the latest gossip."

She studied her sister and frowned. "I wish you could tell me who did this. But I have a bad feeling that you got involved with that group that's been vandalizing gas company property, didn't you?" She sighed and wiped her tears. "I suspect it's the reason you're lying here now. Oh, Oakley, you have to come back. I need you. I love you. I'm sorry I've been a terrible older sister, so involved in my own life that I didn't pay any attention to you."

"You've always been that way." The words came out raspy and barely audible.

For a moment, she thought she'd only imagined that they'd come from her sister's mouth. She stared at Oakley. Those green eyes that Tick had mentioned fluttered open. Oakley did have beautiful eyes. Tilly began to cry with joy as she grabbed her sister's hand.

"Water."

Hurriedly, she pushed the button for a nurse, then struggled to raise the bed enough that she could put the paper straw to Oakley's lips. A nurse rushed in. "She just woke up," Tilly told her, excited as she wiped her tears.

"I couldn't take any more of your blubbering," her sister whispered hoarsely.

Tilly stood back to let the nurse check Oakley and realized she needed to call her mother and let her know. She felt caught between laughing and crying again. Oakley was awake and her old self. The sheriff would have to be notified too, she thought as she called her mother first with the news.

For a moment, she'd forgotten that now that Oakley was awake, her sister could tell them who had shot her. There was no longer a reason for Tilly and Cooper to play detective. It would be over.

Her heart tumbled at the thought, but she quickly tried to rise above it. Cooper would be glad. So would Stuart. Not that any of that mattered. Her sister was going to live; that was all that she cared about right now. Oakley's would-be killer would be caught and put behind bars. Justice would be done. Tilly began to cry again.

STUART KNEW HE was about to make an ass out of himself. When he'd seen Cooper drop Tilly off at this late hour of the night, he'd felt as if he'd been punched in the gut. This after seeing them together earlier?

He'd hoped that Tilly and Cooper butting into his investigation had been a one-off. But he knew now it hadn't been, though he'd never expected to see the two of them coming back to town this late. Whatever they'd been up to, they weren't trying very hard to keep it on the down-low.

That should have relieved his mind. Instead, it made him angry. They were rubbing it in his face. Everyone in town was talking about seeing them together. Cooper hadn't even been back to town for a week, and he'd already come between him and Tilly.

As he walked toward his once–best friend's pickup, he balled his hands into fists, then released them as he neared the driver's side. All the way, he kept telling himself he shouldn't have pulled Cooper over. He shouldn't get into it with him, not like this. However, it was as if he wasn't listening to his logical, sensible self. He was risking his job right now.

But this mix of anger and regret and disappointment was too powerful. Cooper had his window down, waiting behind the wheel, no doubt not looking forward to a confrontation. He was probably hoping this didn't turn into something ugly. Stuart was hoping that himself, and that was what really scared him, because he couldn't see how it wouldn't get ugly the way he was feeling.

"How was your night?" he asked as he reached the cowboy's open window, although that wasn't what he'd planned to say.

"Fine." He could see that Cooper was playing this straight even though he knew that being pulled over had nothing to do with the law. But there was a man in uniform with a gun standing at his window.

"Have you been drinking?"

"I had half a bottle of beer hours ago. You're welcome to do a breath analyzer test if you don't believe me."

Stuart looked away for a moment. "What the hell's going on, Cooper?" He took a breath, trying to hide how upset he was, but knowing he was failing. This was his friend. Once his best friend.

"Nothing's going on, Stu."

"You moving in on Tilly?"

"Nope. Just trying to keep her out of trouble."

"I believe that's my job," he said from between gritted teeth.

"Does she know that?" Cooper asked, and met his gaze.

He swore and slammed his fist against the side of the cab. "Damn it, Cooper. I let you have Leann, but you can't have Tilly."

COOPER FELT HIS heart miss a beat. He wasn't drunk, but the sheriff had definitely had more than a few. "I can't believe you just said that."

"Which part? That I let you take Leann away from me? Or that I'll fight you for Tilly?"

He shook his head. "Let's give this a rest for tonight."

"I'm not going to feel any different tomorrow." His voice sounded hoarse with emotion and rough with whatever booze he'd consumed. He also looked dead on his feet. This case had to be taking a toll on him.

Cooper's heart went out to his friend. "I'm sorry. I'm not trying to make your job harder or come between you and Tilly."

"But you are, Coop. I'm betting you didn't mean to come between me and Leann either."

"I'm not doing this." He started his pickup engine and started to close his window.

Stuart grabbed for him, but the window went up too fast and he had to pull his arm back. They stared at each other through the dusty glass for a long moment before Cooper pulled away. He hoped Stu didn't come after him and was relieved when he looked back to see the sheriff standing in the middle of the road. It was the defeat in his stance that tugged at Cooper's heart.

Clearly, they remembered what happened with Leann differently, but still, Stuart had gotten hurt. Cooper didn't want to ever do that again to his friend. He told himself that he had to keep his distance from Tilly.

As he drove toward the ranch, he felt as if he'd dodged a bullet. Not that this was over. He wasn't as innocent as he'd wanted Stu to believe. He'd kept Tilly at arm's length, but the truth was, if he spent much more time around her, he wasn't sure he could keep doing it.

Earlier, he felt as if Tilly was almost daring him to make a move. It wasn't as if he hadn't thought about pulling her into his arms and kissing her. But he hadn't, even though when he'd looked into her eyes, he'd been certain that was exactly what she wanted. Because she had feelings for him? Or because she wasn't sure what she wanted?

Either way, the two of them together were trouble, something Cooper didn't want or need.

CHAPTER ELEVEN

TILLY HADN'T BEEN in her sister's bedroom in a long time. As she opened the door, she was reminded of a time when their doors weren't closed, let alone locked. When they could call back and forth from their rooms, laughing and teasing. When they would curl up together in one of their beds and talk late into the night about everything from their dreams to the boys they liked to their weddings and the kids they would have.

She hadn't realized how much she'd missed those times as she stared at her sister's messy room in the light of morning. Tilly liked her room neat, everything in its place. Oakley, however, seemed to prefer chaos. There were piles of clothes, magazines and clutter. It felt like she was trespassing, and for a moment, Tilly hesitated.

How could she ever find anything in here anyway? Or was she just afraid of what she'd find? Wading through discarded shoes, T-shirts, pajamas and books, she reached the desk. It was strewn with cosmetics, hair products, perfumes and jewelry. She opened a couple of drawers, but found nothing other than more of the same.

Except taped to one side of a desk drawer was a

list. She realized what she was looking at. Her sister's passwords. Tilly let out a laugh. So like Oakley. She could never be bothered to remember them. She used to have her computer password written on her hand because she was always forgetting it.

Tilly glanced at the list, knowing how upset Oakley would be if she knew. Fortunately, the password for her new phone was at the top. She put the list back where she'd found it quickly. The last thing she wanted to do was break her sister's trust.

As she started to turn away, she caught sight of her sister's bulletin board. It was covered with photos of friends, most making silly faces, most looking tipsy. But the photos, she realized, were old. Was she friends with any of those girls anymore?

She felt as if she'd missed a huge chunk of her sister's life, when she saw the flyer. It was partially balled up on the floor next to her overflowing trash can. What had caught her eye was the company name CH4. She reached for the flyer, flattening it out on an empty spot on the bed. If not for the word *CH4*, she might have thought it was a flyer for some band Oakley wanted to see in Billings.

But as she looked closer, she saw that it was indeed about methane gas drilling. She knew there were numerous organizations in the state opposed to the drilling, but this flyer wasn't on glossy paper. Nor had it been produced by a professional designer. It had been printed on someone's computer in black ink. The grassroots look of it made it seem all that more subversive and dangerous. Printed in large block letters was

DIRTY BUSINESS. There were no data, no facts to back up whatever the organization's claims might be. Instead, there was simply a date and time and the words NO MORE DRILLING.

The date was tonight at 9:00 p.m. Oakley had circled it and written *CH4* next to it. But nowhere could she find where the meeting was to be held. At one of the airport hangars? Seemed unlikely.

She stared it for a full minute before she pulled out her phone, then remembered that she wasn't speaking to Cooper. Her face burned at the memory of last night. What had she been thinking throwing herself at the cowboy? She groaned. Had she really called him a coward? She reminded herself that now that her sister was awake, Oakley would tell Stuart who shot her. There was no longer any reason to look for clues, let alone go to some subversive meeting about methane well drilling. She really didn't even need her sister's password for her phone. The sheriff would get it from Oakley and he'd have whatever he might need to find and arrest her shooter.

Her phone rang. For a split second, her heart lifted at the thought it might be Cooper. It was her mother.

"I leave to go home and shower and change and your sister wakes up?" her mother demanded without preamble. "I'm so glad you called me, though, and grateful she's going to be all right, but I had wanted to be there."

"Has she told you who shot her?" she asked, looking at the flyer in her hand.

"No." She heard something in her mother's hesitation. "She doesn't know. Or at least doesn't remember.

The doctor said, with her concussion, she might not ever recall the time before she was shot and fell from her horse. I have to go. The doctor's here. I haven't been able to reach your brothers. Please let them know if you see them." She disconnected.

So it wasn't over. Not yet. Tilly glanced at the flyer. Then, screwing up her courage, she called Cooper. He answered on the third ring. "Tilly, I'm kind of in the middle of something right now."

"Oakley is awake, but she doesn't remember anything from the hours before she was shot. I'm in her room. I got the password for her phone and I found a flyer for a group called Dirty Business. They meet tonight."

"Great news that Oakley is conscious. I'll call you back in a few minutes. I'm teaching Holly Jo about horses."

In the background, she heard the girl grumbling. She disconnected, her heart still pounding. Cooper had sounded fine. She felt relieved. He'd probably forgotten all about last night. If he called back, then things between them would go back to the way they were. That was what she wanted, wasn't it?

She looked down at the flyer clutched in her hand, needing to reroute her thoughts. She wasn't up to going down that road this morning. DIRTY BUSINESS. Who were these people? She couldn't imagine local ranchers being involved. These were hardworking people who ranched along the Powder River. If they were against the drilling, then they just wouldn't allow the companies to drill on their property. They wouldn't organize to stop all drilling. They'd figure it wasn't their place to tell their neighbors what to do. They would mind their own business and expect others to do the same.

Except the drilling was hurting other people's water supply, she reminded herself, remembering what her mother's methane well had done to the McKennas.

She stared at the flyer again. It couldn't be very many people. So who were they and where were they meeting? Somewhere secret. She still couldn't believe that Oakley was involved. Or that she wouldn't have said something to her if she was. Tilly could under-stand her keeping this from their mother and brothers, especially CJ, who wouldn't mind if the entire ranch was covered in methane wells as long as it meant more money, especially if it hurt the McKennas.

Tilly couldn't shake the feeling that Dirty Business was what had gotten her sister shot, no matter what the sheriff thought.

Her cell phone rang. Cooper? Her heart dropped as she saw that it was Stuart. She let it ring a couple more times, not really wanting to answer it. They would even-tually have to talk. She needed to tell him how she felt, but she was dreading it. He would think it was because of Cooper.

In truth, it was, but it also wasn't. The cowboy wasn't interested in her. But he had made her realize why she and Stuart still hadn't made love after their half dozen dates. His jealousy over Cooper had made her see that he was more serious than she was about their dating. In all fairness to him, she couldn't keep seeing him.

Her phone rang again. What if it was news about her

sister's shooter? "Stuart," she said as she answered the call. She couldn't help still being put out with him after their argument the other night, but she knew it was a lot more than that. She needed to break things off with him, which felt odd since she hadn't really thought of them as a couple. "Any news on my sister's shooter?"

"Was it really all that long ago that my calls were met with more enthusiasm?" he asked.

She felt a little guilty. He was right. The times they'd gone out, she'd had fun with him. He could let his hair down and be quite entertaining. "I'm sorry. I've had a lot on my mind."

"Haven't we all," he said. "Do you know if your sister was dating Pickett Hanson?"

"Pickett?" He was one of the McKenna ranch hands. While good-looking in a rough-edged kind of way, she couldn't imagine Oakley with the good-natured, not terribly ambitious Pickett. "I highly doubt it."

"Well, sometimes there is no accounting for taste or good sense," Stuart said, and she knew he was no longer talking about her sister and the ranch hand.

"Sorry, I'm afraid I can't help," she said, looking around the room. "I have no idea what Oakley's been up to lately." She thought about mentioning the flyer she'd found, but Stuart had already made it clear that he wasn't that interested in CH4 or anything to do with the controversy over methane gas drilling. Like he said, he was following other leads. Did he now think Pickett had something to do with shooting her sister?

"I'll track down Pickett. Maybe he can shed some light on it." His tone changed. "How are you doing?

I'm so glad Oakley is awake and in stable condition. Good that you were with her when she regained consciousness."

Tilly thought about what she'd been telling her sister at the time and flushed with embarrassment. "Did she say anything to you about me?"

Silence, then, "Why would she say something to me about you?"

She skipped over the question. "I didn't ask her about the shooting. I was just so glad that she was all right."

"Tilly." He cleared his throat. "I'd like to see you. I was thinking we could go into Miles City for a movie, dinner, make a night of it. Get out and forget about all this for a while?"

She looked down at the flyer in her hand and let out the breath she hadn't realized she'd been holding. "I can't tonight. I'm sorry." She could hear ice fill the line even before Stuart spoke.

"Maybe some other time." He disconnected, leaving her holding the phone and feeling worse. Should she have told him about Dirty Business and the meeting tonight? Probably, even if he didn't think it was important.

The one thing she couldn't do was put off talking to him. The problem was that he wouldn't want to believe why she was making this decision. He would blame Cooper. The irony of that didn't escape her. Cooper McKenna wanted nothing to do with her. She wasn't even sure he would call her back—let alone help her find out who had shot her sister.

Not that it was going to stop her, though, Tilly told

herself as she tried to ignore the ache in her chest. How long had she felt this way about Cooper? A lot longer than she wanted to admit.

"THAT YOUR GIRLFRIEND?" Holly Jo had asked as Cooper pocketed his phone.

"No. Nor is it any of your business. Pay attention to what you're doing."

She'd groaned, the brush in her hand. "I now know the parts of a horse, and that horses have to be brushed and fed and their stalls cleaned out. Are you ever going to show me how to saddle one?"

Now he studied the girl as she hauled feed and water for the other horses in the stable. She was cute, hard-headed and mouthy. He figured she'd fit in just fine around here. "Okay, go get that small saddle. I'll show you." It was the first real enthusiasm he'd seen in the girl. Also, she actually seemed to be paying attention as he went through the steps.

"Okay, now I get to ride," she said when he had the horse saddled.

"Nope," he said as he began removing the saddle and bridle.

"What?"

"Now you get to do it." He put the saddle and tack down. "Let's see if you were paying attention."

"You can't be serious," she cried. "You had the horse saddled."

"I had it saddled. Now it's your turn." He sat down on a stool near the stall, stretched out his long legs and tipped his hat down as if he was about to take a nap.

Out of the corner of his eye, he watched her lift the saddle that wasn't all that much smaller than her, but to her credit, she managed, then realized there was no way she could throw it up on the horse's back.

"Excuse me," she said pointedly. "I need that stool."

He grinned as he rose and handed her the stool. He thought for sure that once she picked up the saddle and stepped on the stool, she'd be on her backside. To his surprise, she got the saddle onto the mare's back. His father had picked one of their smaller, more docile horses for her.

The mare turned to look at her as she started to cinch the saddle down. "What are you looking at?" she demanded of the horse.

Cooper shook his head, wondering again if his father had any idea what he was getting into. "I'd check that cinch. Remember what I told you—"

"Pull it tighter later. Got it."

She did seem to have it. She put the bridle on and the bit in the horse's mouth. As she finished, she said, "So now I get to ride."

"Nope."

"What?" She sounded on the edge of a major breakdown.

"Tomorrow, same time, same place. I promise, you'll get to ride, but you're not ready yet to go farther than the corral for a while."

Her face clouded, a storm coming, but she said nothing as she started to stomp away.

"But there won't be any riding tomorrow either if you leave that saddle and bridle on that horse," he said.

She'd made it almost to the stable door. She stopped, her back to him. He could see her internal battle going on. Her hands were clamped into fists at her sides, but she turned and walked back, doing her best to ignore him. She got the bridle off, the bit out of the horse's mouth and finally the saddle off, put it and the tack away and took the stool out of the stall.

"Be sure to give your horse a treat after all that," he said.

Grudgingly, she took the apple he gave her and fed it to the horse. "What's her name?"

"Honey. You be nice to her, she'll be nice to you."

Holly Jo nodded, studying the horse for a minute before she closed the stall door and with a sigh walked out. He shook his head as he watched her go. Maybe there was hope. Horses had the power to help any kid willing to accept what they offered.

He pulled out his phone and called Tilly back, all the time reminding himself that he needed to stay clear of her. "Sorry, Holly Jo is a headstrong twelve-year-old hard to rein in. Reminded me of you at twelve years old. Remember that one rodeo where I dared you to stand on your horse and gallop around the arena and you did it?" he asked with a chuckle.

"Got me kicked out of the competition, which I'm sure is why you dared me to do it."

He laughed. "Sorry about that. But come on—you know you were always too big for your britches. Someone had to knock you down a peg or two once in a while."

"I beg your pardon?"

Cooper swore under his breath. This was not the way the phone call was supposed to go. He certainly hadn't meant to be taking a ride down memory lane any more than he'd planned to be joking with Tilly. But he felt bad about the way last night had ended. He didn't want there to be hard feelings between them. He liked her. Their easy banter made it fun, made it easy to be in her company.

He could pretend that they were just friends and that he wasn't attracted to her, or that being around her was making it harder not to do something about it. "You said you found something?"

If she heard the change in his voice, she didn't comment on it. "A flyer from a group called Dirty Business. They're meeting tonight at nine. The problem is, I don't know where. But I think I know someone who might. Pickett."

"Our Pickett?" he asked, sounding surprised.

"The sheriff called earlier. He wanted to know if Oakley and Pickett had been dating. If they had been seen together, I'm betting it had to do with this anti-methane group."

Cooper didn't know what to say. Pickett was a hard-working ranch hand, but also one of the most cheerful and entertaining of the bunch. While he was a hard worker, he seemed to go through life without a care in the world. He certainly didn't seem the type to join some underground group to protest coalbed methane drilling.

"He really doesn't seem the type," Cooper said. "Does Oakley?"

"You have me there. You want me to ask him?"

"If you wouldn't mind." They were back to all business, on solid footing, so why did it make him feel sad? But she had called Stuart "sheriff," if that meant anything.

"No problem. I'll let you know what I find out. And I'm really glad to hear that Oakley is going to be all right."

"But she doesn't remember, and might never be able to remember, who shot her or why."

He'd been hoping that it would be over by tonight—before this meeting of Dirty Business. There would be no reason for Tilly and him to go to the meeting.

They both were quiet for a few moments. "I should go," Cooper said, digging a toe into the dirt floor, feeling uncomfortable, feeling more upset about the situation than he wished he did.

There was no way he was going to let Tilly go to this meeting alone. Tempers were bound to flare. He'd already heard about vandalism of drilling equipment and retribution from gas company workers. He didn't want Tilly in the middle of that—especially if it was the reason one of them had taken a gun to her sister.

"I'll call as soon as I've talked to Pickett." With that, he disconnected, swore and went to find the ranch hand.

CHAPTER TWELVE

TILLY COULDN'T RELAX after her phone call with Cooper. At first he was like he had always been, friendly, teasing, but then she'd felt him pull away. She knew it was because of Stuart. The thought made her angry as she stuffed the flyer into her jacket pocket and headed for the door.

Cooper had made it clear last night that he wasn't interested in her. So did that mean that they couldn't even be friends if it made Stuart uncomfortable?

It was time she took care of things between her and the sheriff. But first she wanted to get her hands on her sister's phone now that she had the password.

In his office, Stuart looked up, clearly surprised to see her after their conversation earlier on the phone. He looked expectant, then a little leery, as if he knew what was coming. "I have a license plate number I hoped you'd look up for me." She'd forgotten about it until she'd found the note on the way into town.

He made a disgruntled face. "That isn't the way things work."

"Also, do you have my sister's phone? I told her I would pick it up for her."

Stuart sighed. "Anything else I can do for you while I'm at it?"

Tilly bit down on a rude retort. They'd gone from enjoying each other's company to this so fast that it scared her. Was it all because of his jealousy over Cooper? She knew her attitude toward him had certainly changed. She didn't think she could put all that on Cooper.

"If you don't want to help me…" She turned to leave, knowing he would stop her.

"Wait." She didn't turn around even as she heard him rise from his chair. "Tilly?"

Turning slowly, she faced him. She kept thinking about Leann Hayes and what her friend had told her. Had Leann gone through this with Stuart, seen a side of him she didn't like? A side of him that worried her? That scared her?

Tilly swallowed as Stuart closed the distance between them, reaching past her and shutting his door. They were inches apart now. If she stepped back, she would be against the door. She held her ground even as he picked up her long braid. He twisted it in his fingers before he met her gaze.

"I care about you," he said quietly. "I'd hoped you and I were headed somewhere."

She pulled her braid free of his fingers and shook her head. "Stuart, my sister being shot has kind of derailed a lot of things."

He nodded and met her gaze. "You don't want to see me anymore."

Tilly swallowed. "I think it's for the best since I

hadn't realized you were more invested in the relationship than I was."

"That's why you weren't interested in sleeping with
me and this has nothing to do with Cooper McKenna?"

"Since Oakley was shot, I've been on an emotional
roller coaster. Right now, I don't want to date anyone,
so no, it isn't about Cooper. I just want to know who
shot my sister and why."

He studied her, making her even more nervous than
when he'd been playing with her hair. She did her best
not to show it, but with his office door closed, it felt
too intimate, and with him so close…

"I shouldn't do this." He studied her openly. "Give
me a minute," he said with another sigh as he reached
for the note in her hand. "Have a seat. I'll be right back."

She stepped to the side in the narrow space and let
him pass as he opened the door and left. She finally
took a shaky breath. She was trembling inside. He'd
scared her, this man she'd known all her life. They'd
been friends—until she went out with him a few times
and he'd gotten so possessive.

Moving over to his desk, she tried to calm down.
She saw her sister's pink glittered phone cover sticking out of a pile of papers. She checked the door, then
hurriedly scooped it up. Even as she was typing in the
password, she kept eyeing the door, afraid he would
come back and catch her.

Why was she suddenly afraid that he wouldn't want
her looking at her sister's phone? Or was she the one
worried about what she might find? Unless the shooting had really been an accident, her sister had been in-

volved in something that had gotten her into trouble. Oakley was still in that trouble with her shooter out there. Maybe next time he wouldn't miss, and it would kill her instead of only wound her.

The phone opened and she quickly began to scan Oakley's calls. Most were from her friends, telling her to get well. She scanned her sister's messages. There were at least a dozen from Pickett Hanson before the shooting. She opened one, but had to quickly shut down the phone and toss it back on Stuart's desk as he walked in the office door.

He didn't speak until he was behind his desk and sitting in his chair. "Tell me again why you want the name of this person."

"He was visiting the pilot, Howie Gunderson. Howie was the one who flew low over the county road the day Oakley was shot. He and Tick Whitaker had seen her and a cowboy chasing her possibly before the shot was fired."

"Yes, I am aware of that. I spoke with Howie and with Tick. I have been doing my job, Tilly."

She didn't rise to the bait. "It seemed suspicious the way he left, as if he didn't want us seeing him there. You know who his visitor was?"

He looked down at the paper in his hand for a moment as if making up his mind. "Jason Murdock from Billings." He looked up as he said it. "That mean anything to you?"

She shook her head. "Maybe it wasn't important, but thank you for checking." Whoever the man was, she had the feeling that he hadn't wanted them to know that he had dealings with Howie and CH4. Why else sneak away like he had?

"He's a private detective." Stuart rose. "I need to get over and see your sister."

"I should take her phone to her."

"Actually, I'll do that," the sheriff said. "There might be evidence on it that will be helpful in solving this case."

COOPER FOUND PICKETT and some of the other ranch hands mending fence out in the south forty. He'd saddled up and ridden out after Deacon had told him where he might find the man. But first the ranch manager had to ask about Holly Jo's horseback lesson.

"I taught her the basics, but she's not ready to ride yet. She thinks she is, but she's wrong," Cooper said. "I'll work with her again tomorrow in the corral."

"That is one stubborn girl," Deacon said. "Better keep a close eye on her."

He wanted to say, "Tell that to my father." The ranch was huge. If the girl wanted to get lost on it, she wouldn't have to go far. He hoped she was smarter than that, but while he'd teach her to ride, he wasn't babysitting her.

"Pickett," Cooper called out now as he rode down the fence line to where the crew was stretching barbed wire. "Need to talk to you a minute."

All of the ranch hands stopped working as Cooper dismounted and led his horse some distance from the others. Pickett followed.

"What you need, boss?"

"It's Cooper, and I just need to ask you a couple of

questions." He pulled off his hat, scrubbed at the back of his neck. The day was hot, the sun glaring in a sky of such deep blue that it hurt to look at it. "Awful hot out here for the end of June."

"You rode all the way out here to talk about the weather?" Pickett chuckled.

He looked back at the others. "Do you know anything about a group called Dirty Business?" He'd been watching the ranch hand's face out of the corner of his eye and didn't miss his reaction. Now he looked directly at him. "Is Oakley in the group?"

He'd caught Pickett flat-footed, and it showed on the man's usual quick-to-smile face. "Your answer has nothing to do with your job."

Pickett nodded and seemed to give the question some thought. "I might know something."

"There's a meeting tonight. Where exactly?" He waited, watching the man struggle. "This also is between just the two of us." He could see Pickett caught between two alliances, maybe more, depending on how close he was to Oakley. Fraternizing with the enemy was definitely frowned upon—on both sides of the barbed-wire fence.

"Down at Bowman's abandoned barn." It was quite a few miles from town. "You planning to come alone?" Pickett asked.

"I'll probably be bringing Tilly Stafford. That okay with you?" He didn't need the man's permission. What he needed was for Pickett not to warn the other members and cancel the meeting.

"'Spect that would be all right."

"Suppose you heard that Oakley regained consciousness. Seems she's going to recover just fine." He saw the man's relief, more relief than he would expect if they were only vigilantes against methane gas drilling. He wondered what Tilly would make of it. Guess he'd have to ask her and let her take it from there, since Cooper had no intention of asking the ranch hand about his love life.

"She saw who shot her?" Pickett asked.

"Not that I've heard. Thanks for your help. Appreciate it," he told the ranch hand as Pickett walked back toward the others. He knew the men would quiz him, curious about their conversation. "And if you see Holly Jo wandering too far from the ranch house, would you let me know?" he called after him.

Pickett turned, smiled. "You bet I will. Already heard she might give us a run for our money."

When Cooper got back to the ranch, he put his horse away and called Tilly. He'd thought about going to this clandestine meeting alone, but Oakley was her sister. If they were going to get any insight into who shot her, he figured people would be more forthcoming with Tilly there. And there was no way Tilly wouldn't want to go.

At least that was what he told himself as she answered the phone. "I know where the meeting is tonight." His throat went dry. He couldn't let her go alone, and he couldn't betray Pickett by sending the sheriff. "You wanna go?"

"You know I do," she said. He tried not to read too much into her tone, but if he had to guess, she sounded pleased. "I've got news as well. Meet in town?"

"No, I think we should meet behind the old gas station on the way out of town. I'll tell you why when I see you. Eight forty-five?"

"See you then."

He disconnected, telling himself he was a damned fool. He didn't like the way he and Stu had left things last night. He couldn't let this escalate. Heading for his pickup, he decided that after tonight it was time to mend some of his own fences.

CHAPTER THIRTEEN

COOPER FOUND THE sheriff just returning to his office. As Stuart got out of his patrol SUV, he took one look at Cooper, slammed his vehicle door and leaned against it, waiting.

"Just stopped by. You'd mentioned having a beer sometime, for old times' sake," Cooper said, walking toward him.

His friend looked up slowly. "A beer?"

"You used to like beer. Or have you switched to whiskey?"

Stu chuckled at that. When they were teenagers, Stu had gotten drunk on some hard-core whiskey he'd taken from his house. It had made him deathly ill. He swore he'd never touch the stuff again. "Think us having a drink would do any good?"

"Can't see how a beer or two would hurt. We could come unarmed, if you think it's nec— Oh, that's right. You're the sheriff—you're always armed." He smiled. "Then again, I remember that you always carried long before you went into law enforcement."

"Maybe you should start."

Cooper shook his head. "I don't think there are that many people in the county who want me dead."

"I wouldn't bet on that." But he smiled when he said it.

"It's almost quitting time."

"For bankers and lawyers," Stu said. "I've got some things I have to do."

"Just give me a holler when you're free."

"How about later tonight?" Stuart asked, an edge to his tone.

"Can't tonight. Family meeting. Not sure how long it will run. You might have heard—we have a new family member. Holly Jo, age twelve. I'll tell you about it over that drink. She's going to turn my father every way but loose."

"Soon, then," Stu said as he headed inside the sheriff's department.

Cooper climbed back into his pickup, wondering if he'd mended any fences or was about to burn down the barn tonight. The family meeting was true. It was what he planned to do after dinner, meeting Tilly for the Dirty Business event. He feared that if Stu found out, it could be the end of their friendship.

But as he drove back toward the ranch, he worried it might already be too late no matter what happened tonight.

HOLDEN LOOKED AROUND the table at his family. None of them appeared happy to be there. Normally, they didn't have family suppers except on special occasions. He couldn't think of a special-occasion meal that they'd had in months. Elaine always made unique meals for birthdays and holidays, but all sitting down together was unusual.

They were busy running a ranch, he would tell her when she complained. The truth was that his grown children had lives of their own. While they still lived on the ranch in the vast old house, they had little to say to each other. His sons knew what had to be done on the ranch and saw to it. The ranch hands were the same way. Especially with ranch manager Deacon Yates, who had been with the ranch for years and ran a tight ship.

The financial part of keeping the ranch afloat had fallen on Holden. That work didn't need to be done from the back of a horse. It meant long hours in this office taking care of the bookwork or on the phone with accountants, bankers, stock buyers and sellers. He missed riding fence, rounding up the cattle, breaking in the new colts. He felt as if he'd lost that feeling of being part of the land.

"How was your day?" he asked Treyton, who merely grunted. "Cooper?"

"Fine."

"Duffy?" His son shrugged. "Bailey?" He had to say her name again.

She quickly hid her phone. "What?"

"How was your day?"

"Fine. Why?"

"Holly Jo?" She had been frowning at her plate, which appeared to have only broccoli on it. He started to comment but stopped himself.

Cooper said, "Holly Jo and I spent some time in the stables learning about horses."

Her head jerked up. "I still haven't gotten to ride a

horse! What's the point of living on a ranch if I don't even get to ride a horse?"

Holden chuckled. "I'm glad you're interested in riding." He was also glad that Elaine had gotten the girl boots, jeans, Western shirts and a summer straw hat. Holly Jo had said she hated the clothing, but she was willing to wear it in the stables if it meant she would eventually get to ride a horse.

"When Cooper says you're ready, I'd love to come with you on your first ride," he told the girl.

She pulled a face and stabbed her fork into a large piece of broccoli, clearly not excited about the prospect. He watched her chewing on the stalk of broccoli for a moment before he looked at Cooper. "I heard Oakley is conscious. Was she able to tell the sheriff who shot her?"

"She's conscious, but because of the concussion, her memory of the hours before that hasn't returned. The doctors aren't sure it will."

"If you'll excuse me," Treyton said after clearing his plate, "I have to get back to work. We're having trouble with another one of our wells." With that, he left.

Duffy finished his meal and excused himself as well. "Date," he said on his way out.

Holly Jo pushed her plate away and started to stand.

"Young lady, please ask to be excused," Holden said.

She stared at him as if in shock. "But they didn't really ask to be excused."

"They're grown men and they did excuse themselves."

She glared at him, the words coming out like thrown stones. "May I please be excused?"

"Yes." He wanted to talk to her about her eating habits, but decided to pick one battle at a time.

"She'll adjust," Cooper said after she'd gone upstairs. "I like her spunk."

"There is a lot of anger there."

"I get it. She has no control over her life. Her mother died, and now she has been forced to come here."

"Some people might not think living on a ranch is such a hardship."

"Have you enrolled her in school yet? Don't classes start right after Labor Day?"

He cursed himself under his breath. "Of course they do. I'll take care of that right away. I didn't even think… Let me know when she's ready to ride. I was serious about coming along. I've missed riding."

Bailey had been secretly staring at her phone, which was partially hidden under her napkin. She rose, excusing herself, leaving him and Cooper alone.

COOPER HAD WANTED to ask his dad how the ranch was doing, but from the things Treyton had said and the new worry lines carved in his father's face, he had a pretty good idea. "Is there anything I can do around here to help?"

"For now, I really appreciate you teaching Holly Jo how to ride. After that, well, we'll see how you feel about being more involved in the daily running of the ranch."

"I don't want to step on Treyton's toes."

His father laughed. "No one wants that."

Cooper hesitated before he said, "I know we talked

about this, but I don't think Treyton has given up on drilling methane wells on the ranch."

Holden sighed. "He and I have discussed this at length. He knows how I feel about it, and I have the last word on the subject."

He chose his words carefully. "You don't think he'd take it on himself to do it behind your back, do you?"

His father looked surprised. "Not if he has a lick of sense." He could see his father's ire rising. "I'll talk to him again." He wanted to bring up again his concern about Treyton visiting the realty company in town, but his father pushed his plate away and rose, saying he had a conference call.

He watched him head for his office, worried about his dad, about the ranch, about what was going on in the Powder River Basin. He worried that Oakley Stafford's shooting was just the warning shot of what was to come.

Especially if he kept hanging around Tilly Stafford. His visit with Stu earlier had been chilly at best. There would be no mending things if Cooper didn't give Tilly a wide berth. Even as he thought it, he had to admit that it wasn't what he wanted—quite the opposite.

Stu said he would fight for her. Cooper had seldom walked away from a fight, especially one he thought he could win. But at what cost?

He groaned at the path his thoughts had taken. But if he kept being around Tilly, he knew what was going to happen, and he thought she did too. Was that what she'd wanted him to say last night? That he wanted her?

Even as he warned himself against it, he was already looking forward to seeing her.

Checking the time, he went upstairs to get ready for the Dirty Business event.

TILLY PARKED BEHIND the abandoned gas station outside of town and got out of her pickup. The summer sun had disappeared behind the rugged hills to the west, but it wouldn't get dark until after nine tonight. No one from the highway could see her vehicle, though, but anyone traveling the road to the barn could. She wondered why Cooper had wanted them to meet here. It wasn't because he was looking for an intimate place for them to meet. No, he was worried. About the talk in town? About their families? Or about the people responsible for Oakley's shooting seeing the two of them meeting?

No, she thought, he was worried about his friend.

Well, he didn't need to worry anymore. She and Stuart wouldn't be dating again. Stuart had taken it better than she'd expected. She was glad she'd cleared things up with him. Not that it would make a difference with Cooper—if that was what she'd been thinking.

Tilly felt a chill even though the approaching night was warm. Were Cooper and she headed for trouble if they kept digging into her sister's shooting? Even though Oakley was going to be all right, was she really safe?

The smell of dust hung in the air. She noticed in the fading light that some of the cottonwoods farthest from the river were starting to turn. This drought was all anyone was talking about. Other than the methane well drilling. They needed a good old-fashioned winter with lots of snow. Would Cooper leave again?

She had no idea why he'd come home to begin with and wondered if he did. She hadn't expected to hear from him after last night. Now she hugged herself and checked the time. He wouldn't stand her up. Not Cooper. There was something so Old West gentlemanly about him that it made her smile.

Still, she felt relief when she heard a vehicle coming down the highway, slowing and then turning. She stayed where she was in case it wasn't him. As she heard his pickup turn in and park, she stepped out into the twilight.

COOPER PULLED UP next to Tilly's pickup. She'd been in the shadows of the old station. The light caught in her blond hair. She seldom wore it down, but she had tonight. It floated around her shoulders. The look of her made him catch his breath, desire a fire in his belly and much lower.

As she approached his pickup, he reached over to open the passenger door for her. He was on edge just thinking about the turn last night's conversation had taken. He didn't want to argue with her. He also didn't want to push her away anymore.

As she climbed in, he caught a whiff of the summer night and the sweet scent he knew was Tilly. Not perfume. Maybe her bath soap or shampoo, but it pulled at him, stirring his need for this woman as if fanning embers.

"You said you had news?" he asked to break the silence as she buckled up and he got the truck moving.

"Good to see you too, Cooper," she said, and laughed almost nervously.

He saw that she wore a sleeveless top, her shapely arms tanned, and a skirt that ended where the tops of her Western boots hit her slim calves. He swallowed, trying to remember if he'd ever seen her in a skirt before. As he drove, she pulled her hair up, reining it into a knot at her nape, exposing a spot of skin so pale and soft looking that he ached to kiss it. He cleared his voice. "You look nice, Tilly."

She laughed again. "Thank you. I heard in your voice how hard that was for you to acknowledge." She reached into the pocket of her skirt. "I have a name on that truck that was parked at Howie's the day we went out there. Jason Murdock. He lives in Billings. He's a private investigator."

"A private investigator?" Cooper repeated. "I wonder who hired him. Maybe CH4 because of the vandalism. Good work. How did you…?"

"The sheriff." He heard the hesitation in her voice. "That's not all. While Stuart went to see about the license plate, I got a look at my sister's phone. Did you know that she and Pickett Hanson are thick as thieves?"

He had suspected as much. Glancing over at her, he asked, "Romantically or just their involvement in Dirty Business?"

"I'd say both. I only got to look at one message from Pickett. But there is definitely something going on between them. It's no wonder she's kept all this under wraps. Our mother would go berserk. I can't even imagine what CJ would have to say about it."

"Because she's involved in the anti-methane-well movement or because she's fraternizing with a McKenna ranch hand?" he asked.

She gave him an impatient look. "It doesn't matter that he's a ranch hand. That would be fine with her. If he didn't work on the McKenna Ranch. As for CJ…" She shook her head. "My brother seems to think he can tell us who we can see and what we can do. Clearly, he can't."

He glanced at her. "You're not just using me to ruffle your brother's feathers, are you?" He'd kept his tone light, but when she responded, hers was anything but.

"Is that really what you're asking?" she demanded. "I don't care what my brother thinks. He and I seldom agree on anything. If you're asking what he'd have to say about you and me?" She looked away. "If there was a you and me? He'd learn to live with it."

Cooper doubted that since he knew CJ. Her older brother had a chip on his shoulder when it came to a lot of things. He was very protective of his family, maybe too protective, and he had a grudge against the McKennas. There was only one person who could keep him in line and that was their mother, Charlotte Stafford, and she seemed to feel the same way about the McKennas—or at least Holden McKenna. "Has your mother said anything about the two of us being seen together?"

"Not really. What about your father?" she said. "Does he know what we've been up to?"

"I don't think so. If he did, his concern would be that we were going to get ourselves killed."

She turned a little in the seat. "Are you saying he'd be fine with us dating?" Was she really going to finally put it out there? Apparently so.

He wanted to say they hadn't gone that far yet, but he saved his breath, pretty sure they'd been headed in this direction for a lot longer than he'd been home. All that passion they'd put into trying to best each other all these years, it had manifested itself into this. He'd known for some time now, and he figured she had known as well—probably even before he knew.

"I honestly don't know how my father would react. I do know that he wants the animosity between our families to stop." He could feel her gaze on him.

"You know what's at the heart of it, don't you?" she asked. "Our parents were lovers."

"You got all this from the local scuttlebutt, so I'm sure it's true," he said.

"It is. They had to sneak around because their families were already fighting. Has your father ever told you why he married your mother instead of mine?" He shook his head. "I suspect it had something to do with his father and hers threatening to send them packing. I think my mother would say that she would have given up everything for him. But who knows if she would have given up the ranch for love. I do know that she never got over him. As they say, there is nothing like a woman scorned."

Or a man scorned, he said to himself, thinking of the elephant in the cab of the pickup—Stuart.

Ahead, he could see mostly pickups parked around the old barn. Lights glowed from inside. Lanterns? It looked like an old-timey church revival meeting. He was relieved that Pickett hadn't put the word out and canceled the event. Then he worried that what they were seeing was exactly what it looked like, some church meeting. But most churches didn't meet in an abandoned barn away from town at night or keep the meeting location secret from everyone but its members. He thought Pickett wouldn't lie to him— except if he thought he was protecting him.

Cooper parked, noticing a large pickup parked some distance away, the license plate illuminated by a shaft of light from inside the barn. The plate number was the same one Tilly had gotten the sheriff to run for her. Jason Murdock, the private detective. What was he doing here? Looking for vandals?

Maybe tonight they would find out. They'd seen his rig parked at Howie Gunderson's, who worked for CH4, and now he was here at the Dirty Business meeting? It wasn't clear which side Murdock was on or what his real business was here in their valley. But if he was looking for the vandals who'd been sabotaging well drilling equipment, Cooper figured he might have come to the right place.

As they climbed out of the pickup, he could hear voices engaged in numerous conversations, some louder than others. But as he opened the barn door and stepped in behind Tilly, a lot of the voices fell silent.

He spotted local rancher Ralph Jones sitting on an old table at the front of the room. Ralph gave him a nod before rising. He held up his hands to quiet everyone. "Just to make sure you're all in the right place, this is a meeting of the anti-methane-drilling group Dirty Business. If you're for drilling, you need to turn around and leave. We're not here to debate. We're here to stop the drilling."

The group quieted. Most had brought lawn chairs and now sat. Some stood against the wall. Pickett motioned for Cooper and Tilly to join him near the front. He'd apparently brought two extra chairs for them. Cooper and Tilly walked through the crowd to join him and sat in the chairs he offered.

"We have a speaker tonight who is going to explain a few things about the wells drying up in our valley," Ralph said. "Phil Bergstrom is a geologist. Phil, the floor is all yours."

Cooper listened with only half an ear as Phil explained about aquifers and the amount of water needed to extract the methane from the cracks in the coalbeds and the harm the abandoned wells were doing to the environment.

"Methane has more than eight times the warming power of carbon dioxide," Bergstrom said. "At least twenty-five percent of today's global warming is driven by methane from what we're doing to our planet."

Bergstrom was preaching to the choir. Cooper had researched the process when the geologists and gas companies had first started drilling in the state. He figured everyone in the barn already knew this. Like him, they could have looked it up online.

He found himself glancing around the crowd of

mostly ranchers and a few of their wives. There were even a few businessmen from town. He couldn't help being surprised at how many people were in attendance. He recognized most everyone, except for a man standing up at the far back. Murdock? If so, he was a large man with a gray crew cut. He wore canvas pants and a black windbreaker that matched his Stetson.

When Phil finished, several people spoke about the deals the gas people were offering. Others talked about how they hadn't been warned that they might not have water on their ranch after the company drilled. Another talked about how the fishing in nearby Tongue River Reservoir had declined since the gas companies had begun drilling in their area. They blamed all the salty water that had been dumped into the river.

Finally, Ralph passed around some more information about who they could call with their complaints. A few rabble-rousers stood up and demanded to know why they weren't running the whole bunch of gas company men out of Powder River County.

The meeting came to a close, but people didn't seem to want to leave. He and Tilly went outside, where a few had gathered to talk and smoke. When Ralph came out, Cooper pulled him aside.

"We're trying to find out who shot Oakley Stafford," he said. "Can you tell me if she's been coming to these meetings?"

"Something we don't do is tell anyone who comes or doesn't come to the meetings," Ralph said. "I'd appreciate it if the two of you would do the same after attending tonight."

"Please," Tilly said.

"Why don't you ask your sister? I heard she's going to pull through," the rancher said. "Don't you have a well on the Stafford Ranch? I understand there might be more drilled."

"That's my mother's doing, not mine," she said.

Ralph shook his head and turned to Cooper. "There's talk of wells on your ranch as well."

"It would have to be over my father's dead body," he said, worried that might be Treyton's plan.

The rancher looked at Tilly. "I'm sorry, but some people have been ostracized after coming to a meeting. We only agreed to meet tonight after one of our members vouched for Cooper. Please don't make me regret it. Talk to your sister," he said to Tilly.

Cooper could feel people watching them with suspicion. "This might have been a mistake," he said under his breath as they walked to his pickup and climbed in. He searched for the man at the back whom he hadn't recognized. The man was nowhere in sight.

As Cooper pulled out to head back to the abandoned station for Tilly's pickup, he saw that Jason Murdock's rig was gone. Apparently, the PI had already left.

TILLY FELT A chill as she looked in her rearview mirror as they drove away. There were no vehicle lights behind them. The people who'd been outside had apparently gone back inside the barn. "I don't think the meeting was over. Did you hear what that one man asked about doing something rather than just talking? Ralph waved him off, but I have a feeling that the ones who are still there are now talking about taking some kind of action right now."

"I caught that too," Cooper said as he looked into his rearview mirror. "I think the geologist's talk tonight was for our benefit. All the information Phil gave us is online. Anyone could access it on one of the many sites about the pros and cons of methane drilling. Plus, I really doubt anyone at that meeting didn't already know all of that."

"Other than trying to get ranchers not to lease their property to the gas company, how do you think they're planning to stop the drilling other than lining up on the county line with guns?"

"Seems several of the drilling rigs have been vandalized. If your sister was involved in that aspect of Dirty Business—"

"I've been thinking about that. I still think we need to check out that ravine Oakley came riding out of according to the pilot and Tick," she said.

"There's nothing over the mountains but the old Smith homestead, and nothing left of it but a few buildings. We aren't running any cattle in that area because of the drought—"

"And the methane well that we drilled on our land close by," she said. "Do you think she was back in there trying to sabotage the gas well? Why else would she have been on your property, unless…?" She seemed to hesitate before she said, "You sure they aren't drilling on your land back in there?"

"There isn't any drilling going on on McKenna property."

"Are you sure about that?" she asked. "Isn't that area a long way from anything on your ranch? Rugged country, rich with coal back in there, right? Only one road in."

She could see him considering it when a set of high-beam headlights flashed on behind them.

"Whoever it is, he came out of nowhere," Cooper said as he kept going but pulled over some to let the rig pass.

"Cooper?" Tilly said when she checked her side mirror and saw the lights growing brighter as the vehicle raced toward them. The driver, though, wasn't moving over to pass. "Cooper!"

"Hang on—it looks like he plans to ram us," he said, and hit the gas. They roared down the dirt road, bouncing over bumps, sending them lifting off their seats even strapped in with seat belts.

The truck chasing them stayed right with them, even though Cooper managed to stay ahead of the vehicle, outmaneuvering the other driver. But ahead in the headlights, Tilly saw the curve coming up where one of the ranch roads connected next to a stand of cottonwoods. Her blood pounded in her ears. If they lost control there—

The flashing lights of a patrol SUV came on from the side road, startling her. As they roared past, the sheriff's department SUV fell in behind what she could now see was a truck tailing them. She heard the siren, could make out the lights through the dust boiling up in the glow of their taillights.

The lights of the truck behind them dimmed as the

driver slowed, then pulled over. To her surprise, whoever was driving the patrol SUV didn't stop. Instead, it sped after her and Cooper.

"Cooper?" she said again, anxiety rising. She'd been relieved to be rid of the driver of the truck who'd been chasing them. But now she wasn't sure they still weren't in trouble if the man behind the wheel of that patrol SUV was who she thought it was.

CHAPTER FOURTEEN

COOPER SWORE UNDER his breath as the driver of the patrol SUV roared up behind them, siren blaring, lights flashing. He pulled off into a wide spot, driving under the limb of a large cottonwood that blocked out the stars.

He put down his window as the sheriff pulled in next to them.

Tilly swallowed, heart hammering. It couldn't be a coincidence that Stuart had been waiting down that road. Which meant he'd known about the meeting. He'd known that she and Cooper would go to it. He'd been waiting for them. Because he knew there would be trouble? She felt as if they'd been set up. But by whom?

Stuart turned off his lights and siren as he put down his passenger-side window and leaned toward them to call across. "You two done for the night? Because I'm ready to call it a day," he said. She looked past Cooper and nodded, her heart in her throat. "Then good night." He hit the gas and roared off toward town.

They didn't move. Cooper still had the pickup in Park. He was staring after the sheriff. "He didn't even stop the driver who was chasing us," Tilly said as the dust settled. She couldn't tell if he was as shaken as she was. At one point, he had started to unbuckle his seat belt as if planning to get out and talk to the sheriff. But he'd apparently changed his mind.

She'd unbuckled hers, thinking she needed to get out, walk around in the fresh night air and calm down.

Cooper looked over at her. "You okay?"

She shook her head and felt tears burn her eyes. Cooper unbuckled his seat belt and reached for her, pulling her across the bench seat and into his arms. She fell into his warm, strong body as if she'd been headed there her whole life. When she looked into his blue eyes, she felt herself smile. She hadn't been wrong. There was something simmering between them that was about to boil over.

He drew her closer and kissed her. She melted against him, her mouth opening to a kiss that felt long overdue. In his arms, she could finally admit how badly she had wanted this. They were both breathing hard when the kiss ended.

Cooper drew back. She looked into his blue eyes and worried he was already having second thoughts. Tilly shook her head. "Don't you dare, Cooper McKenna. If you say you shouldn't have done that, so help me, I will—"

He pulled her to him and silenced her with a kiss, deepening it and seeming to make no excuses for the passion in it. "Tilly," he whispered against her lips. "Damn, Tilly." His hand went to her breast, where her aching nipple pressed hard against his hand through her blouse and bra.

She had no doubt about what would have happened next if a string of headlights hadn't appeared down the road behind them, faintly illuminating the inside of the cab. The meeting had ended.

Cooper quickly slid back under the wheel and threw the pickup into gear. He drove to the turnoff where they'd left her pickup and pulled down behind the old gas station, cut his engine and his lights.

They sat in silence as the stream of vehicles passed on the main road. Tilly's heart was still pounding from the kiss and the earlier terror. Had that been a warning from someone at the meeting? Or was that an attempt on their lives? They would never know, thanks to the sheriff appearing when he did and scaring off whoever was following them. Right now, she was too aware of Cooper, their earlier kisses and his caresses still firing her blood.

He hadn't moved from where he sat, both hands still on the wheel, the silence and darkness enfolding them as the last of the vehicles passed.

"Coop?" She was half-afraid of what he would say, let alone do next. Tell her they could never see each other again? Or make love to her right here in the cab of his pickup? The latter sent a fresh wave of desire rippling through her. She had wanted him for so long without admitting it. Had she just been waiting for him to come back to Powder Crossing? Was that why she hadn't slept with Stuart when he'd tried to initiate sex? Because she'd always wanted his best friend?

He cleared his voice. "Tilly, you don't know how badly I want this, how long I've wanted to kiss you, to make love to you."

"Coop—"

"But I don't want the first time we make love to be in my truck," he said, finally looking over at her. His gaze met hers, burning into her.

Her throat went dust dry. "The first time?"

Cooper nodded. "After that, I'd make love to you on the tailgate if you want, but not the first time." Her heart pounded harder. "And not tonight, not until I talk to Stuart." He shook his head. "If I kiss you again…" He opened his pickup door and stepped out.

She sat for a moment before finding her purse and on wobbly legs got out to walk to her pickup. He opened the door for her, helped her inside, leaning in to kiss her lightly on the lips. "Good night, Tilly." Their gazes locked. Cooper was the first to pull away with a groan.

He closed her door and walked back to his pickup, but he didn't leave until she started her truck and drove out, Cooper behind her all the way out to the turnoff to her ranch.

On the private road to the house, she found herself grinning, giddy and at the same time a little scared. Did she really think they could do this? There was their families and Stuart. She knew the sheriff wouldn't take it well—even though she'd told him that she didn't feel like he did and wouldn't be going out with him again. But she'd said it wasn't because of Cooper, and after that kiss, she knew it definitely was.

Just the thought of Cooper made her ache. It was going to happen. She wasn't sure how, but it had to happen.

COOPER WAS STILL shaken by the time he reached the ranch. Tilly. Just the thought of her made his heart race again. He wanted her like he'd never wanted anything, anyone, and yet he worried that being with her would only lead to heartbreak for them both.

He thought about the story she'd told about their parents. If true, their love hadn't been strong enough to bridge this feud between the families. What made them think theirs would be any different?

They were already pushing their luck. Look what had happened tonight. He hadn't been able to see who had chased them, possibly trying to run them off the road. PI Jason Murdock? He couldn't imagine why. But then again, he had no idea who had hired the private investigator. Someone who wanted to make sure they didn't find out the truth about Oakley's shooting? Or someone who didn't want him and Tilly investigating? Or just some fool redneck from the meeting who didn't want them coming back?

The latter seemed the most probable, since after the sheriff had forced the driver of the truck over, he hadn't done anything more. He'd probably recognized the driver. After all, the sheriff had been waiting down the road. For them?

The Dirty Business meeting alone was enough to make Cooper worry. It was clear that things were heating up between the two factions. The sheriff had known about the meeting. Or he'd followed Tilly to the old gas station, seen them leave together and waited. Then again, he could have known about the meeting all along.

Cooper's head hurt trying to figure out not just who was behind Oakley's shooting, but who they could trust. He couldn't shake the feeling that the sheriff and whoever had chased them might have been in on it tonight. He told himself he was wrong. Stu had been his best friend for years. When Cooper had been arrested for Leann's murder, Stu had still been on his side, helping as much as he could, hadn't he?

Now Cooper wasn't sure of anything. He found himself questioning if he'd ever known Stu. Even if the sheriff and Murdock hadn't been in league tonight, it didn't explain what Stu had been doing on that road at that hour as if waiting for them. There was only one explanation. He'd known about the meeting. He'd known that he and Tilly would attend. So who'd tipped him off? Not Pickett, Cooper was sure.

He had too many questions and no answers. Still, after tonight, Cooper felt as if things had gotten more dangerous. Tonight's close call had felt...personal.

Once in the house, he went straight to his room on the third floor. The rooms were large; each had its own living area and bathroom along with the bedroom. Holden had the old house remodeled as his children had grown so they would want to stay on the ranch rather than leave and get their own place.

He closed the door behind him and stood trying to make sense out of everything, maybe especially what had almost happened between him and Tilly. He could have so easily made love to her tonight right there in the cab of his pickup. He'd wanted her so badly.

Fortunately, good sense had overridden desire. He'd meant it about not wanting to make love to her the first time in his truck. But he had also wanted to come up for air. This was moving too fast. He'd been gun-shy since Leann. How could he not be? She'd killed herself. Because of him?

Wasn't that what worried him? That even though they'd both said they weren't looking for anything long-term, maybe she had lied and been so hurt that she—

He shook his head. He had never believed that she had taken her own life because of him, and yet how did he explain her death? Maybe suicide was unexplainable. How could one ever really know what was going on in the mind of another human being?

The one thing he did know was that he was going to have to put the past behind him. That meant putting Leann and her death behind him.

He saw her favorite book on the shelf where he'd left it. He shook his head as he moved to the shelf and pulled it down. As he did, the worn book spine bit into his finger. He loosened his grasp in surprise.

The book dropped from his hand to the floor, falling open as it did. A half dozen folded sheets of note-paper fluttered out. Blinking, he stared down at them, recognizing the notepaper as the same kind Leann had written her alleged suicide note on.

As if sleepwalking, he reached down and picked up the book and the notes. Unfolding one of the pages, he felt his heart drop. It was addressed to him. He staggered over to the couch and sat down, placing the book next to him as he opened each of the notes. They were all addressed to him, none of them apparently completed.

"What the hell," he whispered as he swallowed, his throat going dry as he read.

Cooper, I wish there was a way to say this, but I can't

That was all she had written. He picked up another one.

Cooper, I wish I wasn't such a coward, but I'm not good at goodbyes. It's not you. It's me. You're th

Again it ended, this time in the middle of a word. He picked up another note, trying to make sense of what he was seeing.

Cooper, thanks for taking me in when I needed a place to stay. But we both know this isn't going anywhere. Maybe this is a mistake but I need to

He put the note down with the others. Were these her attempts at a suicide note like the one that was found next to her body that day? Why practice a suicide note this many times? He picked up the last one.

Cooper, I know you won't approve of what I'm about to do. But I deserve to be happy. Maybe it's a mistake, but what do I have to lose? Maybe this time I'll find lo

He felt a start. *Maybe this time I'll find lo...* She'd scratched out *happiness* and written *lo* and stopped. *Maybe this time I'll find love?* These weren't suicide notes, he realized with a start. She was leaving because she'd found someone else!

Cooper hadn't realized that he'd been holding his breath. Slumping back onto the couch, he put his head in his hands. He had so many regrets when it came to Leann. For the past two years, he'd beaten himself up with guilt, believing that he was the reason she'd taken her own life.

If she'd been leaving for another man, there was no way she would have killed herself. He sat up. Who?

Why hadn't she just told him? He glanced at the notes piled up on his couch. She'd been trying to when… When… When what happened? Her lover had shown up?

He picked up the last note, heart pounding as he realized that if she hadn't killed herself, there was only one other explanation. She'd been murdered.

As the notepaper caught the light, he saw something that stopped his heart dead. Holding it up to the light, he saw the faint pale blue of the large gas company logo, CH4, under Leann's writing.

CHAPTER FIFTEEN

COOPER WALKED INTO the sheriff's office early the next morning, closed the door behind him and turned to face the man he'd once called his best friend. Stu was already on his feet. "If this is about last night—"

"That's another conversation. There's something you need to see."

"I don't have the time to—"

"Make the time," Cooper said, moving to stand on the opposite side of the desk from him. He dropped Leann's book on the desk.

"What's this?" Stuart asked, frowning.

"You don't recognize it?"

"I can see that it's an old book, one that looks as if it needs to be pitched into the trash."

If he'd had any question as to how well Stu had known Leann, he didn't anymore. "It was Leann's favorite book."

Stu's frown deepened. "Seriously, Cooper, I don't have time—"

"She didn't kill herself." He flipped the book open and dumped out the notes.

The sheriff gave him an impatient pointed look. "The prosecutor never thought she did kill herself."

Cooper sighed. "I didn't kill her, but someone did. The man she was leaving with."

"What are you talking about?" He dropped back into his chair.

"Look at the notes."

Stu picked up one and read it. "What are these?"

"She was practicing letting me know that she was leaving. What you found was never a suicide note." He picked up the other notes and spread them out on the sheriff's desk in front of him. "No one practices writing a suicide note unless they aren't serious about killing themselves. She was trying to tell me that she was leaving with someone, someone I wasn't going to approve of."

Stu sighed and read one note after another, making a small pile of them on the corner of his desk. As he read the last one, he sighed again. "She doesn't mention another man."

"It's implied and you know it." He snatched up the notes and read from the most telling of them. "'I know you won't approve. But I've thought about this a lot. I need to leave here and I don't want to go alone. You can't save me, so please don't...'"

"Don't what?" Stu asked. "'Don't kill me'?" Cooper shook his head, wondering why he'd thought this evidence would make a difference with the sheriff. "Maybe she was leaving you for someone else," Stu conceded. "But that seems to only strengthen the prosecutor's suspicion that you killed her."

"No matter our differences, you don't believe that. Come on, Stu. You can't have it both ways. Either she killed herself or she was murdered. If she didn't kill herself and I didn't do it, what does that leave?"

The sheriff sat back, chewed at his cheek for a moment. "You think the man she was planning to run away with murdered her?" He shrugged. "Why would he?"

"Maybe he changed his mind. Or maybe she changed her mind. They argued and things got out of hand."

Stu shook his head. "Or maybe he realized she wasn't the woman for him after she'd been with you."

"That sounds awfully personal," Cooper said.

"I was just spitballing."

"While getting in a few licks of your own." He put the notes back in the book where he'd found them. "Leann didn't kill herself," he said, more to himself than the sheriff. "It never made sense. She and I were friends. I saw how restless she was. She wanted to change her life. She was looking for something that would make her happy— outside of Powder Crossing. Didn't you feel that?"

Stu looked away for a moment. "Who, then?"

Cooper pulled out one of the notes and held it up to the light. "Ever seen this notepaper before?"

Stu took it from him, held it up to the light and frowned. "CH_4."

"How was it that no one questioned, myself included, the paper she'd written her alleged suicide note on was from the gas exploration company that had moved in here two years ago?" Cooper said. "The man had to be someone connected to the company who had access to these notepads."

"You're grasping at straws," the sheriff said as he sat forward, opened a drawer and dug around for a moment. He pulled out a half-used notepad that matched the paper Leann had used. "Don't get excited. The gas company was handing these out like hot dogs. I'd forgotten I even had one."

Cooper thought it could be true, but he wasn't going to let this go. "Find the man she planned to leave town with, and you'll find her murderer."

Stu rose. "Right now, I'm busy looking for the person who shot Oakley Stafford. I'm sure you can understand why that is my priority." He started to step around his desk to leave.

"That the way you're going to play this?" Cooper demanded.

Stu stopped at the end of his desk and sighed. "You sure you want to reopen the case, Coop? The county prosecutor is still convinced that you killed Leann. You'd be behind bars if they'd found even one piece of hard evidence. They reopen the case and dig up that one piece of evidence that makes you look even more guilty, you might be facing life in prison."

"That almost sounds like a threat."

The sheriff groaned. "Not everyone wants you out of Powder Crossing."

"Just you."

"Leave the notes. I'll take them to the prosecutor if you're sure that's what you want, but right now I'm kind of busy trying to find out who shot Oakley Stafford rather than dig up an old closed case."

Cooper hesitated. "I think I'll make copies and leave those with you until the prosecutor wants to see the originals."

Stu shook his head. "Little paranoid?"

"Whole lot paranoid but maybe with good reason."

"You really don't trust me?"

"I used to," Cooper said.

"Funny, I feel the same way. Close the door on your way out."

He waited until the sheriff was gone before reaching over and taking the half-used notepad from the desk. He tucked it into Leann's book and walked out.

It wasn't until he got home that he had a good look at the notepad he'd taken from the sheriff.

The paper was thin. He could see why it left an indentation on the page under it. Holding it up to the light, he almost missed the only word that had been written on the sheet before it.

Leann.

It appeared Stu had started to write her a note but never finished it.

Cooper had almost convinced himself not to continue looking into Oakley's shooting and let the sheriff handle it. But something about seeing that name, ghostlike on the notepad, made him change his mind.

On the way back to the ranch, Cooper called Tilly. "You're right. We need to find out what Oakley was doing in that ravine. Want to saddle up and meet me at the crime scene?"

TILLY WAS SADDLING her horse when CJ walked into the stables.

"Where do you think you're going?" he demanded.

She looked up at him in surprise. "None of your business."

He took a step toward her. "You think I haven't heard about you and that McKenna cowboy? Between you and your sister…"

"What is going on with you?" she demanded, turning to frown at him. "You aren't my father. Stop acting like you're running this ranch. You can't tell me or Oakley what to do."

"That's for sure. Look where it landed her. She could have been killed. She had no business on the McKenna Ranch. So which one of them was she meeting over there?"

"You think Oakley was seeing a McKenna and that's why she got shot?" He said nothing, his jaw muscles bunching, his eyes narrowed angrily. "You don't know what you're talking about."

"Don't I? I warned her to stay away from there and now I'm warning you. I saw the way you looked at Cooper when you were a teenager. He's just toying with you, Tilly. Just trying to rile me up."

She shook her head angrily. "Not everything is about you, CJ. Get out of my way."

"I'm warning you," he called after her as she led her horse out of the stables. "You're just going to get hurt."

As she swung up into the saddle, she saw her mother standing a few yards away just outside the stables.

Charlotte had a worried look on her face as she stepped forward and grabbed Tilly's reins to stop her on her way out. "What's going on?"

Not you too, Tilly thought. "I'm going for a ride."

"Why is your brother so upset?"

"You'd have to ask him. He's been acting stranger than usual."

"Because you've been spending so much time with Cooper McKenna," her mother said. "What did I hear him say about Oakley?"

Why didn't she ask CJ? she wondered, but when she turned in the saddle, she saw that he was no longer in the stables. She turned back and sighed. "He said he thought Oakley was over at the McKenna Ranch to meet one of the boys."

"Is that true?"

Tilly shook her head. "I have no idea. Have you asked Oakley?" She saw at once that her mother hadn't. She thought about Pickett Hanson, the ranch hand who'd been messaging her sister. The one text she'd seen for just a second had looked as if the two of them were close, but maybe Oakley had been seeing one of the McKenna brothers. Cooper probably wouldn't know since he'd been gone for two years. "Is that all?"

Her mother looked as if there was more she wanted to say, but she let go of the reins. "Enjoy your ride."

As her mother stepped back, Tilly spurred her horse. She was going to be late meeting Cooper. She didn't like keeping secrets, but in this case, it seemed the safest thing to do.

THE SUN HAD cleared the crest of the rugged hills to the east as Cooper rode out to meet Tilly. The ravine was a crime scene. Even if the sheriff's department and medical examiner were through with their investigation of the area, the sheriff wouldn't like them going in there.

Then again, Stuart didn't like them doing anything together.

Also, if the medical examiner and sheriff had found anything, Cooper thought they would have heard about it. Still, Tilly was convinced there was something back there to find. Otherwise, what had Oakley been doing in there? Not exactly the place to have a clandestine relationship, even if she and Pickett had something going on.

It felt good to be back in the saddle. He hadn't realized how much he'd missed it. While he'd been away from home for those two years, he'd gotten construction jobs that paid better than rounding up cows. But he'd missed this.

He breathed in the morning air. Overhead, puffy clouds dotted the vast blue of the Montana sky. Here the sky seemed so much larger, stretching from horizon to horizon unobstructed by any structures. He rode along the edge of the Powder River, the water moving slow among the rocks that stood up out of the dark sand that had given the river its name.

Tilly was waiting for him at the edge of the cottonwoods. She'd ground-tied her horse, which was munching the grass, and walked to the edge of the river where she now sat with her face turned up to the summer sun.

The sight of her made his heart pound. She had a classic beauty deeper than skin that humbled him, making him feel unworthy. She deserved better than him. Not to mention that anything between the two of them would be difficult at best. Did they really want to put themselves and their families through that?

Tilly looked up as he and his horse approached. He saw something in those green eyes that struck like an arrow in his chest. He knew then that he'd do whatever it took. He wanted Tilly in his life.

She rose from the rock, picked up her horse's reins and swung up into the saddle with practiced ease. She looked good sitting there, as if perfectly at home. She cocked her head, amusement playing in her expression. Her lips turned up a little at the corners, her eyes bright.

"There something on your mind, cowboy?" she asked.

He looked away, swallowed. How easily she'd read him. He'd have to watch that, he thought. "No, I don't want to discuss the kisses. Isn't that the sort of thing you talk about with your girlfriends?"

She laughed. "You really don't know much about women, do you?"

"Not really," he agreed as he rode up beside her. "But I'm willing to learn," he said, and leaned over to kiss her. "Let's do this."

They rode back through the parklike grass beneath the dark green canopy of cottonwood leaves. The breeze whispered through the branches over their heads. It felt intimate in here, just the two of them. The creak of their saddles, the jingle of the reins, the snort of a horse were the only sounds, as if Tilly was holding her breath and so was he.

"Sure you don't want to talk about it?"

"Nope."

She laughed. "How did I know that?"

He glanced over at her. "'Cuz you know me."

"I do, Coop," she agreed. "I'm willing to get to know you better, though."

He chuckled at that as they broke out of the grove of cottonwoods, and he saw the dark gash of the ravine. "This could be dangerous." He glanced over at her.

"Don't even think about going back in there without me."

TILLY HADN'T KNOWN what to expect when she saw Cooper this morning. She knew that she'd gotten under his skin. She could see that, feel it. He couldn't deny it, not after their kisses last night, not after what he'd said about the first time they made love.

Not that she hadn't expected him to shut down again and try denying what was happening between them. She'd told herself that he couldn't keep pretending there wasn't more than chemistry between them. But she knew that he might try.

Not because he didn't feel it, but because he was scared. Because of Leann? Or because she was a Stafford?

Well, he could keep denying it to himself—but not to her. So she was glad this morning that he wasn't even trying to pretend that last night hadn't happened.

She had watched him out of the corner of her eye as they rode through the cottonwoods. It dawned on her that she wasn't all that was bothering him. This morning Stuart had called her. He'd said he had just wanted to talk to a friend.

"We're still friends, aren't we?"

"Of course," she'd said reflexively. Were they?

"Seen Cooper today?"

"Stuart—"

"Just asking. He was in my office earlier. He thinks he has proof that Leann was murdered." This had surprised her. Cooper had proof?

"This is good news, isn't it?" she'd said.

"He thinks so. He seems to think that she was running off with some man. He wants me to reopen the case. I think that's pretty risky since the prosecutor is still convinced that Cooper is guilty."

"What are you trying to tell me?"

"That you might want to talk him out of opening this old can of worms. That's if you care about him. Who knows what evidence might turn up."

Tilly had seen that he was trying to make her doubt Cooper, make her suspect that he might be a killer. "Thanks for the advice," she'd said, her voice clipped. "I have to go."

"Sure," he'd said. "Maybe I'll see you around."

Not if I see you first, she'd thought. She knew Stuart was just trying to get her to question her feelings for Cooper. Didn't he realize she'd been doing that enough on her own? She was a Stafford. Coop was a McKenna. That alone made even the thought of them having a future together seem impossible.

But she would never believe that Cooper had killed Leann. Though she did wonder why he hadn't mentioned that he'd found evidence about her death. Was he ever planning to tell her?

COOPER WAS QUESTIONING bringing Tilly with him. But now that he had, he knew there was no leaving her behind. They rode across the open expanse to the mouth of the ravine carved over the years in the rising rugged mountains beyond. He felt the early summer heat of the sun lolling overhead. Another hot summer. Another dry one after too many years without enough rain.

A wall of rocks lined both sides of the opening into the ravine, making it a tight fit, just large enough for one horse to pass for a dozen yards before it opened up.

As he eased his horse in, he studied the horseshoe tracks; at least four horses had come through here. One of them had been Oakley's. One track would have been the horse and rider Howie had seen from the plane. Had the sheriff sent men in here on horseback? There were too many tracks to tell.

The land rose, the ravine twisting back into the mountain. Higher up, ponderosa pines dotted the mountainside next to steep cliffs and outcroppings. Everything seemed to glisten in the sunlight ahead, but in the ravine it was dark and cool, the cavity filled with shadows.

It felt peaceful back in here. Yet he felt a chill as if it was almost too quiet. He hadn't heard a bird's song. Even the breeze was silent. The only thing he could hear was the pounding of his heart as he thought of Oakley riding back in here. Why had she?

When the ravine widened enough for two horses, Tilly rode up next to him and reined in. "I saw the tracks. Maybe Oakley was meeting someone back in here."

"Maybe." It didn't look like a place for a romantic

rendezvous, but what did he know? "The other tracks have stopped, buried under fallen dried pine needles." He rode a little farther and picked up only her horse's tracks. "Let's see where this comes out." They rode on up through the ravine and over the top of a ridge. From there they could see the dirt road back into the old Smith homestead, but not any of the buildings.

They dropped into another ravine, this one wider. Someone had been up here on a four-wheeler. He pointed to the fresh tracks and Tilly nodded. It was so quiet, neither of them seemed anxious to break the silence.

Cooper pulled up short as they rounded a bend and the homestead came into view. "Do you see what I see?" he whispered. Below them was a grassy strip of land corded with tire tracks.

"A landing strip?" she whispered back.

"Sure looks that way." It also appeared it had been in use recently. He felt unease crawl up his spine.

As they rode a little farther, Cooper saw what was left of the old homestead buildings. A half dozen outbuildings in varying degrees of condition stood next to the rock foundation of what had been the house. This ranch was one of many that had been added to Mc-Kenna Ranch over the years.

The sun reflected off something shiny on the door of one of the larger buildings. As he rode closer, he saw that someone had put a padlock on the door. "This looks interesting," he said, dismounting. The glass in the windows had been gone for years. But wood had been nailed over the openings. He peered through a crack between two slabs and swore.

"What?" Tilly asked, joining him.

"Unless I miss my guess, someone's set up a meth lab in there." He glanced at the other buildings and the old outhouse that was leaning, but still standing.

"Which would explain the landing strip and the four-wheeler tracks," she said.

He glanced to the west. This old homestead was miles from the nearest highway. With the drought, this part of the ranch didn't have any cattle running on it, making this spot the perfect place for a drug lab. There was little chance that anyone would stumble across it. It was McKenna property, private land. Anyone on it without permission was trespassing.

Had someone gotten permission? He thought of Treyton and hoped his brother had nothing to do with this.

At the sound of a vehicle in the distance, they looked at each other. "Come on," Cooper said. They rushed to their horses, mounting and riding back toward the ravine they'd just come out of. Until they reached the pines, they would be in plain sight.

Maybe the drug makers always stopped by this time of the day. Or maybe there had been some kind of battery-operated security camera on the outbuilding. Cooper mentally kicked himself for not noticing. Too late now.

They were starting up the ravine into the pines when Cooper looked back. Just below them, a large truck pulling a stock trailer came into view.

The driver of the truck stopped, got out and rushed to open the rear of the trailer. Cooper expected horses to emerge. Instead, a large four-wheeler came barreling out, the rider armed with what looked like an AR15 strapped across his chest. Another four-wheeler roared out after him, this man also armed with the military-style automatic rifle.

"We have to get out of here," Cooper said unnecessarily. Tilly was already urging her horse up the mountainside toward the pines. He knew she had to be thinking the same thing he was. This must be what had happened with Oakley. As the men turned the four-wheelers toward them, they gunned the engines and came thundering in their direction.

A horse couldn't outrun a four-wheeler, especially one of these big, powerful machines. His and Tilly's only hope was to go up higher into rougher country where the all-wheel vehicles couldn't follow them. "This way," he yelled, and headed straight up the side of the mountain. He heard one of the engines stop to idle and felt his heart drop.

A spray of bullets ripped across the ground behind them, sending pine bark and wood splinters into the air along with dirt and pebbles. They spurred their horses toward the larger pines. The pine trees were sparse but provided some cover as they reached them.

Cooper could hear the roar of the four-wheelers again. They were going up the ravine off to the left of them. He knew that they had to get up higher on the ridge and into the denser trees before the men broke out of the ravine. If he and Tilly could distance themselves by going through the rough, broken country where the four-wheelers couldn't follow, they might stand a chance.

CHAPTER SIXTEEN

STUART GOT A call from a deputy about a multivehicle accident outside of town. He sent a second deputy out to the wreck, but then a bar fight broke out. With both deputies out at the highway accident, he took the saloon call.

As he walked into the Wild Horse Bar, he saw two men wrestling on the floor. Several tables had been overturned, beer and glass on the floor just feet from them. He recognized the men at once and swore. Boyle Wilson from the Stafford Ranch and Rusty Malone from the McKenna Ranch.

"Knock it off or I'm going to shoot both of you!" he yelled, to no avail. He motioned to the bartender to hand him the baseball bat from behind the bar. Taking it, he jabbed Rusty, who was on top, in the side with the end of the bat. "That's enough!"

The two kept fighting. He jabbed Boyle, who was now on top. "I'm going to start using this bat if you two don't stop." He hit Boyle harder, knocking the air out of him and grabbing the back of his shirt to drag him off. As Rusty started to go after Boyle, the sheriff caught the cowboy in the gut, doubling him over. "Make another move and, so help me, I'll nail you."

Rusty wiped at his bloody lip as he fought to catch his breath and slowly rose. Stuart let go of Boyle but stayed between the two men. "What is wrong with you two? It's too early in the day for this."

"He jumped me," Boyle accused, pointing at Rusty, who immediately went into how Boyle had said some things.

"Stop, both of you," Stuart snapped. He was in no mood for this. Having Cooper storm into his office first thing this morning had set his day off on a bad note already. "I should arrest the both of you for disturbing the peace and let your bosses come bail you out."

"That's not necessary," Boyle said, backing down first. Apparently, he didn't want Charlotte Stafford coming to the jail to free him.

"What about you?" Stuart asked Rusty, who shrugged. "Both of you get out of here. Next time, I'm taking you in."

He handed the bat back to the bartender as the two left. "They cause any damage?"

The bartender shook his head. "Not really. But it's getting worse between those two families," he said with a shake of his head as he put the bat away. "Not just the families, but the men who work for them."

"They've been fighting as far back as I can remember," Stuart said. "Over water, land, love affairs gone bad." He thought of Cooper and Tilly. They were just fooling themselves if they thought they could be together. Maybe Tilly would come to her senses. Or maybe Cooper would force the prosecutor to reopen Leann's suicide case and end up behind bars again.

The one thing he knew for certain was that they could never overcome the long-running feud between their families.

COOPER HADN'T HEARD any more gunfire. Even the sound of the four-wheelers was distant by the time they reached the top of the ridge and headed across the top. They had little choice but to take the south ridge. To the east was a band of sheer cliffs, the top edge marked by large boulders. To the west was more rugged country that dropped back into the narrow valley where the old homestead sat.

He hoped the men on the four-wheelers had turned back but knew differently as he picked up the faint sound of revved engines again. Looking off the cliff side of the ridge, he realized that the two riders must be traveling along what appeared to be a rock ledge some distance below.

Cooper reined in, motioning for Tilly to keep going. "I'll catch up." He could see where the ledge below widened. Once the men on the four-wheelers reached that point, they would be able to pick off him and Tilly up on this ridge.

That meant that Cooper had to stop them before they reached that point. Dismounting, he walked his horse over to the edge of the ridge out of the possible line of fire and tied the reins to a tree. He saw Tilly winding along the ridge through the sparse pines and large rocks and hoped she'd keep going no matter what happened with his half-baked plan.

The four-wheelers were getting closer. He moved back to the edge of the cliff. Looking back, he caught glimpses of the vehicles through the pines below. He stepped to a large boulder balancing on the edge of the cliff. If he could dislodge some of the larger rocks... He tried a couple without success, then found one that gave a little. He waited.

He could hear the four-wheelers growing closer and closer on the rock ledge below. Soon they would be directly under him and the boulder he'd dislodged. He made himself wait a little longer, trying to gauge their distance, knowing he had to activate his plan at the right moment or risk getting shot or completely failing in stopping them.

They were almost directly below him. He sent the first boulder off; it hit other rocks on the cliff, starting a rockslide as it tumbled down toward the ledge and the riders on it. He quickly moved to another boulder and pushed it over the edge. It careered down, the sound of moving rocks almost blotting out the roar of the four-wheeler engines. He worked quickly, sending more rocks off the cliff.

They were directly below him now. He could hear rocks still crashing down as he pushed off yet another. He'd been afraid to look, fearing that he'd only managed to give his location away.

Through the dust and rocks still falling, he finally chanced a look. The first four-wheeler had managed to stay on the ledge, the large rocks missing it. The first rider must have caught the movement and sped up as rocks went airborne over the ledge, missing him.

But as Cooper watched, a large boulder he'd dislodged careened down, striking the second four-wheeler and its rider—sending both off the ledge to tumble down the mountainside.

The rocks continued crashing down. The rider of the first four-wheeler had gone some distance along the ledge before stopping. The man was looking back, no doubt trying to see through the dust and rocks. As the rockslide slowed and the dust began to settle, it was clear that the second rider and his four-wheeler were out of commission.

Cooper saw the first rider look up in his direction and swing the AR15 up. Bullets riddled the top of the cliff, sending rock chips flying into the air. He ducked down, feeling some of the chips cut into his face as he moved quickly to where he'd left his horse. Swinging up in the saddle, he waited until he heard the roar of the four-wheeler before he went after Tilly, staying in the trees as much as possible.

Below him on the mountain, he could hear the vehicle's engine. As the ridge began to drop down to the lowlands, he stopped. The rider on the four-wheeler would have reached a wide spot on the ledge he'd been following. He'd have a clear shot at them. But would he continue on, hoping to stop them?

Or would he go back to check on the other rider? To get help? To let whoever was in charge of the meth lab know that they'd been busted?

Heart in his throat, Cooper listened, relieved when he heard the sound of the four-wheeler's engine growing fainter and fainter until he couldn't hear it at all.

CHAPTER SEVENTEEN

TILLY HAD BEEN TERRIFIED, looking over her shoulder for Cooper. She'd heard the four-wheeler engines, heard what sounded like a rockslide, then the engines stop, then gunfire. Her heart had dropped. She'd been about to turn back when he'd appeared. Relief had brought tears to her eyes. She swallowed the lump in her throat as she reined in under a large ponderosa pine to wait for him.

She couldn't hear the four-wheelers. She didn't know what that meant or what had happened. He rode up to her and reined in next to her. She wiped hastily at tears at just the sight of him. He had some small cuts on his handsome face. But he was all right.

"You okay?" he asked, and she nodded.

"Are they still following us?"

"I don't think so."

"They have to be the ones who shot Oakley."

"Maybe, if one of them had a 270 rifle. The men who fired on us were using AR15s. Let's get off this mountain. We'll go to my house since it's not far from here. I'll take you and your horse home."

She looked at him. "Are you sure that's a good idea?"

"I need to call the sheriff as soon as I can get cell phone service."

Tilly nodded, although she was worried about what kind of reception she would get at the McKenna house. But he was right. It wasn't far. There they would be safe. She thought about that and tried to forget that people had been trying to kill them as she spurred her horse. They rode off the mountain and down toward his family's ranch house.

She kept thinking of her sister running for her life from killers. Oakley had to have found the meth lab. It was the only thing that made sense. Except, like Cooper said, the men who shot at them were using AR15s—not a 270 rifle, which was what Oakley had been shot with. She kept thinking about the other rider Howie and Tick had seen, the one who hadn't followed Oakley. The one who had turned toward either the McKenna Ranch house or the Stafford Ranch property, the same way she'd ridden earlier.

THE MOMENT THEY left the pines on the mountain, the sun bore down on them until they reached the cottonwoods and what relief the thick leaves overhead offered. Cooper reined in his horse to look back. They hadn't been followed. They were almost to the house, safe here in this wooded grove.

Tilly reined in beside him. He could see the green of her eyes accentuated by the dark green of the cottonwood leaves overhead. The sun-dappled ground around them was at odds with the coolness under the canopy. He could see that she was shaken, just as he was. "Tilly."

When the men on the four-wheelers had started

shooting at them, he'd just reacted on instinct. He hadn't taken the time to realize just how much danger they were in—let alone to be terrified.

But, looking at her now, he felt pure gut-wrenching terror at the thought that he'd almost gotten her killed. He reached over to cup her cheek, then leaned toward her, pulling her against him for a moment. The feel of her was his undoing.

"Tilly." That was all he had to say before he was off his horse, reaching up to lift her from the saddle and into his arms. She wrapped her arms around him as he held her tight against him, her feet dangling above the warm soil.

She held on to him as if they were in a fierce storm. They were.

"Those men tried to kill us. Cooper, they tried to kill us."

He cupped the back of her head, pressing her into his chest. "We're okay." It wasn't true, and he suspected she knew that. They'd been seen. They had no idea who was behind the meth lab, but it wasn't those men who'd chased them. The operation had an organized feel to it. Someone higher up was in charge. More than likely someone they knew.

"Even if they didn't shoot Oakley," Tilly said against his chest, "they chased her out of that ravine. It had to be them."

He didn't argue. So who had shot the 270 rifle? The man waiting for her in the ravine, the man on the horse? "You're going to be all right," he told her, not sure of that at all.

Checking his phone, he saw that he had service now that they were out of the mountains. "I have to call the sheriff." She nodded and stepped away as he made the call.

He got Stuart's cell phone first, then his office. Forced to leave a message on both, he told Stu about the meth lab, about the men who'd shot at them, chased them, how one of the pursuers' four-wheelers had been destroyed, the rider injured or dead, and where he could find him. Knowing there was nothing more he could do, he left his cell number and disconnected.

Tilly was standing nearby hugging herself as he looked back toward the rugged mountains drenched in sunshine. They looked so peaceful. Everything about the summer day felt normal. But under the surface...

He stepped to Tilly, pulled her to him again and held her for a few minutes.

"I'm just not used to people trying to kill me."

"Me either." He drew back to smile at her. He told himself that this wasn't the time or the place, but he wanted her with a kind of desperation he knew stemmed from almost being killed. "Let's get you home."

AS THEY RODE into the McKenna Ranch yard, the ranch manager looked up, his gaze going from Cooper to Tilly and back. They rode over to the stables and dismounted.

"You remember Tilly," Cooper said as he helped her down from her horse.

"Ms. Stafford," Deacon Yates said.

"Tilly is fine," she said. "Nice to see you, Deacon."

"I'm going to borrow a stock trailer to take Tilly's horse to her ranch."

Deacon opened his mouth, no doubt to tell him what he thought of that idea. But before the ranch manager could say anything, Cooper saw him glance toward the house.

"Cooper, did you bring someone home for supper?" his father asked behind him as he approached. "Tilly," Holden said as he recognized her. "It's been too long. I hope you will join us. Elaine made pot roast and she always makes too much."

Tilly shot Cooper a look that said, *Rescue me!*

"Maybe some other time," Cooper said, interceding. "I need to take Tilly and her horse home."

His father waved that off. "That can wait. The pot roast can't. Did you have a nice ride?"

Cooper wanted to tell his father about everything that had happened, but in private. "Fine." The meth lab was on McKenna Ranch property, and he was pretty sure it was what had gotten Oakley shot.

"Beautiful day for a ride," his father said.

"I can take care of your horses," Deacon said. "Why don't you go on inside and have some Sunday supper? When you come back, your horse will be loaded in a trailer, Ms. Stafford."

"Thank you, Deacon," Holden said. "It's settled. Come on." He led Tilly toward the house. Cooper looked at Deacon, who shrugged. There was nothing to do but follow Tilly and his father inside.

She'd never known how beautiful the McKenna house was, although she'd heard stories. It was huge, not as rambling as the Stafford house. All white wood and clear glass, the massive three-story house rose above the river, the cottonwoods flanking it, making it look even more majestic.

They crossed the wide front porch, and Holden opened the large door to usher them in. Tilly turned to Cooper and said, "If you don't mind, I need to freshen up."

They were both covered with dust, hot and sweaty. "Me too. I'll show you to the bathroom," Cooper said, and led her down the hall. It wasn't until they reached it and he checked to make sure no one was around that he said, "Sorry about this. I need to tell my dad about what we found when I get a chance."

She nodded. "Sunday supper?" she said, raising a brow.

"I told you. Dad wants our families to quit fighting, though I am surprised he invited you to supper. Maybe this is a start to bringing the families together." Tilly had her doubts about that but didn't voice them. "Go ahead and use this bathroom. I'll go to another one. See you in the dining room."

When Cooper walked into the dining room a few minutes later, he saw that his father had corralled the whole family. He groaned inwardly. No good could come from this, he thought as his father motioned for him to sit next to him across from Treyton. Next to Cooper was an empty chair, no doubt for Tilly.

Before he could sit, Tilly walked into the dining room. Holden stood and cleared his voice loudly. Duffy rose. Treyton started to rise, but then dropped back into his chair as he saw who it was. "No frigging way," he said. Bailey just looked confused, until she saw Tilly. Holly Jo looked up and frowned as if she had no idea what was going on or how unheard-of this was.

"Tilly, I'm so glad you were able to join us," Holden said as Cooper pulled out the chair next to him for her. "I think you know everyone but Holly Jo, the latest addition to our family. Holly Jo, say hello to Tilly." Tilly said hello to the sullen girl, who mumbled something into her empty plate. "Holly Jo, Tilly lives on the ranch next door."

Next door was putting it mildly, Cooper thought as he sat and so did Duffy and their father.

"The men in this family have manners," Bailey said, looking amused. "Apparently, we just needed another woman in the house to bring them out. Except for one male in the family," she said, giving Treyton the stink eye.

"Sorry," Treyton said, shoving back his chair and getting to his feet. "But I can't sit here and pretend this is all right. A Stafford sitting here at our dinner table? After they've tried for years to put us out of business? No, thank you."

"You apologize right now," their father demanded.

But Treyton ignored him. "Who else are you going to bring home? It's bad enough that you brought home your bastard child to live with us."

"Treyton," Holden snapped, but his eldest son was already storming out.

Holly Jo looked up from where she'd been scowling at her plate. "Was he talking about me?" She looked down the table at Holden. "Was he saying that I'm your daughter?" she asked, her voice rising.

"He doesn't know what he's talking about," Holden said. "You're not my daughter. You're the daughter of a friend of mine who has now passed away and wants you to be with us."

"That's a lie," Holly Jo accused. "My mother wasn't your friend. She hated you."

"Holly Jo," Holden said a little too loudly. "We will talk about this when we don't have company."

"Company?" She looked at Tilly. "She's company? Then what am I?"

"You're not company. You're family now, and I won't hear another word."

She shot him a rebellious look. "I'd like to be excused."

"No."

She shoved back her chair. "If I'm family, then I should be able to do what Treyton did, right, *Dad*?"

"I'm not your father."

"Then why did my mother hate you so much?"

"We'll discuss this at another time," he said through gritted teeth, then sighed as the girl stormed off.

"I'd like to hear the answer to that too," Bailey said. "She does look like us. So who is this child who is now…family?"

"At another time," Holden said under his breath. He shook his head. "Again, I am sorry, Tilly. This family hasn't found their manners after all. We'll work on that."

Elaine brought in the food with the help of the other staff.

"There's no reason for you to be sorry, Dad," Cooper assured him. "Elaine, this looks delicious," he said as she put down a huge plate of beef pot roast, potatoes, carrots and onions, and a bowl of homemade warm dinner rolls straight from the oven, given the way they smelled.

"This is beautiful," Tilly said. "Thank you for inviting me to join you."

"Why do I feel like I've missed something?" Duffy asked, looking around the table. "First, family meetings, and now this?"

"Don't be an ass, Duffy," Bailey said. "If you weren't always thinking about women…"

"Unlike my sister who—"

"Not you two also," Holden interrupted loudly. He turned to Tilly. "Again, I apologize for Treyton. He was raised better than this. Also, for the rest of my family."

"It's all right," she said, smiling as if she was amused. "I understand, believe me. If it was Cooper at my family's table, I'm afraid my brother CJ would do a lot more than refuse to eat with him. Treyton's right. Our families are at odds, and we can't pretend that they're not. They have been for a long time. I'm not sure our generation can fix it. But we don't have to continue fighting among ourselves."

Holden smiled. "You're a very smart young woman. I'm glad you're having Sunday supper with us." He looked around the table. "I'm sorry about that outburst, but let's have a pleasant meal. You know Elaine," he said to Tilly as Elaine brought in a large fruit salad in a watermelon bowl. The two women exchanged pleasantries and Elaine started to leave. "This is such a special occasion, Elaine, please join us. Elaine is the best cook in the county and has blue ribbons to prove it."

Cooper saw the surprised look on Elaine's face, but also the pleasure and apprehension at being invited. She started to say something about it just being family, but his father interrupted. "You are family, Elaine. Please take Treyton's place." As she took off her apron and sat, he said to her, "Maybe a prayer?"

Again, Elaine seemed as surprised as everyone else at the table. Holden nodded to her, and they all bowed their heads as she said, "God bless this food, this family and our neighbors and friends. Amen."

Bailey and Duffy looked in shock as their father began passing the food around the table. Like Cooper, he was sure they couldn't remember the last time grace had been said at their table. Then again, he couldn't remember the last time they'd had a guest. He looked at his father with both pride and concern.

What was going on? Cooper knew this wasn't all about Tilly joining them. It had to be the addition of Holly Jo that had brought this on. It seemed his father was trying for a new beginning that he hoped would include peace between the families. While Cooper applauded his efforts, he hoped his father knew that this would be an uphill battle, if Treyton's response had been any indication.

CHAPTER EIGHTEEN

HOLDEN COULDN'T BELIEVE the rebellion he'd witnessed at dinner. He'd lost control as the head of this household. "A house divided cannot stand." The proverb had never seemed truer than now. For years their adversaries had been the weather, the economy and the Staffords.

The ranch had always been his sanctuary. He'd felt safe here, thought his family was. When Oakley had been shot on his ranch… He felt as if he was at war. What he hadn't realized was that there was an underground uprising going on right here within his family.

He looked up as Elaine came into his den. She was petite and slim, everything about her understated, including her beauty. She went straight to the bar and poured him a bourbon. As she handed it to him, he smiled up at her from his chair in front of the stone fireplace.

"Thank you for today," he said as he motioned for her to join him. Only a few years younger than him, Elaine had been his confidante for years. He trusted her with his home, his family, even his life. As usual, her strawberry blond hair was in a knot at the nape of her neck. He'd only glimpsed it down once and had been surprised how long it was. He wondered if she ever truly let her hair down. He hadn't seen it, if she had. She was all business, running her area of the house quietly and efficiently.

"I did wonder what had gotten into you," she said, smiling at him as she took a chair. "If I hadn't known better, I might have thought you'd lost your mind. You shouldn't have asked me to eat with the family. Now your children are going to think that I'm sleeping with you."

He chuckled. "Would that be so bad?"

She said nothing, still smiling, giving him that patient look of hers that said she knew he was joking—just as she had been. A love affair had never been in the cards for them.

"You're my family and have been for years." Again, she said nothing. "Margaret must be rolling over in her grave to see what I've done with the rest of this family. She would have never allowed things to go so wrong. I've made so many mistakes." Like marrying his second wife, Lulabelle. That thought did nothing to improve his mood.

"Today wasn't a mistake, asking Tilly to eat at your table with your family," she assured him. He hoped she was right. She'd always encouraged him to make peace between their families.

"I like Tilly and I think Cooper likes her. But if they were to marry…"

Elaine nodded. "Like she said, it may be up to this generation to settle this old feud between the families."

"Or to continue it. Look at Treyton." He shook his

head. He didn't even want to get into what Cooper had told him about Treyton. Or into Cooper's suspicions about his brother. Holden didn't believe Treyton would go behind his back, but he could be wrong. The thought upset him, making him worry that he really had lost complete control of this family. "Then there is Duffy. I fear there isn't a serious bone in his body, and Bailey…" He took a sip of his drink.

"You're a good father. It's your children who are awful," she joked.

"They are headstrong, that's for sure." He looked at her. Elaine had a quiet quality that he'd come to appreciate more and more. She'd been with him through it all. He knew there could be more between them. Except he also knew she would never make the first move. He was in love with another woman and suspected Elaine knew it. He would never do anything to ruin the easygoing comradery he had with Elaine. He wondered if she felt the same way.

He took another sip of the bourbon. It burned all the way down, sending a needed warmth through him. "You always know what I need," he said, making her smile again.

"When are you going to tell them the truth?" she asked.

"When I have no other choice." He could feel her waiting, her gaze intent on him. "It is hard to admit a part of your life you want to forget. But when it comes to Holly Jo, I hope I'm doing the right thing." He shook his head again before emptying his glass. "I haven't been paying enough attention to what's going on here at the ranch, and it is proving to be a very big mistake."

"We've all made mistakes," she said, waving it off.

He laughed. "Not you, Elaine. You're a saint." He liked the sound of her laugh. "Have a bourbon with me."

She shook her head. "I have my secrets, and you aren't going to try to get me inebriated to worm them out of me." She rose to go to her room off the kitchen. "Don't be so hard on yourself, Holden."

"Easy for you to say." But Elaine had already left the room. He stared into the empty fireplace, already anxious for fall and cooler days, even though it was only late June. He wished he could see the future. With a laugh, he got up to get himself a refill, glad he couldn't see where his life was headed. The future scared him right now, especially as he considered what Cooper had told him about Treyton.

He thought of Cooper. What would Lottie make of Tilly and Cooper spending time together? As if he didn't already know.

AFTER SUPPER, Cooper walked Tilly out to where Deacon was hooking up the horse trailer. He couldn't wait for the two of them to be alone. All through dinner, he'd found himself looking at Tilly, wanting her. There was so much he wanted to say to her. Once they were headed to her ranch, he was damned sure going to kiss her. Hell, he might change his mind and make love to her in the pickup if she was up to it.

"Thank you for earlier today," she said. "I don't

know that I would have gotten out of there alive without you. And I enjoyed Sunday supper."

"That was all my dad's doing. I'm going to talk to him about what happened earlier today, what we found. He'll be upset. He'll want to find out who's behind it. I just hope it isn't anyone close to the families."

She nodded as if it was her fear as well. They lived in a community where they knew everyone. When Oakley was shot, they had both wanted to believe it had something to do with coalbed methane drilling and someone from outside the community had fired that shot.

He didn't want to talk about any of that. He just wanted to get her alone. He wanted Tilly, and by damned, they were going to be together. Just the thought of her naked in his arms was almost his undoing. He knew a spot where they could stop along the river in the trees.

But as he reached the horse trailer, he saw that Deacon had hooked it up not to Cooper's pickup, but his own. "What's going on?" he asked the ranch manager.

"I think it would be best if I took her," Deacon said, and looked at Tilly as if he expected her to back him up.

To Cooper's surprise, she did. "Deacon's right. We don't want any trouble, and I believe there would be if CJ is around. Your father was wonderful tonight, Coop, but he doesn't realize how things really are, and quite frankly, they've been getting worse." She must have seen his disappointment and had some of her own. She leaned toward him and gave him a quick kiss.

He grabbed her, pulling her into his arms, and kissed her passionately. She moaned against him. He swore he could feel her heart thundering like his own. She pulled back, looking as if it was as difficult for her as it was for him.

Deacon had turned away and was now climbing into his pickup.

They stood looking at each other for a long moment before she said good-night and climbed in the cab with Deacon. Cooper watched them drive away, the stock trailer with her horse inside trailing behind.

It had been one hell of a day. As he walked back into the house, he knew that Deacon was right. As his ardor cooled a little, he knew that if he'd taken her home, he would have made love to her in the pickup. That wasn't what he wanted. Not for their first time. But he couldn't take her up to his bed in the house and he couldn't go to her bed in her house. The last thing he wanted to do was take her to a motel, but it might come to that. He told himself that he would come up with something. He wasn't pushing her away. Not anymore.

As he reached the house, his thoughts turned to what they'd found on the ranch earlier. He hated to lay this on his father. But he'd waited long enough to tell him. He hadn't heard anything from the sheriff, but then again, Stu didn't have to call him. He'd left enough information that the sheriff wouldn't have any trouble finding the meth lab at the old homestead. Stu knew this area as well as anyone, maybe better since, as sheriff, he saw more of it than anyone else.

"Dad?" Cooper found Holden sitting in his den in front of the fireplace. "Dad?"

His father stirred, waving him in, smiling. "I'm so glad Tilly had supper with us."

"It was nice of you to invite her. Dad, there's something you need to know." Sitting down, he told him about everything he and Tilly had found on the far side of the ranch.

He could see that the news about the meth lab on McKenna property had struck him hard. "You could have both been killed," Holden said. "Why didn't you tell me as soon as you got back?"

"Because it's on our property. I thought we should keep it between us—at least until Stuart raids the place and word gets out."

"Well, it's not like we have anything to do with it," his father said, and then stopped as if suddenly realizing what Cooper was really saying. "You can't think that Treyton…"

"Or someone else who works for us might be involved? I think it's possible. I also think that it might be why Oakley was shot. She must have heard something about it, went to check it out, and someone tried to stop her from going to the authorities."

Holden let out a breath as if trying to take it all in. "What do you suggest?"

"I already left messages with the sheriff. Whatever he finds, I guess we'll ride it out. What else can we do?"

"You're sure it's a meth lab?"

"That's what they look like on TV. I've personally never seen one before. We must have tripped some security device. Those two cowboys who showed up on the four-wheelers meant business. I didn't have time to even think about taking a photo with my phone."

His father shook his head as if still not wanting to believe it. Cooper knew how he felt. "That isn't all. I found something, evidence that might prove Leann didn't kill herself. I think there was another man she was planning to leave town with. I think he might have killed her." He nodded at his father's shocked look. "I asked the sheriff to reopen the case."

"Oh, Cooper."

"I know. But I have to know the truth. I hate that it will put me and the family back in the news. Also, as Stu pointed out, it might make the prosecutor come after me again."

"Are you sure you want to do this? I'm worried you might go to prison for something you didn't do."

"I need to put it behind me, but I can't."

"Have you told Tilly?" his father asked.

He could see that Holden wanted to ask about their relationship. "Tilly and I…" He couldn't finish. "It's complicated."

"Yes," his father agreed.

"You're worried."

"Just that you might get your heart broken. While I want to end this animosity between our family and the Staffords, I'm no fool. It could take generations."

"I know. Believe me, I've told myself all the reasons I should stay away from her."

"Can you?" his father asked.

He shook his head. "I can't. Not anymore."

"Please don't make the mistake I did. Our families

were so opposed to Lottie and me... I was a coward. I took the easy way out. Don't get me wrong. I know that if I had done things differently, I wouldn't have you kids. So I can't be sorry. But I gave up the love of my life because of this stupid family feud. I would hate to see you do that." His father rose. "We should get some rest."

DEACON WAS UNLOADING Tilly's horse when her brother CJ came out to see what was going on. "CJ," Deacon said without stopping what he was doing. As he brought her horse out of the trailer, she took the lead attached to the halter that Deacon held out to her.

"What the hell is he doing on our ranch?" her brother demanded as Deacon unloaded her saddle and gear, putting them on the ground.

"Deacon was kind enough to help me get my horse home," she said. "I was trying to get home after being thrown earlier." A white lie. "Deacon happened to see me and offered to help."

Her older brother stared at her, not buying the story. "You got thrown from a horse?"

"It happens." She thought about telling him the truth, but she kept remembering what Cooper had said. If she told him about dinner at the McKenna Ranch, she would also have to tell him about the ride she and Cooper had taken and what they'd found.

They had no idea who was behind the meth lab. While it was on McKenna land, that didn't mean that someone from her family or ranch wasn't involved. She was fine with letting the sheriff handle it.

"You sure you can take it from here?" Deacon asked after everything of hers was unloaded.

She knew he wasn't asking about her horse, saddle and tack. He was asking about her brother.

"Thank you. I can handle it," she said. Tilly was relieved when Deacon climbed behind the wheel of his pickup and drove off, no doubt seeing that CJ was looking for a fight and anxious to leave before one broke out.

Deacon had been right. If Cooper had brought her and her horse home, there would have been more than trouble.

"You just happen to be near the McKenna Ranch and the ranch manager just happens to give you a ride home?" CJ demanded. "Do you think I'm stupid?"

"No. I think you're always looking for a fight, though." She was too tired to argue. It had been a strange day. The ride with Cooper had been wonderful at first. Finding what they had had come as a shock, but nothing like those two men trying to kill them. She still believed that the meth lab in the middle of nowhere was what had gotten Oakley shot. Somehow her sister must have heard rumors about it and gone back there to check it out herself.

Tilly knew that when she closed her eyes tonight, she would relive being chased, running for her life. Just as her sister had? She could imagine how terrified her sister had been. She was almost grateful that Oakley couldn't remember.

Only her sister hadn't been alone. She remembered what Tick had told them. There had been a man on a horse right behind Oakley who'd cut off and headed south. Toward the McKenna house? Or toward the Stafford Ranch?

She reminded herself that the rifle that had shot Oakley was a 270—not what those men had been shooting at them with today. So why hadn't the man on the horse come forward after Oakley was shot? Unless he was the one who'd fired the shot. Unless he was now waiting to see if her memory came back. Or would he be afraid to wait and come after her again?

Her only hope was that once Stuart busted the meth lab, he'd find the men behind it. He'd find Oakley's shooter and put an end to this.

She started past her brother, when CJ grabbed her arm and turned her back to him. "There's talk around town about you, little sis. About you and Cooper McKenna. It better not be true."

"You could bring my saddle and gear," Tilly said to her brother as she broke free of him and led her horse toward the stables.

"Do it yourself," CJ said, staring after Deacon through the boiling dust. "I'm going to be watching you, little sis," he called after her. "Stay away from the McKennas. Stay off their ranch. Or you might not be as lucky as Oakley was."

CHAPTER NINETEEN

"I HOPE THIS isn't going to be a daily occurrence," the sheriff said as Cooper walked into the office first thing the next morning.

He closed the door behind him, making Stu groan. "Did you get the messages I left?"

"Sorry, I've been busy. I haven't even had a chance to check my messages, especially the ones from you."

"Tilly and I went for a ride yesterday, trying to trace Oakley's path before the shooting."

The sheriff looked as if he was about to explode. "I have a mind to arrest both of you for interfering in my investigation."

Ignoring him, Cooper continued. "We went all the way up the ravine, over the mountain and down the other side. Your deputies hadn't gone that far."

"Because there was nothing to see but that old homestead," he snapped.

"Someone has moved into one of the large buildings. We found what appears to be a meth lab."

The sheriff rocked back in his chair. "A meth lab?"

"There is also a landing strip there where someone has been flying in and out. We must have triggered some type of alarm, because before we could get out of there, a truck pulling a stock trailer showed up. Two men with AR15s came flying out of the back of the trailer on four-wheelers, fired on us, then chased us."

Stu was shaking his head. "You have to be kidding me."

"I might have injured one of the men. I at least killed his four-wheeler in a rockslide. You don't believe me, go check it out yourself. If you had checked your messages, you would have known about this last night."

"A meth lab, armed killers, all on your ranch?"

Cooper wasn't surprised that would be the sheriff's take. "On the part of the ranch we aren't running cattle on right now. I called as soon as I could and left you messages. I suspect this is why Oakley was shot."

"No kidding," the sheriff said. "Did you ever think I might be on top of this?"

"I sure hope so," Cooper said. Stu wasn't inspiring confidence. Had he really not gotten either message? And if he knew about this, then why wasn't he out busting the thugs running the lab before they could move it?

"Now get out of my office."

Stuart held his head in his hands after Cooper left. He was falling down on his job. He was going to get fired. He was going to lose everything if he didn't snap out of it. Last night... He couldn't believe that he'd driven to Billings, picked up a woman at some bar... He had to quit drinking. He wasn't good at it.

He wanted to blame the job, but he knew that wasn't it. His father had seen this coming. "You always seem to want what other people have instead of being thankful for what you have," his father had told him all the time he was growing up.

It was true. He'd wanted what Cooper had, what Cooper had never appreciated, a huge ranch, a life Stuart would have given his left arm for. Leann had only been a symptom, he could admit now. He'd never really been in love with her. But Tilly, she was a different story. He'd loved her as a friend. He thought it could be more.

"But did you love her because you knew how Tilly and Cooper felt about each other for years?" It was his father's voice making him cringe because he knew there was truth in it.

He realized he'd been angry with his friend for leaving, for giving up his place on the ranch as if it meant nothing to him. When Cooper had returned and started hanging out with Tilly, it had been the last straw.

Rubbing his eyes with the heels of his hands, he wondered if he could feel any lower. His phone rang. He picked up. He swore. Another fight down at the bar. And just when he was thinking his day couldn't get any worse.

TILLY HAD BEEN expecting a call from Cooper, so she wasn't surprised to hear from him so early. "Did Stuart bust the lab?"

"No. He said he didn't get my messages. I think he plans to go check it out himself now. That's all we can do, but there is something else I need to talk to you about. Can we meet?"

She thought about CJ. She didn't doubt he would

be keeping an eye on her. "I've been craving a burger. You know that place in Baker?"

"I do." She could hear the grin in his voice. "Perfect. Why don't I pick you up at the junction outside of town? Ten thirty?"

"See you then." She hung up, wondering what he had to tell her. Yesterday, she could tell that something was bothering him. She'd thought it was the kisses and the discussion of their first time making love. Of course he hadn't wanted to talk about either.

Then last night at his house she'd seen the desire in his eyes, felt it in his kiss and the way he'd squeezed her against him. He wanted this as much as she did. So if that was what he had to talk to her about, denying what was going on, she swore she would deck him.

This morning he'd gone to see the sheriff? She hoped what he had to tell her wasn't about Stuart. She had to quit speculating and go meet him. Maybe it would be good news.

But as she got ready to leave, there was a knock on her bedroom door. Her mother stepped in. Tilly saw her hesitate and felt her stomach drop. "It isn't Oakley, is it?"

"No," Charlotte said quickly. "CJ mentioned that Deacon Yates brought you and your horse to the ranch last night." She waited, letting her mother lead this conversation. "He said you'd gotten thrown from your horse. Are you all right?"

"Just a little sore. I'm fine. CJ shouldn't have worried you with it." She felt the full intensity of her mother's gaze.

"He's apparently heard the same rumors I have about

you and Cooper McKenna." Still Tilly held her tongue. "Matilda, you need to tell me. Are you seeing this Mc-Kenna boy?"

"He's no longer a boy."

"I thought you were dating the sheriff," her mother said.

"We went out on a few dates, yes."

"You're not seeing him anymore?"

"No."

Her mother looked as if she was ready to stomp her foot in frustration. "What is going on? You tell me right now."

"I'm seeing Cooper McKenna. I had dinner with him and his family last night at the ranch. Holden invited me to join them."

"You what?" Her mother grabbed the door frame for support.

"Holden wants to put an end to this ridiculous feud between our families."

Her mother looked aghast. "If you think one dinner will take away all the bad blood and history—"

"No, I don't think one dinner will do it. But it's a start."

Charlotte shook her head. "It's never going to happen."

"Because you won't allow it? Because you can't forgive Holden for breaking your heart?"

"You know nothing about it."

"But I do know. Everyone in this county knows that he broke your heart when he married someone else. He did it because of this stupid feud that goes back years, not because he didn't love you. All it did was add fuel to the flames."

Her mother seemed at a loss for words. "You don't know—"

"I do know that you have never forgiven him."

Straightening to her full height, she met Tilly's gaze with an angry one of her own. "You think it's that simple?"

"No. Love never is. But how long do we have to keep doing this?"

"You can never marry a McKenna."

Tilly didn't know how to tell her mother that it hadn't gone that far. That maybe Cooper had needed to see her today to tell her that they couldn't see each other anymore, because like his father, he couldn't marry a Stafford.

"Are you listening to me? I forbid it!"

She stared at her mother. Did she really think she could stop it? "I have to go. I'm meeting a friend for lunch." It was true. She and Coop were at least friends—if not lovers. Yet.

AT TEN THIRTY, Cooper was already waiting for her. He saw right away that something had happened. She was too quiet, and she was chewing on that poor lower lip. She left her pickup, and they drove toward Baker and the famous burger place.

"I didn't want to tell you this over the phone," he said after they'd gone a few miles.

"You're kind of scaring me, Coop."

"I'm sorry. I'm not trying to. It's about Leann. I'm

still trying to make sense of what I found." He told her about the notes in the book. "I'm running a little scared myself. I need answers, but they could come at a cost."

"Are you okay?"

He knew what she was asking. Were they okay, the two of them? He wished he knew. After his visit with the sheriff this morning, he felt more uneasy about Stu, about the past, about Tilly and this love triangle he'd apparently stepped into.

The problem seemed to be that Stu was the only one who didn't know Tilly wasn't in love with him and never had been. He hated what that might mean, what that told him about his old friend.

Stuart had never been in a relationship that lasted very long, Cooper now realized. He couldn't fault him for that. He didn't have much of a track record himself. But it did make him question what Tilly said her friend had told her. What Leann had said about Stu. Too possessive.

Cooper was so frustrated with Stu, with all of this. Maybe especially frustrated with the fact that the sheriff had been dragging his feet on everything, including busting the meth lab, finding Oakley's shooter, asking the prosecutor to reopen Leann Hayes's case.

He pushed thoughts of Stu away, needing to tell Tilly what he'd found and what that meant for his future. Their future? He told Tilly about Leann seeming to practice how to tell him that she was leaving town. "There was another man she was leaving with, someone she thought I wouldn't approve of, I'm sure of it. Just as I'm sure she didn't kill herself."

TILLY FELT RELIEVED that he'd told her. She didn't mention that Stuart had wanted her to talk him out of pushing to reopen the case. "Then who did kill her?"

"I don't know. Maybe things went sour with the boyfriend, and he killed her. Or maybe there was someone else in the picture, an old lover. I just don't know, but I showed the notes to Stu and asked him to get the prosecutor to reopen the case. He said he's too busy right now with Oakley's shooting. I'm not sure if he will or not. If not, I'll go to the prosecutor."

"The same one who still thinks you killed Leann?"

"I know it's a gamble, but if I'm right, her killer is still out there."

She listened as he told her about how the notes had been written on a CH4 notepad. "But as Stu pointed out, there were a lot of those notepads floating around." She knew that the sheriff didn't think CH4 had anything to do with Oakley's shooting. Did he also think no member of the staff was the lover Leann was leaving town with?

It scared her that Cooper might be arrested again. But it also frightened her to think that someone had gotten away with murder and was still at large.

"You have no idea who the man could be?" she asked.

"Not a clue. Leann and I were friends. It had never been serious."

She was glad to hear that. She'd never been serious about anyone she'd dated either. Coop was another story. Just being around him had always made her blood simmer. When she was younger, she'd thought it was because she'd found him so annoying. Now she knew better. There'd always been a spark between them.

"What's kind of disturbing is the notepaper Leann used to leave me what they thought was a suicide note. Stu had one of their notepads in his desk drawer at the sheriff's department."

"What?" Tilly didn't know what to make of this.

"He pulled it out to show me, saying a lot of people had the notepads. I took the notepad. The last thing he'd written on it was Leann's name, as if starting a note to her. You see why I need answers? It's like everything just keeps circling around CH4—even Leann's death, your sister's shooting—but for some reason, the sheriff isn't interested in chasing that particular lead."

She was almost afraid to ask. "You don't think Stuart…"

"That he was the man Leann was going to leave town with? I don't know. It did cross my mind."

Tilly felt a chill at the thought that the sheriff could be more involved with Leann's death than anyone knew. "But just because he had one of the notepads…"

"Exactly."

She couldn't believe that she'd gone from liking Stuart to being almost afraid of him to not trusting him to the point that she thought he might be dangerous. Might be a killer. She looked over at Cooper. "Do you trust Stuart?"

He glanced at her, then back to his driving. "Right now? Not a whole lot."

They drove in silence for a few minutes. She could tell that he was mulling over everything too. "Supper was really nice last night," she said, wanting to change the subject as they drove through badlands, rocky hills dotted with pines, groves of cottonwoods near the Powder River.

It was a beautiful summer day, the kind that made people want to move to Montana. The blue of the sky was almost blinding. A few puffy clouds dotted the horizon. Overhead, the sun lolled in that big sky, promising another hot day. Summers were short. This one was going fast. She couldn't believe it was almost the Fourth of July.

"I'm sorry about my brother and Holly Jo," Cooper said, as if he too wanted to change the subject that was nagging at both of them.

"What is the deal with Holly Jo coming to live with you?" she asked.

"Who knows? Dad hasn't really explained who she is or why she's there apparently to stay."

"She and Treyton are so angry." Tilly thought of her mother this morning. "We knew there would be some resistance when people saw us together."

He chuckled at that. "You could say that. I heard CJ was waiting when Deacon dropped off you and your horse."

"I was glad we took his advice, and you didn't come with me."

"You do realize we're fighting an uphill battle if we take this to the next step," Cooper said.

"I'm up for the challenge. How about you?" she had to ask, half-afraid of what his answer would be.

He smiled over at her. "I have to be, since I can't seem to stay away from you. All I think about is getting you naked."

"The feeling is mutual," she said as she reached over and put her hand on his thigh.

He glanced down at her hand. "You do realize what that will get you," he joked.

"I can only hope," she said as Baker appeared on the horizon. "You are talking about the best burger within a hundred miles, right?"

"Right," he said as he pulled into the lot, parked and unbuckled his seat belt to reach for her. The kiss was full of promise.

But she didn't deceive herself. Their families would be a problem. They already were. If what she'd heard about Holden McKenna and her mother was true, he'd taken the easy way out by marrying the woman his father approved of instead of Charlotte Stafford, the woman he loved.

If true, she couldn't bear that history might repeat itself. Yet she could understand how hard it would be, and not just for them, but their children, if the two families continued this feud. Worse, she thought of Treyton and her brother CJ. It could get violent. Someone could get hurt. Or maybe they already had, if Oakley wasn't shot by the meth dealers but someone from the McKenna Ranch for trespassing.

"Hungry?" Cooper asked as he ended the kiss.

"Starved." *For you*, she thought. She would not deny

her heart no matter what the future held. She wouldn't be a bitter, unforgiving woman like her mother. But after this morning, she knew it could cost her not just her family, but she feared it would cost her the ranch.

OVER LUNCH, Cooper couldn't take his eyes off her. Tilly was so beautiful, so sexy in an understated way, so confident. That he wanted her desperately was no secret. On the way into town, they'd passed a motel. Their options were so limited other than getting together out in the wild.

He couldn't help being tempted. He had a feeling that she'd be up for the motel, even though it wasn't how he'd wanted to make love with her the first time.

After lunch, they were headed out to his pickup. He put his arm around her and whispered in her ear what he was thinking. "We can leave the pickup here, walk down to the motel…" They knew too many people in this county. If someone saw his truck parked in front of the motel, it would be all over the evening news.

"Yes," she said without hesitation. She met his gaze, and he saw desire bright in those green eyes.

But as they started to turn to walk in the direction of the motel, a car pulled up. Cooper groaned as a local rancher got out, calling to him. They stopped walking as the rancher came over to shake Cooper's hand, ask how long he'd been back, what he was doing in Baker.

Then the rancher recognized Tilly and did a double take before apologizing for not speaking to her sooner. "Picked a good place to get a burger," he said, looking embarrassed.

"I forgot, we're parked over here," Cooper said, telling the rancher goodbye as he and Tilly headed for his pickup.

"What are we going to do?" Tilly said once they were inside the cab of the truck. She stifled a laugh. "This is crazy. It's like the universe is trying to keep us apart."

"Maybe it's for the best. If Leann's case is reopened, I can't be sure what will happen. I'm the last person you might want to be involved with."

"Don't say that. Nothing can change my mind about you, about us, Coop. I want this more than anything. I realized that I have for a long while."

He swallowed. "If I make love to you—"

"*When* you do, yes?"

"When I make love to you, there will be no going back for me. You sure you're ready for that?"

She nodded and smiled. "I'm ready for the tailgate."

He laughed as he started the engine and drove them back toward Powder Crossing. "But no motel, no tailgate today. I'll figure something out."

He was so unsure about so many things—just not this, not Tilly. His heart knew where it had been headed for a long time. They had to find a way.

All day, he'd been hoping to hear that the sheriff had checked out the meth lab at the old homestead. But even after lunch, the drive back to her pickup and the long trip back to the ranch, he still hadn't heard anything.

"Well?" he'd asked in frustration when the sheriff answered his call.

"Well, what? Not that it's any of your business, but we had several emergencies around town. I couldn't get out there."

Cooper swore. "After what happened yesterday, they're going to move the operation."

"Whose fault will that be? If you and Tilly weren't so busy undermining my investigation—"

"Call in more help. Call the Feds. You can't let them get away. These are dangerous people."

"Stop telling me how to do my job," Stu snapped, and disconnected.

He tried to breathe. What the hell was the sheriff doing? Not his job. Cooper wanted to call him back and tell Stu what he thought about him using his anger at him and Tilly to ignore something this important.

He hadn't wanted to go over Stu's head, but now he had no choice. He called the Feds, told one of the agents everything and gave them coordinates to where the meth lab was located.

Stuart would be furious. Cooper was kicking himself for not going to the Feds right away. He just hoped it wasn't too late.

He found Holly Jo mucking out the stalls and grumbling under her breath.

"Heard you got into trouble," he said. She looked up, pulled a face and kept working. He knew his father was now locking the tack room to make sure she didn't take it on herself to saddle up and take off. "I have to go into town, but I'll be back for your riding lesson."

"What is the point if I never get to ride?" she wailed.

He looked up as Pickett came through the stable

door. "Something I think you'd better come see," the ranch hand said, and motioned for Cooper to follow him. Once outside, he saw it immediately. Flames shooting up high into the air on the other side of the ravine that cut through the mountains.

Swearing, he knew exactly what was burning—all evidence of the meth lab and the men involved.

CHAPTER TWENTY

COOPER BLAMED HIMSELF. If he hadn't gotten involved with Tilly Stafford, the sheriff would have done his job. The moment he thought it, he knew this didn't fall on his shoulders.

He caught the sheriff as he was coming out of the building. "What are you doing here?" Stu demanded. His uniform was wrinkled, and he looked tired, beaten down. Cooper had heard that he'd had a visit from the Feds. He hoped they'd chewed his ass good.

"They burned everything, getting rid of the evidence, didn't they? You let that happen out of spite," Cooper said, unable to hold back his anger.

"Unless you want me to lock you up, I suggest you get out of my way."

"You let them get away. Now I'm wondering how much other evidence you let slide—over a woman."

"I don't have any idea what you're insinuating, but—"

"Sure you do, Stu. Leann. I didn't kill her, and she didn't kill herself. The notes prove it. There was another man in her life. She was leaving with him. I wonder what happened. Did she see something in him that she didn't like that day? Or had he changed his mind because he finally had her? He'd finally taken her away from me?"

"You're accusing me of not just covering up evidence, but killing her? You think I was the other man?"

"She said I wouldn't approve and she was right, if it was you. Because she wanted to leave town and you're never leaving here."

"You don't know me."

"You're right," Cooper said. "I don't. I thought I did, but you've now reminded me of things about you that gave me pause that I ignored out of friendship."

Stu let out a bitter laugh. "No one is as perfect as Cooper McKenna," the sheriff said sarcastically. "Good thing you came back to town to save Tilly Stafford. Too bad you couldn't save Leann, though. Isn't that what really bothers you?"

"What really bothers me is that she was murdered, and you don't seem to want to find her killer."

Stu glared at him. "I think I already have. I'm starting to agree with the prosecutor. Maybe I *will* reopen the case. But what will Tilly do without you all those years you're in prison?"

Other people were coming out of the sheriff's department and courthouse as the day ended. This wasn't the place or the time. But Cooper hadn't been able to hold his anger in any longer. He'd felt like Stu had been dragging his feet on Oakley's case, ignoring leads and now letting the men running the meth lab get away.

"I'm going to find out the truth, and not just about Leann's murder, but Oakley's shooting and who was running that meth lab in your county under your nose," Cooper said.

"You get in my way again and I will put you behind bars," Stu said as Cooper turned and walked away. "I mean it, Coop. I'll lock you up and Tilly too."

TILLY FELT SICK when she heard about the fire. She knew at once what was burning. All she could think was that Cooper must be beside himself with anger. He'd called Stuart and told him about the lab. Why hadn't the sheriff done anything? Hugging herself, she feared she and Coop were the reason.

It made her furious with Stuart. It also made her wonder why she'd ever gone out with him. Because they'd been friends, and she had to admit, he'd been fun on the dates. Then her sister had been shot, Cooper had come back to town and she'd seen a side of Stuart that more than disturbed her.

He'd been instantly jealous of her spending any time with Cooper. But, looking back, he always had been jealous of him, she realized. She remembered him making remarks about how lucky ranchers' sons were that they were born into land. Stuart's father had been sheriff in Powder River County. The only land his family had owned was what was sitting under their house. So maybe this wasn't entirely about her.

She'd been so deep in thought that she flinched when her phone rang.

"Coop?" She wasn't surprised to hear the anger and frustration in his voice.

"You've heard?"

"Yes. Have you seen Stuart?" She knew Cooper. He would have gone straight to the sheriff.

"I saw him. How is your sister feeling?" he asked, quickly changing the subject. "You think she's up for visitors?"

She could only guess how the confrontation between the two men had gone. At least Cooper wasn't behind bars. "It will depend on if we can see Oakley without my mother being there. She isn't on the same page as your father," Tilly said regretfully.

"Has she said anything to you?"

She didn't want to tell him how her mother really felt. "Basically that all McKennas will break your heart, ruin your life and steal your silverware and your ranch."

"We do have a couple of your soupspoons," he joked, but she could still hear the residual anger under it.

"I'm headed into town. I'll call you when my mother isn't there."

"Great."

"Coop? I'm not sure how much more Oakley can tell us. You really don't think it was one of the men from the meth lab?"

"I do think Oakley could have stumbled onto the lab, but I don't think they were the ones who shot her. I keep thinking about what she said to me. Buttercup. Are you sure that doesn't mean anything to you?"

"No. Nothing."

"Okay. Call when we can see her alone," he said, and was gone.

As she disconnected, she realized how much she had wanted to believe that they'd found out who'd shot her sister. She wanted to believe it had been meth makers—not someone closer to home. A 270 rifle was so common, anyone could have shot Oakley.

It hadn't slipped her mind either that it would have taken a local to know about the isolated old homestead—and that McKenna wasn't running any cattle in that area because of the well that had gone dry. Or that the well had gone dry because Charlotte Stafford had allowed a methane well to be put in so close to the McKenna Ranch.

Her mind whirring, Tilly drove into town. She checked in at the hospital, only to find that her mother was with her sister. Leaving without seeing either of them, she headed for the sheriff's department, hoping to catch Stuart and put an end to whatever was going on between him and Cooper.

"Tilly?" the sheriff said, getting to his feet. He was smiling, clearly glad to see her. It was the hope in his voice that hurt.

She closed the door and turned to look at him, reminding herself how long they'd been friends. "Maybe I wasn't clear the other day—"

"No, you were perfectly clear. I know. You don't want to go out with me again. You just left out the part about you and Cooper. But I got it. Is there anything else?" he asked impatiently.

"I'm sorry, Stuart."

"Please, don't say anything else."

"I enjoyed the times that we went out, but I didn't feel the way you apparently did...do. I didn't know how you felt until—"

"Until Cooper came home?"

"I guess so. Did you even know how you felt about me before then? Because I don't really think this is about us." He didn't answer. "I think it's about you and Cooper."

The sheriff chewed at his cheek for a moment, not denying it. "So you're serious about him?"

She smiled. "There has always been some strong emotion between Cooper and me. He used to annoy the hell out of me."

"I remember the two of you fighting like cats and dogs. I guess I should have known then there was no getting between the two of you."

"I guess I should have known too. I don't know where this is going, but I want to see. I never wanted to hurt you, though."

"Don't give it another thought. Please."

"I'm sorry that you're hurt."

He sighed and looked to the ceiling for a moment. "I wanted more. Thought in time we might... I was wrong. I'm ready to settle down, and I guess maybe I thought you were too."

"I hate that this has come between you and Coop and that you aren't friends anymore."

"Who says we're not friends anymore? Friends fight, they argue, they disagree, but friendships survive it, the real friendships. I guess we'll have to see if mine and Cooper's is one of them."

"I hope so. I don't like losing friends."

He smiled at that. "It's one of the things that I like

about you. You're loyal to people you care about. Don't worry. We'll all survive this."

She hoped so, but there was such a sadness in his tone, she worried. His phone rang and she hurriedly excused herself. But as she walked away, she knew that whatever was really bothering him ran deeper than her. Maybe even deeper than him and Cooper. She hoped that hers and Cooper's suspicions about him were wrong.

When she returned to the hospital, her mother was gone. She called Cooper.

"YOU'RE GOING TO wear a hole in that floor."

Charlotte turned to see her ranch manager standing in the doorway of the living room, hat in hand, a sheepish look on his face. Boyle Wilson had been a fixture on the Stafford Ranch since he was a teen. She remembered him flirting with her, making her even more aware of the seventeen years between her and her first husband, Rake Stafford.

Before Rake, the ranch had been the Carson Ranch, left to Charlotte as the only child. When she married Rake, the name was changed to the Stafford Ranch. He brought in enough money and know-how to expand the ranch and teach her how to survive as a rancher. She'd given birth to five children before Rake died, leaving her free to run the place the way she wanted.

As she looked around the room, she reminded herself that she'd been born and raised for this life. Just as she'd been born and raised in this rambling house with its worn wood floors and rock fireplaces. Boyle had been around from as far back as she could remember, right through her short second disastrous marriage until today. He'd often told her that he knew her better than anyone.

What he meant by that was that he knew her secrets. He thought that gave him job security. She thought he underestimated her and knew that, one day, he would find out just how much.

In the meantime, as long as he did his job, she kept him close. Just not too close. Even at fifty-five, close to her own age, he still looked at her as he had when he was a young ranch hand.

"What's this I hear about Deacon Yates bringing Tilly and her horse home yesterday?" she demanded.

"I just know what CJ told me. Seems she went riding, got thrown from her horse, and Deacon found her and brought her and her horse back here."

Charlotte tried to breathe. Boyle didn't believe that story any more than she had. Tilly rode better than anyone she knew. But accidents did happen. She just didn't believe this had been one of them. Two of her daughters on the McKenna Ranch? Two of them being rescued by either a McKenna or their ranch manager? "The sheriff called this morning. Said you got in a fight with Rusty Malone at the bar yesterday. I've told you to stay away from him." He was some shirttail relative of her second husband.

"He started it."

"Well, I'm finishing it. Stay away from him. Stay away from the bar, if that's what it takes."

"Anything else, Mrs. Stafford?" he asked sarcastically.

"No." As he turned to leave, she said, "Boyle, see that my horse is saddled." She said it to put him in his place. She was more than capable of saddling her own horse. She would also double-check that he'd done it correctly. Did she really not trust him? The thought made her uneasy.

"I'll get right on that," he said, his look questioning where she was going. But he was too smart to ask as he left.

She pulled out her phone, keyed in the number. When her call was answered, she said, "Meet me at the usual place— Yes, now, please." With that, she hung up. She was still the matriarch of this ranch, and damned if she wasn't going to find out what had been going on right under her nose.

CHAPTER TWENTY-ONE

OAKLEY WAS SITTING up in bed when Cooper and Tilly walked into her hospital room. She burst into a smile and reached for Cooper's hand. "I heard that you found me, saved me," she said, squeezing his hand. "Thank you."

"I'm glad I was there, even though I can't tell you how much you scared me," he said. "It's good to see that you're so much better."

Oakley looked at her sister and laughed. "This explains Mother's foul mood." As Cooper walked over to the window to look out, she motioned Tilly closer and whispered, "Are the two of you…?"

"No," Tilly whispered back. "Not yet."

Her sister laughed again. "Who knew you'd grow up to be the rebel in the family?"

"We want to ask you some questions, if you're up to it," Cooper said, returning to her bedside.

"I don't remember anything from that day at all," she said.

"You don't remember me almost hitting you with my pickup, then?"

She shook her head. "Why?"

"When I found you on the ground after you'd fallen off your horse, you grabbed my arm and said, 'Buttercup.' You were quite insistent. I thought it was the name of your horse and that you were worried about the mare. But when I told you that your horse was fine, you said 'Buttercup' again as if it was important. Once I found out that your horse's name was Cheyenne..."

"Buttercup?" Oakley shook her head, frowning. "I have no idea." She sighed. "It's so frustrating. I'm told someone shot me, you found me and saved me, but I have no idea what I was doing there or why anyone would want to shoot me. I'm sorry." She took a deep breath. "I did hear that the two of you have been trying to find out what happened. Thanks, since I won't be getting out of here for a while yet."

"I know you don't know why you were on the McKenna Ranch or why you came riding out of that ravine that leads to the old homestead," Cooper said. "Your sister and I rode back there. Someone had a meth lab in the larger of the buildings."

Oakley's eyes widened. "You think that's what I found and one of them shot me?"

"We think it's possible, though you were shot with a slug from a 270 rifle. The men who shot at us had AR15s."

"You got shot at?" Oakley cried, looking to her sister.

"We're fine. Unfortunately, before the sheriff or the Feds could get to the lab, it burned to the ground, taking any evidence with it," Tilly said.

"I suppose that could explain what I was doing back in there, if I was looking for the meth lab," Oakley said, not sounding at all sure about that.

"We also suspect that you'd been going to the meetings of a group called Dirty Business," Cooper said. "It's a grassroots organization trying to stop the methane drilling. Pickett Hanson, one of our ranch hands, is a member."

"You really have been digging into my life." She didn't look that comfortable with that revelation. "It's no secret that I'm an environmentalist, a dirty word around these parts. Don't get me started on coalbed methane drilling."

"There is something else. The day you were shot, you weren't alone," Cooper said. "There was another rider either chasing you or with you." Her eyebrows went up. "Have you been seeing someone recently? Someone like Pickett Hanson?"

Oakley grinned and pretended to lock her lips. "I've been busy trying to get our new governor to do something about coalbed methane drilling. I don't think I have to tell you which side he's on."

"You haven't been dating anyone?" Tilly asked.

Oakley shook her head. "I haven't had the time. It's why I need to get out of here. I felt like I was making headway with some of the ranchers in the area. Not our mother or CJ." She sighed. "I swear, they are impossible."

Tilly moved to her sister's side. "I'm so glad you're getting well. I've missed you. When you were shot…" Her voice broke.

Oakley took her hand. "I know we haven't talked much." She glanced at Cooper, then back to her sister, and smiled. "But we will talk. So much to ask."

Tilly laughed and leaned down to give Oakley an awkward hug. "You are incorrigible."

"That's what Mother says. Hey, the next time you come in, could you do me a favor? I need my passwords." She gave Tilly a don't-say-it look. "I have a concussion. Of course I don't remember them. I wrote them down in my desk drawer at home on a piece of paper. Please?"

Tilly laughed. "I'll bring them."

"Don't look at them. Just bring them." Oakley smiled. "Thanks, sis."

Cooper and Tilly left, walking out of the hospital together as the sun hung in a cobalt blue sky. July had come to Powder Crossing. Small American flags on lampposts flapped in the breeze. There was a feeling in the air that anything was possible, Tilly thought. She loved summer, but hoped this year wouldn't be so hot. They needed more rain; it was all local ranchers had been talking about. They also needed an old-fashioned winter with lots and lots of snow.

It seemed to her it was always something. Grasshoppers, heat, lack of rain, wind, hail that ruined the crops or a winter that the cold killed the calves born too early. She didn't understand why people ranched, and yet it was all she'd ever known. All she'd ever wanted to do.

She looked over at Cooper, wondering if he felt the same way. He'd left for more than two years. But he'd come back. To stay?

"What?" he asked, as if feeling her probing gaze.

Tilly shook her head, afraid to ask, afraid of his answer. "I talked to Stuart this morning."

He stopped walking to look at her. "How'd that go?"

"Good, I think. I hope. He's sad. I'm not sure it has that much to do with us. I think he's searching for something." She shrugged.

Cooper nodded. "I know that feeling."

She swallowed, wishing he could say more and hoping he didn't. When he looked at her, though, she saw the answer she wanted in his gaze. Maybe he was through searching.

"I've got to pick up a few things for the ranch," he said. "Then do a horseback riding lesson with Holly Jo."

"I've got things to do too," she said.

"Talk later?"

She nodded. As he walked away, she could tell that he had hoped Oakley might be able to tell them what the word *buttercup* meant and why it had been so important after she was shot.

Tilly reminded herself that her sister hadn't just been shot but had a concussion, a bad one. Maybe she had no idea what she was saying when Cooper found her. Feeling as frustrated as she knew Cooper was, she headed back to the ranch.

Before Oakley's shooting, she'd been working with her mother to learn everything about the financial side of running the ranch. Tilly had grown up calving, rounding up cattle, nursing calves, taking care of the horses and other animals.

But she'd never known about the interworkings of the ranch, something she needed to know if she hoped to one day take over this one. She knew it might mean fighting CJ for not just the ranch, but the heart of the ranch, which she didn't feel he understood.

COOPER CAME OUT of the hardware store to find CJ Stafford waiting for him. The cowboy stood, arms crossed, leaning against the building, his face a mask of fury.

"Whatever it is," Cooper said, "I'm really not in the mood for it today."

CJ shoved off the wall and advanced on him, clearly looking for a fight. "You need to stay away from my sister."

"Thanks for the advice." He started to step past him, determined not to get into a brawl on the main drag of Powder Crossing, but CJ had other plans. He slammed a big palm into Cooper's chest, driving him back a step.

"You think I don't know what you're up to?" the cowboy demanded.

"Not doing this." He tried to step past him again, but CJ caught his arm and swung him around to face him.

Cooper brought the full hardware bag around with him and hit the cowboy in the side of his head. CJ staggered back, reaching for the knife at his hip.

"Don't do it, CJ," said a loud male voice behind the cowboy.

CJ's hand rested on the bowie knife for a moment longer, before he dropped his hand to his side. With a sigh, he said, "Your buddy the sheriff isn't always going to be around, McKenna. Stay away from my sister." With that, CJ strode off, leaving Cooper and Stu alone on the street.

"You just have a knack for making friends wherever you go," Stu said.

"It's a talent," he admitted. "Thanks."

"I just didn't want blood on the sidewalk. After all, it is Main Street."

CJ came roaring past in a Stafford Ranch pickup, giving Cooper the finger.

"Classy," Cooper said.

"But expressive." With that, Stu turned and walked away.

Cooper watched them both go, wondering what the hell he was doing. Also wondering if Tilly had any idea what an uphill battle it would be for the two of them to be together.

HOLLY JO HAD been trying to get into the stables all morning. Every time she went near them, Deacon would appear and she'd be forced to pretend she wasn't planning to saddle up a horse and get out of there.

Now that Deacon was locking the tack room, it made it harder. But she'd just seen Elaine go out to the stables. She was dressed for a ride. If she forgot to lock the tack room door…

Time was running out to make her escape. Earlier she'd heard Holden and Elaine talking about getting her enrolled in school. She would be taking the bus and have to walk to the end of the ranch house road to catch it? They had to be kidding. It was at least a half mile.

"It will be good for her to walk down there every morning," Holden said. "All my kids did. Didn't hurt them."

"She's going to need some school clothes." School clothes, ugh. She could just imagine what Holden would buy her, more Western shirts, jeans and boots like he'd purchased for her so far.

She assured herself that she wouldn't be here when school started in August. This couldn't be her life. The rest of her life, she thought with a groan. She still didn't know how she'd ended up here. At supper Holden had said they would talk about it some other time. But every time she tried to talk to him about it, he'd say, "Some other time."

At the sound of a pickup coming up the drive, she looked out and saw that it was Cooper. She growled under her breath. He'd promised to teach her to ride today. She still hadn't ridden any farther than around and around the corral.

He pulled up beside her and whirred down his window. "Meet me in the stables. You're going riding."

"Outside of the corral?" she asked hopefully.

"Outside of the corral." His window went back up and she ran toward the house to get anything of her past that she could stuff into her pockets. She was getting out of here.

HOLDEN LOVED HOLLY JO's enthusiasm as she focused on saddling her horse. He could feel her excitement and it gave him hope that this might work out, having her here. Raising her, he reminded himself. She was now his responsibility.

He'd picked a good horse for her, an older mare named Honey who had a good disposition. Deacon and Cooper had agreed it was a good choice. Not too large, though she still had to use a stool to get her foot into the stirrup, despite being tall for her age.

"You'll have to use a stump or a log," Holden told her. "But that's only if you dismount or get thrown."

"Thrown?"

"Horses do buck, you know."

She looked at him as if he was teasing and went back to her work. She had so much to learn about ranch life, but there was plenty of time, he told himself. She hadn't been happy to hear that he was going along on the ride with her. He hadn't taken it personally. He couldn't keep putting it off, telling her how it was that she came to be here on the ranch. It was something he wasn't looking forward to telling her or the rest of his family. But it would have to be done, and soon.

"You got her signed up for school?" Cooper said to him as they both watched to make sure Holly Jo was saddling her horse properly.

"Ran into the principal. It's all set," Holden said. "Elaine has promised to help with school clothes. Not sure about taking her to Billings, though. Not sure she can be trusted not to take off."

"Big ears," Cooper said, pointing in Holly Jo's direction.

"I do not have big ears."

"It's an expression." She looked skeptical. Cooper sighed. "It means you're always listening to adult conversations when you should be minding your own business." She couldn't argue that, apparently, because she went back to saddling her horse.

"She seems to be doing better, don't you think?" Holden asked his son.

He made a sound that could have been agreement, but probably wasn't.

"I'm ready," Holly Jo announced, all smiles. She started to lead her horse toward the stable door.

"Settle down," Cooper said. "Dad's going with you." Deacon had saddled a horse for him when he came out after Holly Jo and surprised her, saying he was going with her. "Where are you taking her?"

"Not far," he said. "Don't look so worried. I can handle this."

Cooper nodded but didn't appear convinced. Holden had to admit that he didn't ride enough anymore. He hoped to change that now that Holly Jo was here and so enthusiastic about learning to ride.

The girl stopped by the stool just inside the door and mounted the mare. Cooper grabbed the reins and gave her a warning look. "There's something you should know about my father. He's a lot tougher than he looks. You mess up today, and he'll tan your hide and I won't let you ride again until he says you can."

"Tan my hide?" She laughed.

"I used to tan Cooper's hide. He knows of what he speaks," Holden said as he joined them.

Holly Jo didn't look convinced. "Are we going riding or not?" she asked impatiently.

Holden swung up in the saddle, telling himself he wasn't too old to raise another child, even this one. "We're going to take it slow and easy, got that?"

He waited. "Got that?"

"Got it."

He appreciated the fact that she wasn't afraid. Just the opposite. But she didn't realize the dangers, and no matter how many times she had to be warned, she wouldn't until something happened to her. That was what worried him as they rode slowly out of the yard, headed for the hills in the distance.

"How's it feel?" he asked as they wound their way through a grove of cottonwoods.

"Too slow."

"Ever heard the expression 'You have to learn to walk before you run'?" He looked around, loving the familiar gait of the horse, the smell of the grass and saddle leather, the sun on his back. "Enjoy the view from up here."

Holly Jo said nothing. When he glanced at her, he saw her looking toward the river and the county road beyond the trees. The next thing he knew, she'd dug her heels into her horse, giving it free rein. The mare took off toward the river with her holding on for dear life.

"Pull in the reins," he called after her. But she wasn't paying any attention. He could see the barbed-wire fence between her and the river. Holly Jo and her horse were headed right for it.

He swore and raced after her.

AS HIS FATHER and Holly Jo had ridden off, Cooper started back to the house. He felt as if he'd been beating his head against a brick wall since he'd been home. What had started as simply trying to find out why Oakley had wanted him to know the name Buttercup had turned into so much more. It had taken him to Tilly, and one thing had led to another, as if it had been inevitable.

Only that path had so many pitfalls in it that he'd been dragging his feet. He feared that if he and Tilly went any further, it would only lead to heartbreak. As much as he wanted her—more than his next breath—he wasn't sure it was possible.

Pushing that painful thought away, he tried to focus on what they'd uncovered. So much. Yet none of it seemed to fit together. They still didn't know who'd shot Oakley or what Buttercup meant or why it had been so important that she tell him the day she was shot.

Finding the pilot of the plane that had flown over that day led them to Howie Gunderson and Tick Whitaker and the CH4 gas company. CH4 kept coming up. First with his brother's name indented on the note that Howie had given him. The same notepaper Leann had used to write her goodbye notes to him, then later on, the notepad Stu had in his desk. It was on the latter one that he'd seen the name *Leann* indented on the paper.

Everything they'd found kept leading them back to CH4 and coalbed methane drilling, including the Dirty Business group Oakley had been involved in—until they'd found the meth lab on the other side of the ravine Oakley had come riding out of the day she was shot.

While Cooper didn't trust any of them, he and Tilly hadn't found a link to Oakley's shooting. He felt at loose ends. His father and Holly Jo weren't back from their ride, but Deacon said he'd go look for them if necessary.

Unable to sit still, he drove into town thinking he

might go to the bar, have some nachos and beer, and try to make sense out of everything that had happened since he'd returned home.

But a block away from the bar, he saw a uniformed figure come stumbling out, then weave his way across the street. Cooper sighed, all his instincts telling him to leave the sheriff be as he drove on by pretending not to see him. But as drunk as Stu was, he realized he couldn't let him drive home and he was headed for his patrol SUV.

He swore and made a U-turn in the middle of the street, tires screaming, to go back. He pulled in behind the sheriff's rig and got out.

"I should arrest you for that," Stu said, having apparently stopped to watch him make the turn.

"A U-turn to come back and keep you from driving drunk?" He held out his wrists. "You got your cuffs on you?"

Stu staggered back, bumping into his patrol SUV, then pinging off it to stumble into the pines and sit down hard on the ground.

"You called the Feds," he accused drunkenly.

"You didn't act like you were going to do anything."

"I told you. I didn't get the messages."

Did he believe that? Not really. "Had it been from anyone but me, you would have been out there at first light."

The sheriff merely looked up at him from under hooded eyes. "I wasn't in town. I'd just gotten back, barely making it into the office on time."

Cooper ground his teeth and said nothing.

"Why don't you sit down? You're giving me a pain in my neck," Stu said.

He hesitated, then sat down on the ground, both of them facing the street and the bar across from it.

"We found one of the four-wheelers smashed in the rocks," Stuart said. "There was blood, but no body. We're running DNA on the blood. If we get a match... Thought you'd want to know that I'm actually doing my thankless job. The Feds are taking it from here. I'm sure they'll be a lot more thorough than me."

Cooper chewed on that for a few moments. "You thought any more about asking the prosecutor to re-open the case?"

"Have *you*? You have the most to lose. All those notes she'd started and discarded. Almost as if afraid to tell you her plans."

"Did she tell you her plans when she left you?" he asked.

Stu shook his head, a faraway look in his eyes. "Nope, just left."

No note, Cooper thought. That had to hurt. So Stu also had no idea that Leann came to him just wanting a place to stay for a little while. He and Stuart had never had a chance to talk about it because it wasn't long after that Leann had allegedly killed herself and Cooper had been arrested for murder. Now he saw that Stuart could have jumped the gun on arresting him because he was too emotionally involved.

"I never asked you what happened between you and Leann."

"Kind of late to ask that now, don't you think?" Stu said.

"No, I think it's finally really relevant."

"Why don't you run across the street and get us a couple of beers?" the sheriff said, and pulled a face. "I'll be here when you get back. Since I'm not driving, another beer won't hurt me."

Cooper rose and held out his hand. It took Stu a moment before he dug into his pocket, pulled out his keys and dropped them into Cooper's palm. "I'll be right back."

Stu was pretty much where he'd left him, on the ground, but he'd moved to lean his back against an old tree stump. Cooper handed him a beer and sat down next to him before opening his own.

Clearly Stu had been thinking about the question Cooper had asked him, because he began to speak without opening his beer. "I came home one night and what little Leann had at my house was gone. I'd asked her to move in with me, but she'd refused. That should have been a clue, huh." He twisted the top off his beer and took a drink. "I called her when I saw her things were gone, and she told me she'd moved on and that she'd been thinking about it for some time." He raised his gaze to look at Cooper. "That's where you come into the story."

"I hope you realize I didn't know any of this. She and I had crossed paths a few times. Each time she'd been with someone else at the bar. When she showed up at my door, I asked her about you and she shrugged it off, saying you two were just friends. I didn't go after her. She needed a place to crash for a few days while she made up her mind about something. I offered her my couch."

"But she ended up in your bed."

"The couch hurt her back."

Stu laughed. "Big surprise."

"She knew I wasn't interested in her. Looking back, I realize now that I was in love with someone else."

"Tilly." The sheriff said it like a cussword. "How convenient."

"Not convenient at all. Come on, Stu. There are so many reasons why Tilly and I..." He shook his head. "I always liked her. I'd never really spent any time alone with her. At the competitions she was so singularly focused. But I liked that about her. She wanted to win. I wanted to win too, so I understood. We were from families that didn't get along." He laughed. "That's putting it mildly. Too much history there, I guess."

"I want Tilly," Stu said, sounding drunker even though he'd set his fresh beer in the grass beside him.

"That's up to her."

He shook his head. "She's already made her choice."

"This isn't a competition. I didn't want this any more than I wanted Leann."

"Is that why you killed her? Because maybe the man in her life was me and you couldn't stand her coming back to me?"

"Were you the man in her life?"

Stu looked at the ground, not answering.

"I know you don't believe I killed her. Come on,

Stu. We've been friends for too long. You've known me my whole life. Do you really think I'm a killer?"

"I don't know," he said dismissively. "Maybe I've never really known you." He picked up his beer and took a drink.

"I guess there are some things we're never going to agree on," Cooper said. "But it makes me sad that we're at odds over it."

"Do you really think you'd be happy with Tilly?" the sheriff asked. "With staying in Powder Crossing? You always said you weren't a rancher. What are you, Cooper?"

The question hurt because, in this case, Stu was right. He hadn't been sure who he was or what he wanted, and he should have been. "I think I've been looking for something."

Stu let out a bitter laugh. "And now you've found it, and it just happens to be my girlfriend."

"Tilly isn't your girlfriend. She's a woman you dated a handful of times."

"Yeah, but what if you hadn't come back to town? What if we dated a few more times? What if she fell in love with me?" They fell silent for a few minutes. Stu stared at the beer bottle in his hand. "Tilly's too good for you."

"I know."

"Would be nice to go back in time, though, wouldn't it," Stu said. "Knowing what you do now. Change things. Then again, maybe not."

Cooper considered that. "If I could go back and rewrite history, I'd make sure the Staffords and the Mc-Kennas never started feuding."

"Who's dreaming now?" Stu said. "Might want to rethink that. The way I heard it, your father and Charlotte were quite the hot item. If they'd stayed together, you wouldn't be here."

"I guess that's the point, huh. We can't rewrite history. You are my friend. You were Tilly's friend. If we're all going to live in this town…"

"Can't see how that can happen. Can you?"

"You planning on leaving?" Cooper asked, realizing that his friend hadn't answered earlier about whether or not he was the man in Leann's life that she was leaving with.

"No, as a matter of fact, I'm not." His gaze locked with Cooper's. "But I think one of us needs to." He finished his beer, handed Cooper his empty bottle and pushed himself off the ground to stand swaying on unsteady feet. "You taking me home or what?"

THE MARE SPOTTED the fence and reacted by rearing up just feet from it. Holly Jo went off the back, coming down hard in the dirt. The horse ran a few feet away from the fence and stopped.

Holden raced up to the girl, leaped off his horse and went to her. "Is anything hurt other than your pride?"

She looked as if the fall had knocked the air out of her. All she managed to do was shake her head as he helped her up.

"You're sure nothing's broken?" he asked.

"I'm fine," she finally said as air returned to her lungs.

Pulling away from him, she walked over to where her horse stood. Grabbing the reins, she began to beat the horse with them, yelling, "You stupid, stupid horse!"

Holden came up behind her, grabbed the reins and snatched them out of her hand. "If I ever see you hurt another animal on this ranch…" He looked into her face, anger and pain twisting it, and dropped the reins to pull off his belt.

Her eyes widened in alarm. "You wouldn't dare," she said.

"Like hell. I think you need to know what that horse felt." He struck her across her denim-covered legs, once, twice, three times, the same amount she'd hit the horse— just hard enough that she felt it. He saw tears shine in her eyes, but she held them back by sheer stubbornness, he was sure. He put his belt back on.

"You can't make me stay here," she cried. "I don't care what you promised my mother." He walked over and picked up her horse's reins. "I'll run away!" she yelled at him.

"And I'll come find you and bring you back," he said over his shoulder as he walked her horse over to his. "And, believe me, you'll regret it."

Turning back to her, he watched her kick a boot toe at the dirt, tears coming now as frustration won out. "She hated you! She hated your guts!" she yelled. "She said you killed my dad!"

"I did," Holden said. "It was an accident. I lost my temper. I did something stupid. I hated myself for it. I promised your mother I would make up for it and I have tried, and I will keep trying. Now get on your horse and apologize to her. Honey is a nice, gentle mare who deserves better. I gave her to you because I knew she would be good to you."

"She threw me off!"

"She threw you off because you tried to make her run through a barbed-wire fence. She was smarter than you. She saved you both. You owe her." He waited as the girl walked over to the horse, laid her hand on its neck and mumbled something he couldn't hear. "Give me your foot." He hoisted her up into the saddle. She reached for the reins, but he shook his head. "Your mother wanted you here. She trusted me to take care of you. That's the way it is. How good or bad it is going to be is up to you."

He mounted his own horse and led hers back toward the stables. He glanced back only once to make sure she was still there. He could tell that she'd been crying. His heart went out to her. He thought of his own father and the way he'd been raised. Turned out, he was a lot like the old man, good or bad.

Deacon came riding out when they were almost back to the stables. He looked worried, even more so when he saw Holly Jo's horse being led and the girl's tearstained face. "Everything all right?"

"It will be," Holden said as he dismounted and helped Holly Jo down. "Now put your horse away," he said to her. "Brush her, feed her and make sure she has fresh water, and maybe she'll forgive you."

"Are you ever going to let me ride her again?" she asked, her voice breaking.

"You live on a ranch. Of course you'll ride your

horse again once she trusts you again," he said, and went to take care of his own tack and horse. "That's if you want to."

"I want to."

He smiled to himself, hearing something in her voice that gave him hope. He was probably wrong; he often was. But he wanted this to work out. He wasn't one to break a promise. As he'd told Holly Jo, he owed her mother, he owed her daughter. He'd do whatever he had to to keep that promise.

But he worried. If she wanted to run away, would he be able to stop her? She had no idea what the world was like out there. A girl of twelve on her own? He shuddered to think of it. Which meant he had to convince her to stay. Problem was, he didn't know how to do that.

Probably taking his belt to her hadn't helped, but if she was going to stay, she wasn't going to be abusing the animals. Of that, there was no question. He'd seen too many cowboys beat their dogs, their horses, often their wives. It made him sick to his stomach to see animals mistreated like that. It had gotten him into more fights than he should have taken on—including the one that had gotten Holly Jo's father killed.

CHARLOTTE REINED IN her horse as she saw the rider waiting for her. When she'd heard about the meth lab on the old homestead, she'd felt gutted. She had no doubt that it was what Oakley had been doing on the McKenna Ranch when she'd been shot. That old homestead had been part of the Smith Ranch. Her best friend growing up had been Margie—right up until Holden had married Margaret Louise Smith and all that land was added to the McKenna Ranch.

She'd never forgiven Holden. Or Margie. It wasn't in her nature to forgive. At least that was what her mother had told her, and apparently it had been true. Even when she'd heard that Margie was sick, she hadn't been able to bridge what she'd seen as an unforgivable betrayal. She'd been stuck on the other side even as Margie died, making it impossible to grieve alone. Regret was a hard pill to swallow. She'd had to learn to live with it, shifting all her anger and regret onto Holden.

Now it was as if the past refused to die, taunting her with soured memories and tormenting her with the precious ones she still couldn't let go of as much as they hurt.

Elaine looked up as Charlotte rode into the trees to join her. They'd been meeting like this for years— since Margie had fallen ill. Elaine had taken pity on her one day when they'd run into each other in town at the store.

Charlotte had asked about Margie as if the words came flying from her heart against her iron will. Elaine had told her and begged her to forgive and contact Margie herself. "It's your chance to put the past behind you. Do it for yourself," Elaine had pleaded. "Do it for Margie."

But Charlotte hadn't been able to. Instead, she'd called Elaine, who gave her updates. When Margie died, Elaine had called and asked to meet.

That day, Elaine became her friend, the only true one she counted. Charlotte had cried over Margie's death, the death of their friendship, the death of any hope of changing the lonely, desperate life she'd made for herself. Elaine had shared her own grief in losing Margie, who'd been a friend to her.

"Thank you for meeting me," she said now to Elaine.

"You heard about the meth lab?"

She nodded, met her friend's gaze and swallowed. "That has to be why Oakley was shot coming from that ravine."

"It does seem so," Elaine said. "You do know that Cooper and Tilly went back in there looking for evidence. They're the ones who found the meth lab and called the sheriff."

Charlotte hated that she knew little of what her offspring had been up to, unfortunately. She'd heard the rumors about Tilly and Cooper and let her daughter know how she'd felt about it—for all the good it had done. "Have you heard if the sheriff found anything?"

"Unfortunately, the lab burned, I believe, before the sheriff could get out there." Elaine took her hand. "Cooper said those men at the meth lab fired on him and Tilly."

"Oh, my heaven," she said, feeling sick. "They could have been killed."

"The men were using military-type semiautomatic weapons, AR15s, Cooper told his father. But, Charlotte, Oakley was shot with a bullet from a 270 rifle."

"How do you know that?"

"I overheard Cooper telling Holden. He thinks someone else shot her," Elaine said. "That's why deputies collected all the rifles from the family and the ranch hands. I heard they took yours as well."

She nodded, remembering how furious CJ had been. He wanted to get their lawyer to demand they be returned. She'd refused, only making him storm out. "It's ridiculous. No one from our ranch would have shot my daughter." Elaine said nothing. "Can this get any worse?"

"I think we both know it can," her friend said. "If the sheriff is getting close to making an arrest, we need to be prepared."

Charlotte huffed. "How do we do that? I always thought the worst thing that could happen was when I heard that Holden was marrying Margie."

Her friend touched her arm. "Margie's been dead now for more than twenty years. Twenty years, Charlotte."

She didn't need to be reminded. It wasn't like she didn't know what Elaine was saying. But there were some things in life a person never got over. "Thank you for the news," she said, and picked up her horse's reins to leave. "You'll let me know if you hear anything."

"It's not too late."

She chuckled since this was something she'd been hearing from Elaine for years. "It is way too late, and now with all this… There are some things even I can't get over, let alone undo." Her life was a web that she'd woven herself into and was now trapped. She met Elaine's gaze. "I'm just sorry that I dragged you into—"

"You didn't drag me in. I wanted to be here for you. It's what Margie had wanted as well."

Strange, Charlotte thought, how it was Margie and their mutual loss of the woman they had both loved that had brought them together. She swung up onto her horse and rode back toward her ranch with a sense of foreboding. It was as if she could feel the past breathing Hell's fire down her neck. All her mistakes were coming for her—and the target painted on her back.

CHAPTER TWENTY-TWO

STUART HAD TO ask again. Not just because of the raging hangover that had his head throbbing and his stomach roiling this morning. But because he couldn't believe, maybe didn't want to believe, what the lab tech was telling him.

"We ran all of the 270s we took from the two ranches. It is definitely this rifle." He held it up in the evidence bag with the label on it from where the rifle had been taken. "Once we realized the slug taken from Oakley Stafford matched the slug from this rifle, we checked it for prints. It's definitely CJ Stafford's rifle, and his prints on the trigger show him as the last user."

The sheriff rubbed a hand over his face. "Why would he shoot his own sister?" Stuart demanded.

"Guess you'll have to ask him when you see him."

COOPER WOKE THE next morning determined to talk to Jason Murdock. If the PI had tried to run him and Tilly off the road the other night after the meeting, he wanted to know who paid him to do it.

He'd driven through town and hadn't seen Murdock's truck. He hadn't seen it, he realized, since that night. Maybe he'd gone back to Billings. He was driving past the hotel when Tick Whitaker came out and waved him over. Cooper put down his driver's-side window.

"Haven't seen that girl of yours for a while," Tick said.

Tilly would love being called a *girl*. "The young woman in question isn't my *girl*, and I wouldn't call her that to her face."

The geologist laughed heartily. "She is a firebrand, isn't she? I was just thinking of her when I saw you driving past. There was a man in the bar the other night asking about her and her family, especially her mother."

"What man?" Cooper asked.

"Said his name was Jason Murdock. After he left, I asked who he was and was told he was a private investigator. I guess he'd been asking questions around town about a man named Dixon Malone. Used to be married to Charlotte Stafford. Apparently, Dixon disappeared some years ago and hasn't been seen since."

Seemed odd anyone would be looking for him now. "Did he say who'd hired him?"

Tick shook his head. "I noticed that a lot of people clammed up in the bar. I heard Tilly's name mentioned. Got the impression everyone liked her. Just thought she should know."

"Thanks," Cooper said. Tick didn't seem like such a jerk when he wasn't drinking. "I'll let her know." He wondered if Rusty knew anything about this. Rusty and Dixon Malone were shirttail relatives. He'd never understood exactly how they were related, but maybe he'd better find out. He couldn't imagine Rusty hir-

ing a PI after all these years to investigate what might
have happened to Dixon, though.

STUART KNEW THAT he couldn't send a deputy out to the
Stafford Ranch to pick up CJ. He was going to have to
do this himself. He hoped CJ wouldn't put up a fight
and would simply come along peacefully. Maybe he
should have brought a couple of deputies with him, he
thought as he left town.

What he couldn't understand was why CJ would
have shot his sister. Once he had, why hadn't he come
forward? He had to know that he would be found out.

Then again, Stuart had found most suspects didn't
turn themselves in. They waited, hoping they'd get
away with it, right up until they were caught.

As he drove out to the Stafford Ranch, he was still
having trouble believing CJ had shot Oakley. He kept
telling himself there had to be a mistake. He'd been so
sure it had been someone from the McKenna Ranch
who'd taken a potshot at her. Someone like that hothead Rusty Malone.

But the evidence didn't lie. Oakley had been shot by
a 270 rifle belonging to her brother. CJ's fingerprints
were still on it. Now all Stuart needed was a confes-
sion, and he could wrap up at least this case.

He still had the meth lab to deal with. The Feds were
out there combing through the ashes. With luck, they
would come up with something that led them to the
culprits. They wouldn't even need the sheriff's help.

After the past week, he was ready to take off his
badge and hang up his gun. Problem was, what would

he do? Leave Powder Crossing? He chuckled. Cooper had been right. He was never leaving here. His boots were covered with too much of the red dirt from these hills. He couldn't leave, even if he wanted to.

Just as he couldn't quit the one job he'd thought he'd been pretty good at and maybe could be again.

Pulling through the gate, he drove up to the sprawling house and got out. All on one level, the house had been added on again and again from the original small one that John and Ruth Carson had lived in with their only child, Charlotte. But after they passed and Charlotte married Rake Stafford, a man seventeen years her senior, the family had grown and so had the house. She'd gotten pregnant with five children in less than eight years. Rake had been her age now, fifty-two, when he'd died from a fall from his horse, hitting his head on a rock.

After Rake died, Charlotte had added more rooms as her children required more space, with rooms going off in different directions until the original house was part of a sprawling complex of glass and wood and rock.

Stuart had always wanted to see inside the house, but had never been invited in. While he and Tilly were dating, he'd hinted a few times, but it was clear he wasn't going to get an invitation. He didn't take it personally since, from what he'd heard, Charlotte Stafford practically lived as a recluse.

He walked up to the door again thinking he should have brought at least one deputy with him. He knocked and waited, then knocked again.

Ryder Stafford opened the door, brushing back a

lock of long blond hair out of his green eyes. "Yes?" Behind him, Stuart got a glimpse of the living room with its rock fireplace, worn wood floors covered with equally worn Native American rugs and worn leather furniture. A bear rug hung on one wall next to a large whitetail deer head. "Yes?"

"I need to see CJ. Is he around?"

"He and Tilly left about five, ten minutes ago."

CJ and Tilly? That struck him as odd since the two were always at odds with each other. "Do you know where they were headed? Because I didn't pass them on the county road into town."

Ryder shook his head, but then seemed to remember. "I thought I overheard Tilly say she had to get to the hospital to bring Oakley something."

"Is there anyone else home who might know? It's important." Stuart couldn't shake the sliver of dread that had embedded itself just under his skin.

Ryder turned back to the empty room for a minute. "Sorry. My mother's gone for a ride. Brand's been gone with the ranch hands checking cattle since early this morning. I could ask our cook, though I really doubt they told her where they were going."

"It's okay. If you see either of them, would you give me a call?"

"Sure," Ryder said, and closed the door.

As Stuart walked back to his patrol SUV, he called Tilly. Her phone went straight to voice mail. He left a message. "I know who shot Oakley. Get hold of me right away and don't say anything to CJ."

"WHO'S THAT? COOPER?" CJ snapped as Tilly quickly put her phone away.

Don't say anything to CJ? Stuart knew who had shot Oakley. Her heart was pounding. All her instincts were on alert—just as they'd been when CJ had insisted he drive her into town to the hospital in one of the ranch trucks.

She'd argued that it wasn't necessary, that she was more than able to drive herself into town. She didn't mention that she was taking Oakley her list of passwords. She hadn't looked at them as she'd kind of promised. Frankly, she didn't care. But she knew her sister was waiting for them.

That was why she couldn't understand why CJ had insisted on taking a back road. She'd been thinking, *Does he have to drive so fast?* when she'd gotten the message from the sheriff.

"CJ, where are you taking me?" she asked as she looked up and realized he'd turned off on yet another road. They were now headed not for Powder Crossing but for Miles City. "I told you, I need to get to the hospital." He was starting to scare her—especially after Stuart's cryptic message.

"We're going to Billings."

"What?" Tilly had her sister's password cheat sheet in her pocket. She took it out. "CJ, Oakley's waiting for this. I promised her—"

"Forget about Oakley!" he yelled. "This is all her fault!"

She stared at him, seeing how tightly he was holding the wheel. The set of his jaw was worse. "What is all her fault?" she asked quietly, her heart in her throat.

All his anger seemed to burn out as quickly as it had flared up. He scrubbed his arm over his face and looked away from her. "She just wouldn't listen."

Her pulse drummed in her ears, and she felt dizzy as she watched her brother driving too fast on the narrow dirt road. "CJ, pull over." He shook his head. She glanced down at the paper in her hand and realized that Oakley had written her password list on CH4 notepaper. How many of these notepads were floating around?

One of the passwords jumped out at her. *Buttercup?* It was one of Oakley's passwords? For what?

CJ sped up, taking a curve in the narrow dirt road too fast and throwing her against her door.

"I can't go to Billings. I have to see Oakley."

"I told you to forget about her. She's fine." He glanced over at her, tears swimming in his green eyes. "I have to get out of town, out of the state, maybe out of the country."

Tilly swallowed, suddenly even more afraid at the emotion she heard in her brother's voice. Her pulse thundered in her ears at the expression on his face. When she spoke, her voice came out in a whisper. "What did you do?"

He wagged his head, looking miserable. "I warned her and warned her. She just wouldn't listen. Someone had to stop her."

Realization struck like a slap, stinging and sharp, bringing tears to her own eyes. "Oh, tell me you didn't."

He looked at her, swallowed, and the words poured out of him. "I saw her go into that ravine. I waited for her. When she came out...I thought she was headed for their house. I meant to fire just a warning shot..." He broke down, no longer capable of talking through his sobs.

"It was an accident," she said quickly, noticing that he seemed to be driving even faster and more recklessly. "Oakley's fine. She's going to be fine. Once you tell the sheriff what happened—"

"No." It came out a growl. He wiped his sleeve over his face again and regained control of his emotions, but he was driving more dangerously. The pickup lifted off the road as he hit a bump and came down hard, making him fight to keep the vehicle on the road. "I can't go to the sheriff." He shot her a look. "Mother can never know."

"She will know, CJ. It's going to come out. You can't run from this."

He didn't answer, his knuckles white on the wheel as he gave the pickup even more gas.

Tilly looked at the road ahead. He was driving recklessly, not in his right mind. She had to stop him before he killed them both.

STUART JUMPED BACK into his patrol SUV. If CJ and Tilly left only five or ten minutes ago, he should have passed them on the main county road—unless CJ turned off on one of the cut-across roads that would take him to Miles City and the interstate and several major airports.

In which case, he wasn't headed into town to the hospital. He was making a run for it.

He alerted his deputies as he roared out of the ranch road onto the county one. He hadn't gone far when he saw Cooper's pickup coming down the road toward him. He made the decision in an instant. Whirring down his window, he waved him down.

"CJ was the shooter. It was his rifle. He has Tilly in one of the ranch pickups. I think he's headed for the interstate—I just don't know which crossroad he took. He's only about ten minutes ahead of us."

Cooper didn't hesitate. "I'll take Little Bear Skull Creek Road."

"Okay, I'll take Castle Rock, but, Coop, don't try to take him by yourself. Call me. You should be able to get cell phone coverage out there."

Stuart took off to the next road that would cross over to Highway 59 and take CJ to Miles City and the interstate. They had to stop him before he reached there. He called his deputies, told them to head to Highway 59 and set up a roadblock for a Stafford Ranch pickup headed north.

Behind him, he saw Cooper turn around in the middle of the county road. He lost sight of him, dust boiling up behind his SUV. As he passed Little Bear Skull Creek Road, he saw Cooper turn. He questioned getting his friend involved. Cooper wasn't the law. But CJ had Tilly. If he ran across them, he might be able to talk some sense into CJ. Or at least get Tilly away from her brother.

That was what had him worried. Why had CJ taken

Tilly with him? Why not just jump into a ranch truck and make a run for it alone?

Because he was planning to use her as a hostage to help him get away?

Stuart swore as he made the turn onto Castle Rock Road. He couldn't bear to think of how badly this could end.

CJ HAD TILLY. Cooper raced down the narrow windy dirt road without any thought to his own safety. All he could think about was getting Tilly away from her brother.

CJ had shot Oakley. It made no sense. Why would he do that? He was a loose cannon, no doubt about that, and he had one hell of a chip on his shoulder. But shoot your own sister?

He watched the road ahead, telling himself that if he was CJ, this was the road he would have taken—the first one to the west. The county road got little traffic. This one even less. Cooper wasn't worried about running into anyone as he took the curves at breakneck speed. He figured CJ would be doing the same thing.

Hadn't the cowboy realized that once the lab ran a test on his rifle he would be caught? Had he been trying to buy time? Or had he just been afraid and didn't know what to do?

That sounded more like it. Now he was on the run—with Tilly. He certainly hadn't thought this out—or maybe he had by taking a hostage with him.

Tilly. He felt such a rush of fear. If he lost her now… He pushed the thought away, but the fear stayed. He should have kissed her more, he should have told her what he was feeling, he should have made love to her so she knew how much she was loved.

But CJ was the perfect example of why he'd been afraid that if he and Tilly went any further, they would only get their hearts broken when they were forced apart. Holden wanted peace between the families. But he also had to know what an uphill battle it would be. It might make things worse. Tilly's family might disown her. If CJ had shot his own sister because she was on McKenna land…

Cooper fought to control his temper, half-afraid of what he would do if he caught up with them. *When* he caught up with them, he told himself. He'd want to strangle CJ with his bare hands. He'd have to because Stuart hadn't given him back his guns yet. That wasn't a welcome thought.

As he came over a rise, he saw something ahead that sent his heart thundering. Dust. There was another vehicle on the road about a quarter mile ahead. He pushed down on the gas, flying around the curves and dips in the road.

Cooper just needed to see if it was them. It had to be, he told himself. He came over a rise and spotted the pickup ahead, getting a good look at it as CJ made a turn to the right. Cooper could see the Stafford Ranch logo on the side. He started to make the call to the sheriff.

His desire to get his hands on CJ without any interference from Stuart made him hesitate, although he had no idea what he was going to do when he caught up to them.

With a curse, he made the call. "He's in front of me," he told Stuart. "We're almost to a connecting road to the north. You should be able to catch us there if you come south."

"Got it. Follow, but don't confront. You hear me, Coop?"

"Loud and clear." But he made no promises.

STUART HOPED HE hadn't made a mistake enlisting Cooper's help. When he reached the dirt road south, he turned, hoping to see CJ and Tilly headed for him. He'd radioed his deputies. They were on their way. He figured CJ would be armed. The eldest Stafford male was always a little dangerous. Now, with CJ on the run, it was going to take a very careful, calm approach, which was one reason he didn't want Cooper confronting CJ.

He hoped Cooper hadn't gone rogue and tried to stop CJ. There was no telling what the cowboy might do if confronted. Stuart feared CJ had taken Tilly for that very reason. Would he really use his sister as a shield? As a hostage?

The sheriff reminded himself that CJ had shot his younger sister. Whether it had been an accident or not, he'd almost killed her.

He tried to relax, but he still hadn't seen the Stafford Ranch pickup and he was almost to the turnoff that would connect with the road both CJ and Cooper were traversing. His anxiety was growing by the minute. What had happened? He hated to think. *Damn it,*

Cooper, he thought. *We already have one out-of-control cowboy. We don't need another one.*

As he came to the turnoff, he didn't see either Cooper or CJ. What if CJ had turned and headed south instead of north? He slowed, debating what to do. Cooper said he had spotted them. He knew this area better than anyone. If CJ had gone south, Coop would have called.

Unless, he thought with a groan, he'd let his feelings for Tilly overrule his common sense.

TILLY CAUGHT A flash of light in her side mirror. The sun reflected off a vehicle's windshield on the road behind them. Cooper?

She couldn't believe her eyes. But then the pickup dropped down over a rise and disappeared. The pickup was the same color as Cooper's, but how could he…?

"CJ, please," Tilly said. "Stop and let's talk about this."

"It's too late." He shook his head.

"Well, at least slow down. We can figure this out." She checked her mirror. No sign of the pickup. Had she merely imagined it? Wished it and Cooper into being right now when she needed him the most? "You just have to tell the truth. You weren't trying to hurt Oakley. It was an accident."

He seemed to drive even faster. "When Mother finds out…"

"You think she hasn't made mistakes in her life?" Tilly demanded. "She'll understand. Everyone will understand. It was an accident. It wasn't your fault."

He looked over at her as if he couldn't believe what

she was saying. The front tire on his side of the pickup dropped into the shallow barrow pit and pulled hard to the left. The tires dug into the loose dirt at the edge of the road, and the pickup began to fishtail. CJ fought to regain control of the truck but he was going too fast.

Tilly hung on, too scared to even scream as the pickup began to roll.

CHAPTER TWENTY-THREE

COOPER FELT HIS heart drop to his feet as he came around a curve in the road and saw the Stafford Ranch pickup. He stared in horror as he slammed on his brakes and jumped out of his vehicle to run toward the truck now resting in the middle of a field beside the road. Windows broken, the cab top crushed, the truck looked as if it had rolled numerous times before it had finally come to rest sitting on its tires.

He fell to his knees beside the passenger side of the cab and bent to look inside, terrified of what he would find.

Blood. It seemed to be everywhere.

Tilly's blond hair was streaked with it, her body still. With trembling fingers, he reached in to carefully ease her hair away from her face. She was breathing. His fingers rested on her temple. He felt a pulse. He could hear a vehicle coming. The sheriff? He pulled out his phone and called 911.

"There's been an accident," he told the 911 operator. "We need an ambulance. At least one injured." He gave her the location as the patrol SUV came into view. He pressed his hand to Tilly's cheek, promising that he would never let her go if she would just live.

He stayed with her as the sheriff arrived, then his deputies, followed by an ambulance. He finally had to step away as the EMTs and Jaws of Life went to work to get her out of the truck.

As he stood there, he saw that CJ was conscious and screaming for help inside the wreckage. Cooper hadn't checked on him, wanting to stay with Tilly. But he knew that wasn't the only reason. He'd been half-afraid of what he would do to him.

"They're getting Tilly out," Stuart said beside him. "I figured you'd want to follow the ambulance to the hospital."

He nodded, feeling hollowed out at the sight of her on the stretcher. His throat had gone dry, and he doubted he could speak even if there were words. He'd never been in this kind of pain, nor felt so helpless.

"I'll need to write up a report at some point," the sheriff said. "Did you see them roll?" He shook his head. "You hadn't caught up to them?"

He glanced at him, knowing exactly what he was asking. Did Stu really think he would have jeopardized Tilly's life by chasing CJ? He swallowed. "I hadn't caught up to them yet. I doubt they even knew I was behind them. That answer your question?"

"I had to ask."

Cooper met his gaze. The truth was that he hadn't known what he would have done if he had caught up to CJ's pickup.

CHARLOTTE COULDN'T BELIEVE both of her daughters were now in the hospital, her older girl now possibly fighting for her life. Just as crushing, CJ had been driving the truck and had apparently also been injured. She could lose both of them and she had no idea what had happened, just that it had her running scared.

Her world seemed to be coming apart at the seams, unraveling a piece at a time as if the fabric of her life had become rotten. The thought made her realize how true it might be, and she knew she was to blame.

She didn't believe in karma, but maybe she was getting what she deserved for the role she'd played in all of their lives. If so, it was only the beginning. Karma wasn't through with her yet. Not even close.

She walked into the emergency room and saw her daughter lying on a gurney. Not her beautiful Tilly. There was no sign of CJ. Surely he hadn't— Her knees went weak. A nurse rushed to her to tell her that CJ had been taken up to surgery.

Tears flooded her eyes. She grabbed the wall for support, awash in her sins that had wrought this. A doctor and nurse were working on Tilly. All she heard was *surgery* before the two began to roll her away. She rushed forward to touch her daughter's arm before she was gone, the nurse saying something about waiting for word.

As she turned, she saw Cooper McKenna. He sat in a nearby chair, his head down and resting in his hands, hands covered in blood. Her daughter's blood? Her nails bit into her palms. She took a step toward him, knowing only that there had been an accident, desperately wanting to put all the blame on this McKenna and all the rest of them.

"Mrs. Stafford."

The sheriff's voice stopped her. She turned slowly, suddenly feeling too light-headed. He took her arm. "Let's go down here where we can talk."

"Who did this?" she demanded the moment he lowered her into a waiting room chair and closed the door so they had some privacy. "I saw that McKenna—"

"It wasn't Cooper."

She looked up at him then, saw something in his eyes. This man was about to rip out her heart. She braced herself, straightening in her chair as she reminded herself who she was. "Tell me everything," she said, and then wished she hadn't.

COOPER LOOKED UP as someone tapped his shoulder. He didn't know how much time had passed since he'd been told to sit down and wait. He blinked up at the nurse.

"I'm waiting to see Tilly Stafford," he said.

The nurse nodded. "All I can tell you is that she's out of surgery."

"She's going to be all right?"

The nurse gave him a reassuring smile. "I'm sure the doctor can tell you more."

He felt as if he could finally breathe a little. "Can you tell me what room she's in?"

"She's still in recovery. You won't be able to see her until tomorrow."

He nodded, reminding himself that he wasn't family, that he would have to sneak in to see her when her mother wasn't around.

As the nurse walked away, he stood, rubbing the

back of his neck. It was stiff from hours in the chair. Tilly was going to be fine—she had to be. His relief was followed quickly by his anger at CJ. The bastard had better not die, because Cooper wanted a piece of him.

When he saw the sheriff coming down the hallway, he waited. Cooper met Stu's gaze. "She's going to be all right, isn't she?"

Stuart nodded. "Mild concussion, abrasions, broken forearm that had to be set."

He took a ragged breath, let it out. "CJ?"

The sheriff seemed to hesitate. "He suffered a lot of abrasions, some broken ribs and a severely fractured left leg. He also has a neck injury and right now has no feeling in his lower extremities."

"Will he ever walk again?"

"They don't know at this point. They're trying to assess the damage right now," Stu said. "Let me guess. You're hoping he can walk again so you can beat him up."

Cooper chuckled. "You think I wouldn't go for his throat even if he was in a wheelchair?"

"No, I don't think you would—even if he can walk again. You want to be with Tilly? You can't beat up her older brother."

"Even the one who tried to kill both of his sisters?"

Stu pulled a face. "Both were accidents, though..." He held up his hand to keep Cooper from interrupting him. "He was responsible for both. Maybe he's learned something from this."

He snorted and Stu laughed. "Yeah, he's still CJ Stafford."

"Yeah," Cooper said as he saw CJ's mother crying down the hall. Crying with relief that her daughter was going to live? Or crying because her son was badly injured and going to prison? Or was he? "She'll get him off if there is any way in hell."

Stu followed his gaze down the hall before looking at Cooper again. "You going to be all right?"

"Sure, I'll be fine." But he didn't feel fine. He remembered being on the ground next to Tilly when she was trapped in the wrecked pickup, promising that if she lived, he wouldn't let anything come between them.

He hadn't realized what an impossible promise it had been, but he did now. Not that it would stop him. But as Stu had pointed out, it would force him to rein in his ambivalence. He'd have to be a lot more diplomatic than he was by nature. He'd have to tread lightly if there was any hope of bridging that gap between the families. How else could he and Tilly survive even a relationship—let alone a marriage and children?

It was going to take a better man than he was right now, he thought. Because he still wanted to go for CJ's throat. Hopefully, he'd get over that impulse before the cowboy got out of jail.

CHAPTER TWENTY-FOUR

COOPER KNEW HE wouldn't be able to see Tilly until morning. As he climbed into his pickup, his stomach growled, reminding him that he hadn't eaten all day. He didn't feel hungry, but he did feel lost and he had no desire to go home right now.

He drove down to the Wild Horse Bar, took a stool and ordered a burger and a beer. It was quiet and cool, not even many of the regulars here at this time of the evening. Things would pick up later, but right now he pretty much had the place to himself. He did notice that Deputy Ty Dodson was sitting at a table in the corner with a friend. Cooper hoped he stayed there.

"Rumors are running wild," Eric, the bartender, said as he poured him a draft and set it on a napkin in front of him. The man was young, early twenties. He'd worked for the Stafford Ranch until he was fired for allegedly hitting on Oakley, speaking of rumors.

Eric leaned on the bar. "Is it true what I heard about CJ Stafford?"

"What did you hear?" Cooper asked.

"That he shot Oakley, almost killed Tilly when he wrecked his pickup, and now he might not ever walk again."

Cooper shook his head. "News to me." The way rumors traveled in this county truly amazed him. Then again, he suspected Deputy Ty Dodson had probably been spreading a few.

"Can't say I'm surprised, knowing what I do about that family," the bartender said. "Heard a private investigator out of Billings has been asking a lot of questions about Charlotte Stafford's husband who disappeared."

Cooper pretended he hadn't heard that. "What kind of questions?"

"That maybe Dixon Malone never left here. At least not alive. Strange no one has seen or heard from him."

Cooper sipped his beer. "Who'd care enough to hire a private detective?" he asked, scoffing.

"Dixon's daughter from his first marriage."

That was news. "I guess I never knew that he was married before."

Eric nodded, looking pleased with himself to be sharing the news. "The PI's asking everyone who has any kind of connection to the Staffords."

From the kitchen the cook called, "Order up!" and the bartender went to get Cooper's burger.

"Now it's got people wondering about Charlotte's first husband, the old guy, Rake Stafford, the one she had her kids with. People are questioning now if he really did die of natural causes." Eric lifted a brow as he set down the burger before reaching under the bar for ketchup and mustard. "With her second husband missing and her first one dead and buried...might have to dig the old guy up and see just how natural his death was."

"Sounds like a whole lot of speculation," Cooper said. "And very little evidence of wrongdoing."

"Maybe," Eric said. "But if they find out that Dixon Malone never left the Stafford Ranch, well, kind of opens up a whole can of worms, doesn't it?" He laughed at his own lame joke.

Fortunately, a patron down the bar called to Eric for another drink. Cooper devoured the burger, finished his beer and left. He'd heard the rumors for years. Everyone wanted to make Charlotte Stafford a killer. Or maybe they just wanted to see her knocked off her throne. The fact that she was so seldom seen, yet had so much power in the county without leaving her ranch, made her a target.

But now a PI was looking into her second husband's disappearance. Sometimes where there was smoke, there really was fire. He certainly hoped not, though.

THE SHERIFF MADE it official as soon as CJ came out of surgery. He found Charlotte in her son's room, with two attorneys. She was on the phone when Stuart walked in. He could hear her making plans to have CJ flown to a facility that specialized in neck injuries.

He read CJ his rights over the objections of his mother and the attorneys.

"Oakley isn't filing charges," Charlotte said indignantly.

"Well, the county is, Mrs. Stafford," Stuart told her. "It was a shooting. Your son fired at his sister and hit her. I'm sure your lawyers will be talking to the prosecutor. Meanwhile, I'm just doing my job. It's the law."

She huffed and turned her back to return to her phone call. Her attorney started to argue, and Stuart held up his hand. "I'll let your lawyers fight it out." With that, he walked out.

CJ would probably never get more than a slap on his wrist. If his mother had anything to do with it, her son wouldn't even spend a minute behind bars. CJ wasn't talking on the advice of his attorneys. But according to Tilly, CJ told her that he'd fired a warning shot when he'd caught Oakley on McKenna property, thinking she was meeting up with one of the McKenna boys after he'd warned her to stay away from them.

Unfortunately, it sounded like something the trigger-happy CJ Stafford might do. That he might never have to pay for what he'd done wouldn't sit well, especially with Cooper. But his friend had lived in this county long enough that he should know that Charlotte Stafford got what she wanted. It was no secret that she would move heaven and earth to protect her eldest son.

As Stuart was leaving the hospital, he saw Cooper drive up. He walked over to his friend's pickup as Cooper put down his window. "How do you feel about getting a beer? I picked up a six-pack on my way here."

"You know, I really could use one."

"Your new deputy's down at the bar, so let's not go there."

Stuart saw that gleam in Cooper's eyes that he'd missed seeing for a long time. "You weren't suggesting the fire tower?"

Cooper grinned. "Got to admit it did cross my mind. It's been a long time."

"Too long."

"Hop in."

They said little on the drive up into the mountains to the fire tower. They used to come here as kids after getting someone to buy them a six-pack of cheap beer. They would sit on the top deck, legs dangling over, and take in the view as they talked about sports, girls, school, girls, horses and girls.

Tonight they climbed the winding stairs up to the top as they had done so many times before. The wind rocked the large nearby ponderosa pines, playing a melody in the branches that was both familiar and at the same time a little melancholy.

As they sat down on the deck, their legs dangling over the side, Stuart was painfully aware that they weren't kids anymore. They weren't worried about things that now felt so irrelevant. The issues in their lives felt huge, life changing, scary.

Cooper popped open one of the cans of beer he'd bought and handed it to him. He opened one for himself. "To us," Cooper said, holding it up in a toast.

They touched cans and Stuart repeated, "To us," and took a drink.

Stuart looked out at the valley now shaded in twilight. He still loved it here in the Powder River Basin. His father used to call it God's country. He could never see himself leaving, even though he probably should.

"Charlotte's having CJ flown out to a special hospital for neck injuries," Stuart said, wanting to be the one to give him the news. Cooper said nothing. "I guess some would say he's paying a hell of a price for what he did."

His friend scoffed and shook his head. "What *is* the price for almost killing both of your sisters?"

They fell silent again as if neither wanted to get into the bigger issues.

"Do you remember when Dixon Malone disappeared?" Cooper asked.

He looked over at him in surprise at the abrupt change of subject. "Not really. Why?"

"That license plate number Tilly had you run for her? Jason Murdock is a private eye from Billings. Apparently, he's in town asking questions about Dixon Malone's disappearance. Rumor is that he was hired by Dixon's daughter from another marriage."

"After all this time, huh." Stuart took a gulp of his beer and sighed as he looked out at the growing night. "It's always something, isn't it."

Cooper chuckled. "I thought that was why you became sheriff. For the excitement."

"That and the money." He watched lights blink on across the valley. "You thought any more about asking to have Leann's case reopened?"

"I've thought about it. I haven't changed my mind."

Stuart nodded. "I can talk to the prosecutor. He's going to be inundated by Charlotte's attorneys for a while, but after the dust settles, I'm sure he'll be happy to reopen it."

They drank, listening to night fall around them. Stuart leaned against the log railing, feeling his age. He remembered his father one time saying he'd felt old in his thirties. But it had passed. Stuart hoped it passed soon, as he finished his beer and Cooper handed him another one.

CHAPTER TWENTY-FIVE

"BUTTERCUP." IT WAS the first word Tilly said to him when she opened her eyes and saw Cooper sitting next to her hospital bed. He'd sneaked into her room after her mother had left to find her still sleeping, but he hadn't wanted to wake her.

Buttercup? He fought the feeling of déjà vu since that was exactly what Oakley had said. He figured it was the drugs talking.

"Hello, beautiful." She had scratches and abrasions on her face, a cast on her right arm, but he'd never seen a more wonderful sight than those green eyes of hers open. "How are you feeling?"

"I'm groggy, but I'm okay," she said, returning his smile. "You heard about CJ?" He nodded. "I can't believe he shot Oakley or that he's hurt so badly after wrecking the pickup. Mother says not to worry, that she's taking care of everything, including having him flown out to a special hospital."

"I'm more worried about you," he said. *"Buttercup?"*

"That's what I've been dying to tell you." They both cringed at her use of the word *dying*. "I was on my way to the hospital when CJ insisted he drive. Oakley had asked me to pick up her list of passwords. She can never remember them, so she kept them written down on a paper in her desk drawer at home. I promised not to look at them, but CJ was driving so crazy. I'd forgotten I even had the list." She looked at him, took a breath. "Sorry, I'm rambling." She motioned to the cup and pitcher next to her bed. He got her some water and helped her drink it.

"It's all right. You should be resting."

She shook her head as he put the cup back on her bedside table. "I looked down the list and saw the word *buttercup*. It's one of her passwords."

A password? "For what?"

"That I don't know. You need to take the list to her. I think I stuffed it into my jacket pocket just seconds before the pickup rolled. I have no idea where my clothes are. Maybe a nurse has them."

"Don't worry. I'll find the list and talk to Oakley. You just need to rest." He leaned over and kissed her.

"Coop," she said, grabbing his shirt in her fist and drawing him to her again.

He knew what she wanted to ask. He could understand why she was worried. He'd been worried that this could change things between them. "I love you, Tilly Stafford."

Tears filled her eyes. "I love you, Cooper McKenna. I had a dream about you and me. It involved the tailgate of your pickup."

He grinned. "As soon as you get out of here and are up for it."

"Oh, I'm up for it. Does this mean you're through fighting it?"

He nodded. "I can't wait to make love to you."

"What the hell are *you* doing here?" Charlotte Stafford cried from the doorway.

"Visiting the woman I love," Cooper said as he gave Tilly another quick kiss and turned to leave.

Her mother looked as if she might explode as she strode past him to her daughter's bed.

"I don't want to hear it, Mother," Tilly said as Cooper left the room, closing the door behind him. His boots felt lighter on his feet as he headed down the hall to find Tilly's jacket and the passwords before visiting Oakley's room.

All the way, he couldn't help but wonder why a password had been so important to Oakley that day after being shot.

HOLDEN STOOD IN the doorway of the stables watching Holly Jo. He couldn't hear what she was saying, but she was definitely murmuring something to her horse as she groomed the mare. Her movements were slow, almost loving, and he felt a tug at his heart.

He'd been beginning to think he'd made a mistake by bringing her here. He'd promised he would take care of her. That didn't mean that he had to bring her to a ranch where she didn't want to be and force her into his lifestyle instead of her own. He'd been having doubts since their ride together. He'd known that she'd thought she would just take off on the horse and never look back. Was she that desperate to get away?

But watching her now, he felt such a ray of hope

that he wondered how he could ever have thought of not keeping her here.

"Interested in going for a ride?" he asked as he approached.

She looked up in surprise. "Really?"

"No more stunts like last time?"

"I promise," she said excitedly. "I promise. I think Honey wants to go even more than I do."

He smiled at that. "She does look like she could use a little exercise. We should saddle the horses." The girl was all smiles now.

They walked their horses out of the stables. She went over to the corral and used the railing to climb up on her horse by herself. Turning, she grinned at him. He could see the pride in her eyes.

"Nice job," he said as he swung up into the saddle. They rode out across the pasture toward the foothills. He felt the warm morning summer breeze on his face and looked over at Holly Jo. Her expression was one of bliss. He smiled, thinking he'd never felt more alive than at that moment.

They stopped in the trees to let their horses get a drink from the creek. He didn't want to spoil this easy peace between them, but he also wanted to talk to her about a few things.

"Are you looking forward to school?" She shot him a disbelieving look. "I think you'll enjoy it. You'll meet other kids your age. You'll make friends." She didn't look convinced.

He changed the subject. "I've noticed that you don't

seem to like a lot of the food we eat. I was wondering if there is something Elaine can buy that you might like."

"It's okay. Elaine talked me into trying some beef. It's not bad. I think I could like it."

Holden smiled. "Better than broccoli?"

She gave him a sheepish look. "I don't really like broccoli."

"I noticed you didn't eat much of it."

"If I'm going to stay here, what should I call you?"

It was a good question, one he hadn't considered. "What would you like to call me?"

She shrugged. "I suppose Holden. You're really not my dad?"

"No, but I wish I were. I'm glad you're staying with us."

Holly Jo looked away. "I'm not sure I belong here."

"I think you do and so does Honey."

She laughed at that as she stroked the mare's neck. "You shouldn't believe everything Honey says."

He laughed and they turned back toward the house, him promising that they would ride more.

"Can I learn to do tricks on Honey?" she asked.

"We'll see." He told himself to enjoy this moment because it wouldn't last. He was smart enough to know that there would be tantrums, crying, yelling and threats to leave. After all, Holly Jo was just at the beginning of her teenage years.

He remembered what he'd gone through with Bailey. Just the thought of his daughter reminded him that he hadn't seen much of her lately. He hated to think what she might be up to. He tried not to worry as he looked over at Holly Jo. Right now, he had a good feeling about the future and he was determined to hang on to it.

AFTER LEAVING TILLY'S ROOM, the sheriff went down the hall to visit Oakley. He figured she'd already heard that it had been her brother who shot her. But Stuart needed to make it official. She was sitting up in bed when he stepped in.

"I figure you've already heard," he said. "I'm sorry."

She nodded. "I knew how CJ felt about a lot of things. I should have known I was pushing him too far. He just seems to think that he's now the man of the house and that we all have to do whatever he says. That's not going to happen. I hope he learned something from this."

Her attitude surprised him. He'd known Oakley a long time. This young woman was strong and determined. But he also knew her brother CJ. "You're taking this awfully well." He wasn't completely sure that he believed it.

She laughed. "I'm not taking it that well. When I see him, I'm sure I'll have a few things to say to him. With him injured, it will limit how angry I get."

"How's your mother doing?"

"You haven't seen her?"

"Actually, I did just see her."

Oakley groaned. "Then I'm sure you have a pretty good idea how she's taking this. CJ is her hope for the future. She keeps thinking he's going to change because she is planning on him running the ranch one day. For such a liberal, strong, independent woman, it kind of amazes me that she thinks CJ should run the ranch. How can she not realize that Tilly's the one who loves the ranch and will take care of it? I can't say the same for my brother. He's all about money and power. But then again, so is my mother."

"I'm sorry about the problems with the family."

"Oh, you haven't seen anything yet." Her gaze softened. "You know about Tilly and Cooper." He nodded. "I have no idea what Mother will do."

"You're not interested in running the ranch?" he had to ask.

She shook her head. "I'm not sure why I've stayed here this long."

Stuart thought he might know. "Do you mind if I ask if you're involved with Pickett Hanson?"

She smiled. "I like Pickett. But he's not the only man I'm interested in, if I'm being honest. And in case you're wondering, my brother CJ wouldn't approve of either of my choices."

He realized she wasn't going to share any more of her personal life with him. Wasn't his business. But keeping peace in this valley was. "I heard you're getting out of the hospital pretty soon."

"Thank goodness. I'm going stir-crazy in here."

"I'm going to need a formal statement from you." She started to say that she wasn't pressing charges. "I've heard you're not pressing charges. But in the case of a shooting, the county will. CJ will face charges."

She shook her head. "We both know that my mother will get him out of it."

"I'll send a deputy by with some paperwork." He tipped his Stetson, wished her well and left.

He could foresee a long legal battle ahead, but CJ would get off easy. Not that it would end the trouble in that family. His best friend was in love with a Stafford, there was a PI in town asking questions about Charlotte's last husband who'd disappeared, and if he'd read Oakley right, she wasn't just interested in a McKenna ranch hand. He figured there wouldn't be any peace in that family for a very long time.

He just hoped it didn't boil over and require the law to step in.

Down at the office, Cooper was directed to the head nurse who found Tilly's clothing and jacket. All had been covered with blood and bagged. He dug in her jacket pocket and found a scrap of paper with a list of passwords on it. He scanned them as he walked to Oakley's room. The word *buttercup* jumped out at him, but there was nothing after it that explained what the password was for.

He hoped she would be able to solve at least one mystery that had been driving him batty since she'd ridden her horse onto the road that day. He tapped on her door before peeking in. He didn't want to have a run-in with her mother. He'd barely escaped the last one.

Fortunately, Oakley was alone. "I have something for you," he said as he stepped in.

"I hope it's not flowers. I'm not dying."

He laughed. "I can see that you're recovering." She

was so much like Tilly. He never appreciated her sense of humor until now. "It's your passwords." He handed her the handwritten list.

She looked at him suspiciously. "Did you memorize them?"

"I can't remember my own passwords, so I'm certainly not going to try to memorize yours." She laughed and glanced at the sheet. "But I do have a question. Remember when I found you?" She didn't remember. "I told you when I found you that all you said was 'Buttercup,' and I thought it was the name of your horse and that you were worried about your mare."

"Oh, right, and I can't remember why I said that."

"Apparently it is one of your passwords."

She looked at the sheet again and laughed. "It is. It's actually not my password. It's CJ's. I stole it so I could look at his phone occasionally to see what he's been up to. He leads a very boring life."

"So that day you were shot, were you trying to tell me who shot you?"

She shrugged. "I don't know. Maybe. Truthfully, I can't imagine why I said that to you."

"You were pretty adamant that I remember the word *buttercup*. Did you know it was your brother who shot you?"

"I must have. But why didn't I just say his name?" She frowned. "I don't remember any of it."

He wondered if even then she was covering for her brother. "You know the county is going to press charges even if you don't."

"That's what the sheriff just told me."

"You don't hold a grudge?"

"Of course I do. Don't you think I'm going to make him pay the rest of his life? But I can't press charges against my brother. I already told the sheriff. I think we all just want to forget it."

Good luck with that, he thought.

"Well, I'm glad you're feeling better and that you're getting out of here pretty soon. I know your sister will be glad too." He turned toward the door, when she stopped him.

"You and Tilly?" She grinned, not waiting for him to confirm it. His expression must have given him away. "I'm not surprised. I always thought you two had some kind of chemistry between you. You aren't worried about the families?"

"I'm always worried about the families," he said with a chuckle. "But you can't stop true love, right?"

She didn't look so sure about that. "I hope that's true," she said, and he suspected that she wasn't talking about him and Tilly anymore.

As he left the hospital, he heard a helicopter land in the field behind it.

CHARLOTTE FOLLOWED THE gurney with CJ strapped to it to the helicopter, even though she was told it wasn't necessary.

"I will be the judge of that," she'd snapped. She'd already been told that she would have to drive to Billings instead of accompanying CJ on the chopper. For what she was paying, she should have been able to fly the damned helicopter, she thought.

She had seen the expressions of the nurses and Doc Hammond. She'd overheard one of the nurses tell Doc that Charlotte Stafford seemed to think she owned the hospital.

Doc had laughed. "In a way, she does. She pays the taxes that keep this hospital running. She and Holden McKenna and the other large landowners around here. I've always thought she'd make a good general if we ever went to war again."

She'd taken it as a compliment. Now she reached into the helicopter to take her son's hand. Motioned back by the pilot, she let go, ducked under the rotating blades and stumbled back toward the hospital. She stopped, shielding her eyes as the chopper took off, hiding her tears.

Her baby was hurt so badly that he might never walk again. How would she ever get through this? She kept watching the helicopter until it disappeared from view. Then, pulling herself together, she straightened her shoulders and put on her stern expression before going back inside to pay her bill. After, she'd head home and pack for the drive to Billings, then fly on to a specialized care facility. She had no idea how long she'd be gone from home since Doc had told her that CJ's recovery could be a long one.

WHEN COOPER RETURNED to the ranch, he could hear what sounded like an impromptu rodeo going on down at the corrals. He walked over to find Holly Jo hanging on the side of the corral railing, watching. He joined

DARK SIDE OF THE RIVER

her as Pickett performed some basic horseback tricks to the cheers and jeers of his fellow ranch hands.

"Can girls do that?" Holly Jo asked.

He considered her, seeing a gleam in her blue eyes. "A most famous trick rider was a woman named Connie Griffith. She's in the National Cowgirl Hall of Fame."

Holly Jo's eyes widened with wonder. "Can you teach me to do that?"

He wondered what his father would say. But if Holden was here right now and could see the look on this girl's face, he couldn't say no. "I can do a few tricks." He thought of Tilly, who was even better at trick riding. "I also know a cowgirl who could show you a few things too."

"Please?" She said it as if it hurt to form the word, let alone that she might get her dream crushed. For days she'd fought everything about ranch life, from the food to living out in the sticks. He suspected that the only reason she'd originally wanted to learn to ride a horse was to leave. He wasn't sure when that had changed or if it would last, but he thought it was a good sign that her staying here might work out.

"I'll make a deal with you," he said. "You make more of an effort to eat the food Elaine cooks, including the beef—"

Her face lit up. "I ate some. I did. It wasn't…terrible."

He couldn't help but laugh. "You do that and I'll think about it."

"Cooper, I want to be able to do horse tricks more

than anything in the world." She said it with such sincerity.

He kept looking at her for a long moment, knowing he'd already made up his mind. "I'll have to ask Dad. You could get hurt. If you do, he'll blame me."

She grinned. "Then I guess you better make sure I don't get hurt."

HOLDEN SENSED THAT something had changed when he sat down to supper that night. For starters, all of his offspring were here along with Holly Jo. Even Elaine looked surprised, giving him a questioning look. He had no idea.

As the food was passed around, he saw Holly Jo take a little of everything on her plate, including a tiny piece of roast beef. He saw her shoot a look down the table at Cooper, who gave her a nod.

He wanted to ask what was going on, but he thought there was something to that old expression, let sleeping dogs lie. Whatever had caused this rare occurrence, he didn't want to do anything to ruin it.

Holden listened as Bailey and Duffy joked with each other. Even Treyton seemed to be in a good mood, discussing the building of the new barn with Cooper. All of it made him wonder at the change, though. His ex-wife, Lulabelle Braden McKenna, would have said it was the position of the stars.

Just the thought of the fiery redhead always made him question his good judgment. He'd married her right after Charlotte's first husband had died and she'd quickly married Dixon Malone. Her marriage had lasted less than a year. His hadn't made it much longer.

He was still embarrassed and didn't need a psychiatrist to tell him why he'd proposed to the sexy, loud, long-legged city girl. She was the extreme opposite of Charlotte Stafford. She'd instantly hated ranch life, having thought it was like the Western romances she read.

"I thought we'd wear Western clothes and go places, like Vegas and New York, once in a while," she'd said, pouting. "I hate living out here in the middle of nowhere. You never told me it was so…boring."

Just when he'd thought that things couldn't get any worse, Lulabelle had ended up in a hair-pulling fight at the grocery store with Charlotte. He hadn't been there, but he'd been told that the fight was a draw before the manager at the store got between them and broke it up.

He felt himself flush at the memory of the second-worst mistake he'd ever made.

"What do you think, Dad?" he heard Cooper say.

Assuming they were discussing the new barn, he said, "Sounds good to me."

Holly Jo let out a cheer and then quickly took a bite of the roast beef. Holden watched, wondering what he'd just agreed to as the girl chewed for a few moments. Everyone was watching her expectantly. He wouldn't have been surprised if she had spit it out.

But she swallowed and nodded. "It's not all that bad," she said about the prized beef they raised.

There were chuckles around the table at that. "Glad to hear it," Holden said, unable not to smile as he watched the girl eat the rest of the food on her plate. Something had happened, and he had no idea what. He looked at Cooper, who merely grinned.

He told himself he didn't want to know, didn't need to, as he listened to Treyton's plans for the barn and Cooper offering his suggestions, which his eldest son took without comment.

For several years, Treyton had been saying it was time to let him run the ranch. Holden wouldn't go that far, but he did see how this younger generation might be able to step into his boots at some time in the future. It gave him hope, especially when it came to Holly Jo, who was now asking Bailey questions about horse riding.

"Glad you agreed to letting Holly Jo learn some horse-riding tricks," Cooper said, almost making him choke on the roast. "It's something she wants pretty badly. If you don't mind, I thought I'd get Tilly to help. She's always been better at it than I am."

Holden didn't know what to say as he looked down the table at his ward. He heard Treyton murmur something under his breath about the Staffords. Trick riding? "You just make sure she's careful." Even as he said it, he knew they were a waste of words. This was Holly Jo they were talking about.

"I told her if she got hurt, you'd blame me," Cooper said, still grinning. "She said I better not let her get hurt."

"She's right." His words didn't carry his concern about only Holly Jo's trick riding but also whatever was going on with his son and Tilly Stafford. He liked the young woman, thought she was a fine partner for his son.

Still, he knew Charlotte wouldn't agree. He considered riding over one day and talking to her about it. It was a terrible idea, but it made him smile to himself. No matter how it went, he did like seeing her.

Then he was reminded that she wasn't at the ranch. He'd heard that she'd flown from Billings on to Minneapolis, where CJ would be treated for his neck injuries.

He told himself that she'd be back. She wouldn't be able to stay away long. He would see her again, he thought, and smiled to himself, refusing to think of the day when that might not be true.

STUART HADN'T REALIZED how late it was. He looked up from his desk and the pile of paperwork he'd been wading through. He rubbed his temples, his head aching. He heard the front door of the sheriff's department open, heard the dispatcher say something, and the next thing he knew, a woman was standing in his doorway.

He recognized her as the new nurse who worked at the hospital. She was holding a take-out container. The smell of the food made his stomach growl. He couldn't remember the last time he'd eaten. He'd been so busy, it had skipped his mind.

Stumbling to his feet, he said, "Hello." He wasn't sure what was going on until she stepped in.

"We met at the hospital earlier," she said. "You probably don't remember." He did remember. She had a heart-shaped face, big brown eyes and a wide, friendly smile. "You looked dead on your feet, and I wondered if you had remembered to eat. When I saw your patrol SUV still in the parking lot and your light on… I hope you don't mind I brought you supper."

He glanced at the container as he went around the end of the desk to take it from her. Shoving the paperwork aside, he set the meal down. "Thank you, but I hope you're planning to join me, because I'm sure that's more than I can eat." He looked at her. "While I do remember you, for the life of me, I can't recall your name."

She smiled and stuck out her hand. "I'm Abigail Creed."

"Nice to meet you, Abigail. Please join me." He pulled up a chair for her, feeling not quite as tired. "So, what brings you to Powder Crossing?" he asked as they sat down.

"The job. It's part-time, which is perfect," she said as they helped themselves to the food. "I'm a photographer when I'm not a nurse. This area is beautiful. I'm trying to get a collection of photos together for a showing around Christmas."

He realized it was the way she said it, as if she'd rehearsed the words. He told himself she'd probably told so many people her story that it had become rote. But at the same time, he found himself looking at her more closely.

He'd often said that he'd gone into law enforcement because he'd followed in his father's footsteps. But he suspected it was because of the way his mind and instincts worked.

But right now, he hated both. All his instincts were

telling him that this pretty, charming, sweet and thought-ful young woman was leaving out something very important about why she'd come to Powder Crossing.

CHAPTER TWENTY-SIX

THE POWDER CROSSING Fourth of July Rodeo was more than a Western tradition. It was an excuse for cowboys and cowgirls from across several counties and even states to gather. Pickups would be parked a mile down on both sides of the dirt road from the fairgrounds to accommodate the crowds. Trucks and stock trailers lined up in the fields around the rodeo grounds for a quarter mile.

Food trucks came from all over, along with vendors selling cowboy hats, bolo ties and horse tack, as well as jewelry and fancy Western shirts and boots.

Because the town was so far from anything, the three-day event brought in campers, trailers and tents that now spread out as far as the eye could see. Cowboys were lined up six-deep at the makeshift beer garden that had been set up at the edge of the arena. Country music played from a loudspeaker in the two-story building where Doc Hammond would be doing the announcing—unless he got called away to patch up someone at the hospital.

The air filled with excitement, and dust rose along the road and drifted toward the mountains.

From up on the mountain, Cooper had a bird's-eye view of the fairgrounds as he parked his pickup.

"Can I take the blindfold off now?" Tilly asked impatiently.

"Soon," he said as he got out and ran around to open her door and help her out. "Just a little longer." He led her away from the truck and into the pines. "Okay, you can take it off," he said as he untied the bandanna he'd used.

He checked her expression and saw tears in her eyes.

"Oh, Coop," she said, looking from the tent he'd erected in the pines to him. The breeze flapped open the tent's door, offering a view of the air-mattress bed inside all made up with sheets and a quilt. He'd brought a couple of small stumps inside and picked up candles. A cooler sat in the corner with her favorite wine, and beer for him. "It's perfect."

He drew her to him, kissing her with longing before drawing back. "It's not too late to back out."

She laughed. "It's been too late for a very long time." She cupped his face and pulled him down for another kiss. "But the tailgate would have been just fine."

He laughed at that as he swept her up in his arms and carried her awkwardly into the tent. He put her down, gently aware of her arm in a cast and her other injuries. Then he zipped the tent door closed and joined her on the bed.

His heart raced as he looked into her green eyes. "I love you, Tilly."

SHE TOOK HIS hand and drew him closer. She was amazed at the trouble he'd gone to setting this all up so they could be together, away from prying eyes, alone at last—and not in his pickup.

"I can't believe this," she said, looking around the tent. "You've thought of everything."

"I'm sorry I spent so much time pushing you away. It was the last thing I wanted."

She touched his handsome face, gazing into his blue eyes. "Didn't your stepmother believe in destiny?"

"Lulabelle? You are not going to bring her up at a moment like this." They both laughed. He brushed a lot of her hair back from her face. "You think we were destined to be together?"

She nodded. "I do."

"I do too." She felt a shiver of desire as he ran his thumb pad over her lower lip. The tip of her tongue grazed his thumb; her need for him was almost painful as his fingers trailed down her throat to the opening of her Western shirt.

She leaned back, arching against his touch as his fingers dipped farther to caress the tender flesh above her breasts. Her heart began to beat more wildly as he slowly unsnapped her shirt. He bent down to push aside her bra, baring her breast as he sucked her already pulsing hard nipple into his mouth.

Groaning with pleasure, she reached to touch him, but he pulled back her hand and shook his head. He suckled at that aching nipple as his fingers brushed over her stomach down to her jeans. She felt him unbutton them, and then his fingers slipped under her panties where she was already wet.

She writhed under his touch as he gently stroked

her. His fingers pressed harder. Pleasure was a spiral that spun higher and higher until she cried out with the release. Unable to stand it any longer, she tore open his Western shirt, desperately wanting to feel her skin pressed to his. It was awkward with her arm in a cast.

He eased her clothes off, working around the cast, then rolled her over onto him. Their kisses grew more demanding. She reached again for his jeans. This time, he let her unbutton them. He wriggled out of them, and she did the same, stripping off her panties as she watched him remove his briefs.

They stared at each other, now completely naked—except for her cast. "Tilly, you are so beautiful."

"I was just thinking," she said on a sigh, "how gorgeous you are."

He laughed and carefully leaned over her as he said, "No going back, Tilly."

She knew exactly what he was saying. She felt the same way as she pulled him to her with her free hand. Below them on the mountain, music played as they moved together in an age-old primal dance that left them both sated and smiling.

Later, they made love yet again. This time fireworks began to go off, casting flashes of brilliant light that seemed to fall like stars over their tent. They lay wrapped together, the tent door open, and watched the Fourth of July celebration going on below them on the mountain.

Tilly noticed that Cooper had gone silent. She pulled back to look at him. "Having second thoughts?"

He rose from the bed and pulled on his jeans. For a moment, she thought—

But then he knelt down beside the air mattress and said, "If we're doing this, then let there be no mistake about my intentions." He met her gaze. "Or yours. Tilly Stafford, will you marry me?"

She blinked in surprise. He'd said that once they made love there would be no going back for him. But she'd never imagined this was what he had in mind.

For a moment, she couldn't speak as he pulled out a little velvet box from beside the bed.

"It was my mother's. I asked my dad if I could have it. He was delighted, though concerned, of course. But if we are going to do this, then I want to make it official. Will you marry me?"

"Oh, Coop, yes," she cried as he took out the ring and she held out her hand as he climbed back up on the mattress with her. He slid the ring on her finger. It fit perfectly, and she realized he'd probably asked Oakley and had the ring sized.

She looked from the ring to him. "I don't care who likes it—I want to marry you. I'm *going* to marry you." She tried to throw herself into his arms, but only managed to hit him with her cast, nearly knocking him to the tent floor. He pulled her close, laughing as the night exploded in fireworks around them.

STUART HAD ALREADY heard about the engagement. News traveled at the speed of light in this county. But Cooper had stopped by before the Fourth of July to tell him in person.

"If she'll have me, I'm going to ask her to marry me this weekend."

"That's kind of quick, isn't it?" he'd said.

"We've known each other our whole lives. I think we've been dating most of that time. I know it looked like we were fighting and hated each other, but you know what they say about love and hate."

Stuart had laughed. "You two are made for each other. Good thing you're both fighters, because I think you're going to have a battle ahead of you. Sounds like your father will be fine."

"He gave me my mother's ring. Treyton doesn't know yet."

"Yeah, that should be interesting when he finds out. But what about Tilly's mother?"

Cooper had shaken his head. "I guess we'll see. She's in Minneapolis. Don't know when she'll be back. I'm sure someone will let her know."

"Well, congratulations," he'd said, and had pulled his friend into a hug. "I wish the two of you the best."

"Did I hear something about you and the new nurse in town?"

"She's also a photographer. Says she might open a small studio here." Stuart didn't mention the feeling he had when he was around Abigail. He kept hoping he was wrong.

He and Cooper had parted as the friends that they were.

Before word moved through the sheriff's office about the engagement, he'd announced it himself. Everyone gave him concerned looks as if afraid he was taking it hard. He wasn't. He'd seen it coming and was determined to put the past behind him. At least that was what he told himself.

"Those two are meant for each other," he told his staff, hoping that would be the end of any speculation.

Then the FBI had dropped by with an update on the meth lab and he'd gotten busy. There wasn't much new. The Feds just warned him that they expected whoever had been running the lab would relocate—probably somewhere in Stuart's jurisdiction. He'd already figured that out himself and would be keeping his eye out for it.

The prosecutor was moving forward on Oakley's shooting. Stuart had thought about mentioning that Cooper wanted Leann's death case reopened, but he held off. Right now the prosecutor was tied up with the legal wranglings of Charlotte Stafford's attorneys.

If Cooper still felt the same way later, Stuart told himself, he'd do it. But right now he thought it best to give it a little more time as he tied up loose ends in his office. Reopening Leann's case would mean uncovering the identity of the man she was planning to leave town with. Stuart wanted to put that off as long as possible.

CHAPTER TWENTY-SEVEN

OAKLEY WIPED AT her tears as she pulled Tilly's left hand closer. "It's a beautiful ring. It was his mother's?"

Choked up herself, all Tilly could do was nod.

"I'm so happy for you," her sister said. "Have you told Mother?"

"She's busy with CJ. I'm sure she's probably heard, because she hasn't been taking my calls."

"Did you leave a message with the good news?" Her sister laughed when she saw that Tilly hadn't. "Chicken. Not that I blame you. I'd put off hearing what she has to say about it as long as I could too."

It wasn't just her mother. There was CJ's reaction to the engagement to worry about as well. She hated to even think it, but she was glad he wasn't around to spoil her happiness. She already knew what his reaction would be. "Mother already said she wouldn't allow it."

Oakley nodded as if not surprised. "What could she do to stop you? You're old enough to know your own mind. CJ is going to go apeshit, though."

"You have such an elegant way of putting things," Tilly said, and laughed. Laughing felt good, especially with her sister.

"She hasn't disowned you yet, so maybe there's hope." Oakley didn't look hopeful.

"You want to tell me?" Tilly asked.

Her sister looked up in surprise. "About what?"

"Everything?"

Oakley smiled at that. "I do want to tell you, but—"

The hospital room door opened, and the doctor and nurse came in.

Tilly gave her sister a quick hug. "We'll talk soon," she said, and left.

She hadn't told a lot of people about the engagement because of the reaction she knew she would get. Everyone knew about the McKenna-Stafford feud. She'd told some of her friends. Her closest friends had moved away from Powder Crossing, going on with their lives. They stayed in touch online.

Tilly would put it on social media once she'd told her family. She wondered who Cooper had told. He called every night and morning. They talked about everything but their families.

She waited until the nurse and doctor left before going back into her sister's room. "So what's the word?"

Oakley smiled. "Not quite good as new. I'll have a scar, but I get to go home tomorrow. I can't wait."

"I can pick you up," Tilly offered.

"No need. I've got a ride." She looked at her little sister askance, making Oakley laugh. "It's not what you think. Brand offered to pick me up. I know, surprising, huh, that our brother offered. While it is probably out of the goodness of his heart, I suspect it has more to do with the new nurse working here." She shrugged. "I don't mind. I like helping out true love every chance I get."

Tilly still found herself studying her sister. Oakley had been living a secretive life that had almost gotten her killed. But the big question was why CJ had shot her. Nothing he'd said before he'd wrecked the pickup made any sense. All her instincts told her that he'd lied about why he'd fired that shot. She just hoped it wasn't because Oakley had discovered the meth lab. Then again, it could have been because of her involvement with Dirty Business. She doubted, though, that it had anything to do with CJ thinking she was meeting someone on the McKenna Ranch.

It worried her. Oakley had been living a dangerous life, and none of them had been aware of it. Soon her sister would be going back to it. Tilly had no doubt about that as she said, "Okay, I'm going to head home, but we are going to talk soon."

"You worry too much about me when you're the one you should be worried about. When Mother sees that rock on your finger…" She shook her head but smiled. "Just remind her that she would have married Holden McKenna if he hadn't chosen someone else."

"Oh, that sounds like the perfect thing to remind Mother of when she'd be having a coronary over my engagement to Cooper," Tilly said. "'Bye. Call if you need me."

As she left, she knew that her mother probably had already heard about the engagement, but she doubted she would call—even to tell Tilly how disappointed she was or to make threats.

No, Tilly knew that there wouldn't be a showdown between her and her mother over this until she returned to the ranch with CJ—and who knew when that would be?

As she stepped outside into the Montana summer, she decided to enjoy this time. She glanced down at the ring on her finger. She was marrying Cooper McKenna, and she couldn't be happier.

Her step felt light as she walked to her pickup. She was in love and right where she wanted to be.

"YOU MISSED THE RODEO," Holly Jo said when Cooper found her down at the stables. "Everyone was looking for you at the Fourth of July celebration."

He doubted that. "I was busy."

"Treyton was really mad. He said you were probably up to no good with Tilly Stafford."

Treyton needed to keep his mouth shut around Holly Jo and her big ears. "You want me to teach you a trick or not?"

"Yes." She closed her mouth, but he could tell she had all kinds of questions brewing.

After her lesson, he left her to put everything away under Deacon's watchful eye and walked up to the house. He found his father in his den.

"Knock, knock," he said, tapping on the open door. "Got a minute?"

"For you, always. Have a seat."

"I just got Holly Jo started on a couple of horse tricks. She's taking to it quickly. We might have created a monster. She keeps saying she wants to be a cowgirl in the Hall of Fame like Connie." He held up his hands. "My bad. I mentioned Connie to her."

His father chuckled. "Thank you for doing what you are with her. I wouldn't have the patience."

"It does take patience," he admitted with a grumble. "But that wasn't what I wanted to talk to you about. I gave Tilly the ring and asked her to marry me. We're engaged."

Eyebrow rising, Holden said, "That was quick."

"I suppose that's what people will say, but I think it's been percolating for years." Cooper got to his feet, feeling a little disappointed at his father's response. "Just wanted you to know."

"Congratulations," Holden said, rising and reaching for his hand to shake. "She's a delightful young woman. I'm honored for her to become part of our family."

"Thank you," he said, shaking his father's hand. "I was worried that you——"

"No, no," Holden said quickly. "I was just surprised you popped the question so quickly after I gave you the ring. You have my support."

Cooper nodded, pleased. If his father had been against it, he would have been another hurdle to leap over——not just now but in the future. "It means a lot to me."

"I hope you and Tilly will make your home on this ranch," his father said. "You're welcome to live here, there's plenty of room, but I suspect you'll want your own home."

"I think we'd be more comfortable in our own home."

Holden nodded and smiled. "My thought exactly. Take your pick of whatever acreage you'd like. I've always planned to build homes for my children here on the place once they married. I put money aside."

"Thank you." He couldn't help being surprised.

"And please stay here after the wedding until your home is ready. I know Elaine would love it, and I would too."

Holden did look so happy that it made him feel as if this was all going to work out. He and Tilly would bring these families back together. They would end the feud.

As if his father knew what he was thinking, he said, "I'm not buying trouble, but I hope you and Tilly won't be too disappointed in Charlotte's reaction or those of other members of both families. It won't be easy, son, but I'm determined to do what I can. I want you two to be happy. You both deserve that.

"I can see a brighter future for this family," Holden said, a little misty-eyed. "Why not? We're going to have a famous cowgirl trick rider in the family." He met his son's gaze. "Not to mention grandchildren one day."

"Whoa," Cooper said. "One day far in the future. You're too young to be a grandfather."

Holden laughed. "You make Charlotte Stafford a grandmother at this age, and you're really asking for trouble."

They both laughed as Cooper left to go see his bride-to-be. Just the thought put a smile on his face. He thought his father might be right about that brighter future. Maybe love could conquer all. This cowboy certainly wanted to believe so.

* * * * *

*You can read more about
the McKennas and the Staffords in* River Strong
by New York Times *bestselling author B.J. Daniels,
available December 2023 wherever
Canary Street Press books are sold.*

HARLEQUIN PLUS

Try the best multimedia subscription service for romance readers like you!

Read, Watch and Play.

Experience the easiest way to get the romance content you crave.

Start your **FREE TRIAL** at
<u>www.harlequinplus.com/freetrial</u>.